'Miller is a pellucid, evocative writer: he brings alive the thick fogs over the Thames, the dreary winter countryside, the lamp-lit London streets . . . A beautiful evocation of a few months of this womaniser's life'
Marianne MacDonald in the *Observer*

'Full-bodied yet razor-sharp . . . Period detail, which so often reveals only that the writer has commendably and carefully studied a contemporary portrait, in Miller's hands takes us into the heart of 18th-century London so that we can almost smell and touch it . . . its fetid atmosphere almost making the reader itch'
Katie Grant in the *Spectator*

'An elegant and gripping entertainment that gives the first-time reader a difficult choice: do you linger over Miller's sensuous images and felicitous prose, or simply surrender to a fast-paced storyline and turn the pages? . . . It is hard to believe that this is only his second novel. He is already a formidable artist and technician, so skilful that all one notices is a seeming absence of technique and style. His writing is vivid, precise and constantly surprising. It reads easily, suspends life until it is read and is a source of wonder and delight'
Hilary Mantel in *The Sunday Times*

'Andrew Miller's forte is painting verbal landscapes, laying the words just so. At times it's like a fine miniature, delicate with atmosphere and smoke and gleam'
Eithne Farry in *Time Out*

'I was thoroughly amused, stimulated, entertained and instructed by the whole book . . . I don't think I've read anything which has brought 18th-century London so powerfully to life'
Jonathan Coe

CASANOVA

ANDREW MILLER

SCEPTRE

First published in 1998 by Hodder and Stoughton
A division of Hodder Headline PLC
A Sceptre Paperback

10 9 8 7 6 5 4 3

A CIP catalogue record for this book is available
from the British Library

ISBN 0 340 68210 8

Typeset by Palimpsest Book Production Limited,
Polmont, Stirlingshire
Printed and bound in Great Britain by
Clays Ltd, St Ives plc

Hodder and Stoughton
A division of Hodder Headline PLC
338 Euston Road
London NW1 3BH

For PW and DK

No'vel. A small tale, generally of love.

From Samuel Johnson's Dictionary

PART ONE

The door opened: light washed in from the corridor. The figure of a servant unlatched the shutters, folding them back and standing there, rubbing his hands together, looking out over the snow-dusted roofs of Dux. Behind him, the old man in the chair with the dog at his feet stopped his sobbing, his babble, and sniffed at the daylight.

'You have a visitor, *mein Herr*,' said the servant, turning from the window and regarding the old man as though he were looking at a figure in one of Count Waldstein's great tapestries which hung in the draughty halls below, a man of thread, so lank and worn one would not have been amazed to see the back of the chair through his chest.

'A visitor?'

'A "lady", *mein Herr. Sehr schön.*'

Bolder now, for the count was away and Feldkirchner, the major-domo, called the old man a freak, a relict – and cruder names than that – the servant winked, kissed the air and slipped out of the room while the old man, fighting off blankets and gravity, pursued him to the door, fists waving like the horns of a furious snail.

'Pot-washer! Jacobin! Your master will hear of this, you hedge-creeper! . . . And what about a fire, eh? You want me to freeze to death? A pox in your nose!'

But his rage was pointless. He was shouting in Italian, or more precisely in Venetian, and these barbarians did not understand him. For the thousandth time he resolved to learn a selection of the most obscene epithets in German or Czech, the sort of language that went straight through a man's liver like a good Toledo blade. Then perhaps he would have some respect, though of course it was too late for such revolutions, for miracles.

He shook his head and tottered to the window. Smoke crept from a dozen chimneys, and the snow, which had stopped during the night, had begun to fall again, covering the delicate writing of birds' feet on the windowsill and spiralling down into the market square, where against the bodies of the geese the flakes appeared grey. There was a splash of red down there too, where something had been bled.

Today, it seemed, was market day, a feast day too perhaps, for the puppeteers were there with their puppets made of bones and wire, and their old mule that carried them faithfully from Olmutz to Hubertusburg. There was a time when, leaning on a cane, he had liked to go down to see them, for there was something very diverting in their shows. In his honour – he had always been treated kindly by such people – they had performed a marionette version of the *commedia dell'arte* with Dottore and Brighella and Arlecchino and, of course, Captain Spavento, who could not wear a shirt because the hairs on his chest bristled so with indignation. It had made him laugh, but it had made him cry also, idiotic old men's tears thick as amber which he could not stop.

And this was where he must end his days! This Bohemian boneyard, tangling place of the winds – though it was true that on certain days in spring and summer a breeze sprang out of the south-west and for half a day he could taste that other world of flowered balconies, of colonnades in purple shadow, of afternoons so long one could live an entire life in them wrapped in the arms of some beauty, breathing her hair, her breath in warm tresses on his chest . . .

No. It did no good to think of women now, though occasionally he still dreamt of them and when he woke there was a bump in the sheets where a little blood had found its way to his jargonelle. Better the nights when sleep was a mere excision of consciousness, a rehearsal for the death he was no longer hiding from. Dreams, which had once consoled him, now only taunted him.

On the table, among the rubbish there, he discovered the remains of a hard-boiled egg. He examined it and broke off a piece of the gelid white, slipping half into his own mouth and feeding the rest to his fox-terrier bitch, Finette, fondling her ears and slowly, stiffly, bending to kiss the clipped velvet of her skull.

'Did that house-lizard not say we have a visitor?'

The animal gazed at him, not stupidly but as if filled with intel-ligent regret that she could not reply to him other than with sniffs and tail-wags and affectionate growls. The old man shrugged. He was not expecting anyone but people still came, visitors, whose names he did not recognise, could not remember, welcome because they sometimes brought presents – wine, mascarpone cheese, even crayfish which he adored and which the cook made into a soup for him. Then they sat politely, listening to his stories and nodding their heads, prompting him to be indiscreet, though who there was left to be indiscreet about, who of all those he had known still alive to blush, he could not imagine.

He had the whim to put on a good coat. There were still one or two that the moths and the damp had not destroyed. And those papers which gave his room the look of a deranged stationer's office, it was time he tidied them away; the servants would never do it. He wiped his nose on his sleeve and, gratified to have had these thoughts, modest flights of the mind which reminded him that he was still – however tenuously – a citizen of the world, he immediately picked up the papers nearest to him, shuffled them and squinted at the heading on the uppermost.

'THE DUPLICATION OF THE HEXAHEDRON DEMON-STRATED GEOMETRICALLY TO ALL THE UNIVERSITIES AND ALL THE ACADEMIES OF EUROPE.'

Beneath this, in place of the promised monograph, there was a list of his possessions that had gone missing since he had come to this den of magpies to take up the position of castle librarian; and below that, a dozen pages explaining how, with a judicious blend of grifting and arithmetic, one might be sure of winning the state lottery in Rome or Geneva or anywhere – not that he himself ever had much luck with them.

He gathered the papers in his arms like laundry, but rather than stuffing them into one of the drawers or kicking them under the bed – supposing there were any room left there – he carried them to the hearth and dropped them in among the chill of the ashes. Then, striking a spark into the lint of his tinderbox and touching a match to the embers, he ignited them.

WOOMPF!

How hungrily they took the fire! Blue and orange lips swallowing the ink, the pulp, the fine looped hand, the sentiments ('Unico Mio Vero Amico . . .'); the French, the Italian, the black and the red wax. He watched it a moment, half afraid, then went for more fuel: love letters, Latin treatises, appeals for money, for an audience, for a position. Bills of every description, a disproportionate number from tailors and wine merchants. All on to the pyre, blazing up the chimney into the iron skies of Bohemia. He searched in the cupboards, in chests stamped with the Waldstein arms, in the pockets of suits he had not worn in months, in years. Finette, her plum-coloured eyes brilliant with lights, followed him about, intrigued by this new activity. Soon, the room was almost warm and still he uncovered new material to burn. A manuscript entitled 'Delle Passioni'. A creased and yellowed copy of a Gothenburg gazette. An old passport into Catalonia – '*bon pour quinze jours*' – 1768. Remember Nina Bergonza whose mother was also her sister?

Why had he not done this years ago? He felt like those balloonists who threw out bags of sand to send their air boats, their little air gondolas, soaring again. He had himself once planned to fly over the Alps to Trieste and thence to Venice. The thought of drifting in through a sea mist over the Golfo di Venezia and dropping rose petals or dog turds on the inhabitants had quite intoxicated him for a month, but the winds had all been northerlies and everyone had stolen from everyone else and the scheme had failed, as so many others had.

Into the flames he thrust a dozen pages of poetry and the first chapter, the only chapter, of his great *History of the Republic*. Letters from Henriette, letters from Manon Baletti. A libretto intended for the composer of *Don Giovanni*, never delivered. Cryptograms, memoirs, dream diaries. Laundry lists. Recipes for stuffed peppers, for jellied pig's feet. There was no end to it! His life had turned to paper and now he was turning the paper into air, into silky black ashes. Then just as it seemed there could be no more left to burn other than an old newspaper or a limp, elegant banknote from a currency as defunct as the king or emperor printed upon its sides, he found, wedged into the toes of his riding boots – the boots a gift from the nymphomaniac Duchess of Chartres for curing her of her acne – yet another parcel of letters, seven or eight of them, held together with a rust-coloured garter, and these too he was on the point of incinerating when some thrill of unease made him pause and bring the letters up to his nose, that trusty organ, one of the few that had not yet betrayed him. He sniffed, flared the wings of his nostrils and detected, through the overlaying scent of aged and supple leather, a perfume of summer jessamine, so faint, so frail, that at the second sniff – sniff? – the second passionate inhalation, it was gone, like a face in a tobacco cloud.

He tugged the top letter from the grip of the garter, opened it, turned it, his eyes travelling down over the deliberate and girlish hand to the signature at the bottom. A single 'M', tall as a thimble.

Monsieur, you will be glad to know that your parrot was recovered from the roof of a brewer's house in Southwark and that the man made a present of it to his wife, a very large and jolly woman as I understand . . .

He squeezed the parchment in his fist, crushed it. Memory, like a thousand-petal bloom, unfolded. Marie Charpillon, her mother, her aunts, her grandmother (poor woman! May God forgive him!) blew into his brain like luminous pollen, complete, perfectly there, as if he had seen them only an hour before instead of more than thirty years ago. With them came Jarba and the great man-shadow and Goudar. And London, that bruised honeycomb of a town, that voracious city that had chewed him up and spat out his bones. Ah! Such shocks of recollection, how dangerous they were, tugging at the frayed lacing of the heart . . .

Finette whimpered. On frequencies denied to men she heard the footfall of the dead, smelling their spoor of cobweb and grave-dust. For several moments her master had the appearance, the awful stillness, of one of the mummified bodies at the Capuchin church in Palermo. Then he stirred again, shuddered and went to the fireplace, but when his visitor arrived, coming in silently and unannounced, he was still posed irresolutely in the snow-light, the letters seized in his hand.

'Signor Casanova?'

Something in her voice, as if a finger had lightly brushed the hairs at the back of his neck. Slowly, he turned to her.

1

Imagine him now: thirty-eight years of age, big chin, big nose, big eyes in a face of 'African tint', a guardsman's brawny chest and shoulders, stepping down the gangplank in Dover harbour behind the Duke of Bedford, with whom, after a gentlemanly wrangle, he had shared the expense of the voyage from Calais, each of them paying three guineas to the captain of the brig. Servants lugged the men's cases, stacking them on the quayside.

'In-ge-lan! In-ge-lan!'

'England indeed, monsieur,' replied the duke in the faultless French one would have expected from the British envoy to Fontainebleau. 'And may your stay here prove to be an interesting one.'

They stood a moment, settling themselves on *terra firma*, recovering their land-legs, inhaling a breeze of salt and caulking tar and fish guts. A half-naked boy, holding his mongrel by its scruff, stared at them – their stiff coats, tight gloves, their sword hilts glittering in the sunshine – as if they had been lowered out of a cloud on creaking ropes like the heroes of a village pantomime. Casanova stared back; the insolence of wealth at the insolence of poverty. Such children were everywhere, of course, a kind of transient human trash, yet he could never look at them without seeing himself, half-witted son of the dancer Zanetta, running through the *calli*, gaping at red-cloaked senators, at gilded foreigners, at ladies tottering in their jewelled clogs. From his pocket he took a small coin, a scrap of silver, and balancing it on his thumbnail he flicked it to the child. The coin bounced on the cobbles and rolled into a puddle of yesterday's rain. The boy, still staring at the men, felt for it with his fingertips. Casanova turned away. He was determined to have no unpleasant thoughts for as long as he was able.

In the customs house he gave his name as de Seingalt, the Chevalier de Seingalt, a citizen of France. Lies, of course, or something like them, but it pleased him to dream up names for himself; it was also politic. Europe – the parts of it that counted – was a small place, and in his travels he had met at least half the people of influence in the entire continent. 'Casanova' was in too many documents, too many secret reports and in the minds of too many people he would rather not encounter again. As for his being a French citizen, well, he was, in the loosest sense, in the employ of a minister of Louis XV who, during a supper of buttered lobsters and wild doves on a purée of cooked artichoke hearts, had desired Casanova to learn what he could about the English which might be of use to a foreign power – shipping, scandals, disaffected Tories. And since, in addition to this, he was in permanent exile from the Venetian state for corrupting the youth of the Republic; for preferring the playwright Zorzi to Abbé Chiaria in a year when the Red Inquisitor was head of the Chiaria faction; for freemasonry and cabbalism and driving the Countess Lorenza Maddalena Bonafede mad, the description was not, perhaps, without some slender basis in fact. These days everyone was reinventing himself. It was almost expected.

With a moist flourish of the pen he signed 'Seingalt' in the Register of Aliens. The official blotted the ink with sand, leaned back in his chair and smiled, coldly.

'It is just,' he said, 'a formality, monsieur. You are free to pass.'

The Duke's machine was waiting in the street outside the customs house. Casanova, having arranged for his numerous packing cases to follow on the first available wagon, accepted the Duke's offer of a lift into London. It was warmer now. They took off their coats and opened the tops of the windows, just an inch or two or the dust from the road would choke them. His Grace, a very orderly sort of man whom Casanova had never surprised in the Allée des Soupirs at the Palais Royal or in any other of the notorious walks of that notorious area, immediately began a history of the County of Kent from Earliest Times until the Present Day, but Casanova, though nodding his head and occasionally exclaiming politely, heard no more than a few words. He was looking out at the green whorls of English fields and English woods, at the enchanting chalky blue of the English sky, and wondering if this tilled and agreeable little country might not be just the place for a man to revive himself, to shake off those morbid dawn vigils, those nights when it seemed some demonic lapdog crouched on his chest, panting into his face; those lugubrious moods that had troubled him ever since Munich like a cough one could never quite be rid of . . .

Munich! Where every card had been a losing card and that little dancer, La Renaud, had stolen his clothes and his jewels and infected him with a vile disease. Exquisite pain. A fever that had made him roar like a lunatic in a thunderstorm. And what the disease had started the doctors almost finished with their Latin, their drunkenness, their dirty knives. In the end he had saved himself with a strict regimen of milk and water and barley soup. Two and a half months of it. Double vision, tooth-rot. The most terrifying exudations.

In time the wasted muscles had recovered. Walnuts cracked once more between his fingers, and to the casual glance he did not look much altered by the experience. And yet, he wondered, what was the true cost of such a battle? What percentage of a man's deep reserves were consumed by it? It felt sometimes as if the world had closed in on him, the horizon tightening like a tourniquet. He needed peace, a span of quietude in which to find himself again; serenity. I am, he told himself for the third or fourth time that day, in the prime of my life. He found it strange, however, disquieting, that he should need to remind himself of this as often as he did.

They arrived in the West End of London at dusk, parted with expressions of mutual esteem, and as the Duke's carriage glided away into the evening the Chevalier was seized with that delicious vertigo which always followed upon arrival in a strange city with his purse full of gold, that sense of being softly pressed upon by a mysterious abundance. On the subject of cities he considered himself the expert – he who had seen so many – and claimed he could tell everything simply from the pace at which the people walked, the condition of their animals, the number and behaviour of their beggars, the various stinks that constituted the particular and distinctive air of the place, like the nose of a wine or the intimate whiff of a petticoat. London, filtered through the fine inner reticulum of his head, had a smell of damp mortar, of mud, roses, brewer's mash. Of coal-smoke and pastry and dust.

In Soho Square he lounged under the windows of the Venetian residency, long enough – so he hoped – for Zuccato, the Resident, looking down at the traffic of the square, to notice him, alive and tolerably well in London, indifferent to the censure of that distant and longed-for republic.

He puffed out his chest and strolled through the gardens in the centre of the square towards the house opposite. He was calling on an old friend, one with whom, somewhere in the past and under other skies, he had spent some passionate hours: Madame Cornelys – also known as de Trenti and as Rigerboos – widow of the dancer Pompeati, the same Pompeati who had destroyed himself in Venice by ripping up his stomach with a razor.

She received him in the drawing room on the first floor. The lamps had not yet been lit and Casanova could not tell, not until he was close enough to bow over her hand, how kindly or otherwise the years had treated her. She wore a gown and underskirt of dark and lighter blues and on her face a little paint, a little powder. She was still as thin as she had ever been, thin as a boy, but a boy now whose body had been hardened in the kiln of hard living.

They complimented each other. Each remarked how the other had not changed at all. The years had simply passed them by!

How young she looked. How well he seemed, and prosperous too. They laughed. She said the darkness flattered her. Her gaze mirrored his: between them, the reflex of concealment was pointless. Whatever would not be said – and much would not be said – there could be no important secrets.

They walked, arm in arm, and stood at one of the tall windows overlooking the square. With etiquette satisfied they began to speak of old acquaintances, of Marcello and Italo, of Frédéric and François-Marie and Fyodor Mikhailovich. A sombre roll-call of names, of briefly conjured faces, for too many had already fallen victim to the riptides of disaster: sputtering, clutching their throats, their hearts, bleeding in a park at dawn or cleaning a pistol with the barrel in their mouths. Fleetingly, in the guise of melancholy, their old intimacy surfaced. The evening seemed to pull at them, to seduce them with the onset of night. They fell silent. For two or three minutes, as they watched the light receding over the London rooftops, a golden shawl dragged over church spires and chimney pots and patterned by the flight of small birds, the Chevalier entertained the idea of embracing her, of carrying her to the *lit de jour* behind them for the brief consolation of pleasure, the copulatory anodyne. Then clocks chimed and servants came in with lights. The couple at the window stood apart.

She made her money now by throwing parties for the Quality. One great dinner a month for which a two-guinea ticket must be bought in advance. She led him to the banqueting hall, holding up a candelabra to show the expanse of polished table where five hundred guests could all sit down together. She said there was not another like it in the city.

'You must be doing well for yourself, my dear Teresa.'

'I should be,' she answered, looking at him through the candle-tips, 'but everybody robs me. The workmen, the traders, the servants. My receipts last year amounted to twenty-four thousand pounds but I have hardly a penny for myself. What I need' – she turned away – 'is a sharp man to look after my interests.'

Casanova looked the length of the hall. This was his first offer in London and not one to despise, yet he knew immediately that he would not, could not, accept. Her luck was out; he could smell it on her breath. Her gratitude would be of the poisonous variety and in the end he too would cheat her. La Cornelys and her parties – the vileness of which he could readily imagine – were precisely what he had not come to London for.

'I am sure you will find such a man,' he said.

'No doubt,' she answered, as though drawing the nib of her pen through his name, dismissing him.

In the drawing room, where coffee was served in the French manner, Casanova was introduced to Cornelys' daughter. Her name was Sophie, and a quick subtraction of the years – a calculation he had performed on many occasions – showed that he himself might be the girl's author, that a line could be traced from the creaking bed, the shout, the last careless thrust, to this cool-eyed child in her cap and gown. She spoke well in both English and French. She played the piano. She sang. She danced. She was ten years old. He danced with her then covered her face with kisses. It was a wise father who knew his own child. Her skin was as delicate as honeysuckle, and when she stood before his chair they stared into each other's eyes as though trying to see themselves. She would, of course, never know all her brothers and sisters. Most he did not know himself, but he had reached the age where on the main streets of any town from Bruges to Famagusta he imagined that he saw them, casting flirtatious glances at him, smiling at him with his own lips. It should perhaps have reassured him but it made him feel diluted, tugged at.

It was the eleventh day of June 1763.

2

For a fortnight he lived beneath Cornelys' roof, then, no longer able to ignore her reproachful stares, her prattle about the servants, the fear on her skin when she left the house in case she should be seized by her creditors, Casanova rented a residence of his own in Pall Mall at twenty guineas a month. The house had four floors, each with two rooms and a closet. Everything was scrubbed, folded, ready to be lived in. There were carpets, mirrors, china services, a set of silver plate, an excellent kitchen and plenty of good linen. To the rear of the house was a little garden with a brick privy and a pond where a stone Cupid gazed at the lily buds.

He was assisted in his negotiations by a Signor Martinelli whom he had uncovered at the Orange Coffee House opposite the Haymarket Theatre, a resort for rascally Italians where Martinelli, sitting by the window oblivious to the gangs of *vongole* sellers, disgraced *confidenti* and professional husbands, had been correcting a manuscript as though he were in the library at Padua University. For fifteen years he had lived among the English like a learned bedbug, a man full of quiet industry who had, it seemed, weathered the storms of his life and achieved at last that tranquillity Casanova longed for. His latest venture was a new translation of the Decameron for which subscription tickets were a guinea each. Casanova bought a dozen. He had a reverence for writers which he could never quite overcome.

When they had settled business at the house, Martinelli guided the Chevalier across the town to the Royal Exchange on Cheapside. Here, among the hustle, the polyglot babble, the quick clasp of hands, the shaking heads, the clink and sniff of business, the eyes that settled on one's apparel, one's company, measuring, assessing, marking down in the ledgers of memory one's particular face and estimated fiscal mass, Casanova acquired a servant, a young educated black man with shrewd polite eyes, a forehead of licked coal, a slender, somewhat female presence in a suit of brown fustian and a scarf, a crimson scarf, like a flame at his throat.

'Your name?'

'I am called Jarba.'

'You speak Italian?'

'When I was a boy, signore, I lived in the house of an olive merchant in Palermo.'

'And the French tongue?'

'Yes, monsieur. In Bordeaux I was for five years footman to the wife of a lawyer.'

'No doubt you also speak good English.'

'Indeed, sir, I do, for I served as valet to an English sea captain and went to sea with him and every night read to him from his Bible.'

'What became of your sea captain, Jarba?'

'He died.'

'In his bed?'

'He drowned.'

'Then I should like to hear the circumstances.'

'We were bound for the Guinea Coast, monsieur, with a cargo of glass and brass wire and cloth. Storms blew us far into the west and then the winds deserted us and we drifted for many days. There was sickness. The men were too weak to pull the ship from the boats. We shot cannon to wake the wind and my master prayed in his cabin but the wind did not come back. Some said it was because our trade was evil. Some said the captain was cursed. There were strange lights, monsieur. The sailors saw sea beasts with human faces and ghost ships with crews of weeping men. One morning when the sea was like oil the captain called me to his cabin. He blessed me, gave me his spyglass to remember him, then went on to the deck, climbed the rail and dived into the sea. He did not come to the surface again.'

'You tried to stop him?'

'He did not wish us to stop him.'

'He was insane?'

Jarba shrugged.

'What age was this unfortunate man?'

'Of about the same age as Monsieur.'

Jarba was hired and found for his new employer a French cook who was stood in the atomic bustle of the crowd with his pans and ladles, claiming, for anyone who would hear it, that he had once cooked a chicken fricassee for the Queen of France.

Now, considered Casanova, travelling home behind the damask curtain of a sedan chair, the house keys in his pocket, I have burrowed into the city. I can live and dine like a gentleman. Everything is good. The world is good. He wished however that he could somehow unremember Jarba's captain, for he was afraid that he would dream of him, of his long swim to the floor of the ocean. He was afraid that he would begin to admire him.

3

Despite once spending ninety-seven days in solitary confinement in the prison of the Doge of Venice, solitude was not an art that Casanova had ever mastered. Alone, shifting around the pretty rooms of his house, he found himself engaged by voices that spoke to him in muffled, insistent tones, as though he had inside his head a dozen hooded men on a scaffold, confessing, accusing ... And how hard it was to see this great city all around him like an unopened present! Who were these people who strolled outside his door, who drove in their carriages through the gates of the grand houses opposite? The lure of good company, of any company, was too hard to resist. He held out for a week, then gave in, his resolve shattering like a pane of sugar-glass. La Cornelys provided the introductions, grudgingly at first, as if he might somehow steal these people from her for her precious list of names was her true collateral, but in the end, with a blink and a sigh, she scrawled the necessary letters and Casanova, not without some nagging sense of cheating on himself, began to make the acquaintance of the town.

In drawing rooms, casinos and opera boxes, the married women studied him as though he were a moth looping around the light of their lamps. Their daughters, high-coloured, obsessed with caste, looked at him as a cat looks at a spider. The old men talked of law, of ancestors and of the cost of their mistresses. The young men, droll and vicious, went to the inns with him for oysters and champagne. Only violence seemed to soothe them, these illustrious boys, violence and gambling, though they were all poets, had all visited the Colosseum in Rome. Many had even been in the Serenissima, but Casanova could not quite consider them to be civilised.

In spite of this, or because he was charmed by their restlessness, their cruelty, the imbalance in them engendered by the times or the breeding habits of their elders, one of these young men, Lord Pembroke, became a kind of friend. His lordship was rich, fashionable and handsome. He had himself shaved three times a day so that his consorts – he could not, he claimed, bear to see the same woman two days in a row – were never scratched by his beard.

One sultry dusk at the end of June, his lordship called at Pall Mall to admire Casanova's new house. The Chevalier had been sitting reading by the light of the sunset, crossing and uncrossing his long legs, twisting in his seat. The little book on his lap, open like some mysterious leathery-skinned fruit with a delicate musty pulp (and how often he wanted to eat books, to devour them physically!) was Ovid's *Metamorphoses*. The moment before the bell rang he had come to the story of Peleus's pursuit of the sea nymph Thetis, and how, in the bay of Haemonia, he had wound his arms about her and clung to her as she changed into a bird, into a tree, and finally into a spotted tigress, at which point the hero, out-raped, fled along the beach, his lips bloody with splinters, his mouth choked with fur and feathers . . .

'Seingalt,' said the young lord, circling the room with a glass in his hand and looking as cool as if he wore a suit of dock leaves, 'you have done very well for yourself here.'

'I trust your lordship will do me the honour soon of testing the skill of my cook?'

'With the greatest pleasure. But tell me, are you not lonely?'

'Lonely, my lord? Why should I be lonely?'

He opened his mouth as if to laugh at the idea, but it was no good. Despite the people he had met – and meeting people was never the cure – he was, he realised, at that particular instant, as lonely as he had ever been in his life. But had he begun to look lonely? He had a horror of that. He could not bear the thought that Pembroke might have seen so easily through his social poise. He gathered himself, and in a voice he hoped would suggest some enigmatic largeness of soul, a profound indifference to the needs of more ordinary men, he said, 'I intend to spend my days surveying the town and my evenings reading.'

His lordship made a face. 'I did not take you for a reader, Seingalt. Reading is for those who have neither the wit nor the money to enjoy themselves in other ways. What of girls?'

'Girls, my lord?'

'Have you had much success? I will give you tickets and you may send out for them.'

'They will come to my house?'

'Of course.'

'That would be . . . most convenient.'

Why not? Nothing weakened a man more than abstinence. In this manner he could satisfy his curiosity as to what the women of the place kept beneath their aprons without having to endure the conceit of some baronet's daughter who would squint at him over the top of her newspaper as though he were a house painter. Sending out was no doubt the modus operandi of the future. It would suit him perfectly.

His lordship, supplied by Casanova with the necessary implements, wrote out the tickets. A girl's name, where she might be found, her price. Some were four guineas, some were six. One was twelve.

'Who is this one, my lord?'

'She is the mistress of a man who owns a silk-throwing mill in Derby, but he makes use of her only once a month.'

'I see,' said Casanova, distracted by a great topaz-coloured fly squatting on the young man's sleeve, which, until it crawled, he had taken for a jewel.

'In this city,' said Pembroke, 'everything is easy for a man who has money and is not afraid to spend it. Remember that, Seingalt.'

The Chevalier bowed.

Next evening, as the clocks with their tiny hammers chipped away at the hour, Casanova dropped his book on to the floor, took one of Lord Pembroke's tickets and sent Jarba out to bring back the girl. He waited for them at the window, thinking how happy he would be if instead of this stony northern street with its population of strangers, he saw on the other side of the glass the moonlight swarming on the Grand Canal, and the prow of a gondola, like a man praying, parting the patchwork water, curving towards the steps of his house . . .

The girl, when she arrived, was not a girl at all but a woman who, by the skin of her hands and neck, was several years the Chevalier's senior. She had kept herself tolerable with ceruse, chalk dust, kohl and mastic (much as he himself had done). She had neither the French nor the Italian tongue. He peeled her a pear, fed it to her. She began to cry. She was crying and eating the pear and talking all at the same time. 'What is she saying?' asked Casanova.

'She says,' answered Jarba, polishing a glass, 'that the gentleman reminds her of her mother.'

The next was brought. She supped with the Chevalier. She spoke some words of French. She had once had a friend. From France.

'Where in France, my dear?'

'Yes, monsieur. From France.'

He kissed her wrists. She asked: 'What will you give me at dessert, monsieur?'

When they had finished their food she perched on his knee, stroked the end of his nose and spoke a whore's baby-babble, baby-croon. Her trade had killed the sex in her. She stank of boarding houses, of bad dreams. Casanova nodded over her shoulder to Jarba. Jarba showed her into the street.

The twelve-guinea girl pleased him least of all. She had the face of one corrupted in childhood. Her smile was charming but in five years the weevils of vice would have hollowed her out entirely. He toyed with her yet he was afraid of her, of what they shared, their

– so it struck him – almost incestuous connection. He counted out her money. She clipped on her earrings and dropped her fee into her purse. She enquired if the gentleman would like the names of some accommodating boys.

'Boys,' said the Chevalier, 'I only eat in season.'

They stared at each other a moment. She said: '*Bonne chance, monsieur.*'

'*Vous aussi,* mam'zel. *Vous aussi.*' Though luck, as they both knew, would not be enough.

4

No more ticket-girls. With them one got precisely what one expected, precisely what one did not wish to get. The happy ones were deranged and the sadness of the others was too infectious for a man of any intelligence to stand it, even briefly. One could go to them only by taking into one's heart a kind of determined brutishness, or by drinking oneself to the necessary pitch of dullness. He had been a fool to accept Pembroke's offer. Better to sort these things out for himself.

He decided to advertise.

'SECOND OR THIRD FLOOR TO BE LET, FURNISHED, TO A YOUNG LADY SPEAKING ENGLISH AND FRENCH, WHO RECEIVES NO VISITORS EITHER BY DAY OR NIGHT.'

Jarba translated, and the notice, written out in large letters, was placed in the parlour window. Later, it appeared in the *Gazetteer and London Daily Advertiser*, 5 July 1763.

In the first week there were ninety-two applicants. Runaway wives, courtesans, mad women, and girls newly arrived on hay wagons from the shires, who, by some miracle, had not yet fallen into the hands of the pimps and bagnio scouts. With Jarba and Mrs Feaver, his cronish housekeeper, Casanova interviewed them in the dining room. The auditions were conducted in French and this immediately eliminated a great number. Others were rejected for being too brazen or too shy. He was most pleased with those who showed the greatest ingenuity in their attempts to deceive him; he knew well enough what it was to play a part, to live on nothing but words, but none of them was the creature he had in mind. Soon, what had seemed such a delightful idea began to stale. When the doorbell jangled he groaned, and when they came into the room he did not wish to meet their eyes. He was glad when the flood slowed to a trickle, when at last the river dried up entirely.

'It appears,' he said to Jarba one evening whilst Jarba enter tained him by making a bestiary of shadows on the parlour wall with his hands and a candle, 'that this advertisement has served only to make me ridiculous. I am sure the whole town is laughing. Do you not think I should have chosen the very first who came?'

'Or the very next,' replied Jarba, tilting his head towards the partly open window through which, suspended in the summer-night air, came the sound of light feet approaching the front door.

She was in her early twenties, dressed in a gown of pink silk. Her hair, the palest lemon-gold, was plaited and gathered into a soft knot on the crown where it was trimmed with a white feather pompom. Her face was very pale, her eyes too; pale grey on pale blue. She was hard at first to really see; one had to look at her then clench the gaze. In truth, one had to stare at her. Jarba brought in a bowl of oranges. She peeled her fruit skilfully, a continuous coil of pith and rind. She said two shillings a week was all she could spend. That, replied Casanova, was precisely the sum he had in mind.

'On Sundays,' she said, 'I go to the chapel of the Bavarian ambassador.'

She said: 'Pray, do not introduce me to anyone.'

She paid for a week in advance and as she took her leave the Chevalier said:

'You will dine with me now and then? It is terrible to dine alone. And you will save money.'

She moved in. She had few possessions: a dozen gowns, an ivory chess set (on which she played with great skill, checkmating the Chevalier in four moves); a volume of Milton in English, Ariosto in Italian and La Bruyère's *Characters* in French. Her name was Pauline, a Portuguese whose life story took several days to tell, for it was full of complications, of cruel uncles, lost fortunes and storms at sea. Casanova, with a fatherly, a priestly inclination of his head, listened patiently, particularly to the history of her romance with the Count A who, for reasons never entirely apparent, had visited her every day in her father's house in Lisbon disguised as a lace seller. The recollection made her blush. Casanova understood her completely. She was the healthy kind of hysteric and her pleasure would lie in the scandalised witness of her own seduction. Her sisters were all successful nuns, prim ecstatics, and she herself would have done well in the cloisters, St John of the Cross floating over her cot at night, a cicisbeo in a hair shirt.

He read to her from Ariosto, the adventures of Ricciardetto and Fiodespina. He wondered if he were falling for her: he told himself that he was. How long, how many years since such liaisons had been more than a game, an itch, a kind of false money? They ate together, paid each other extravagant compliments. They had their portraits made by the most fashionable painter of miniatures in London. Sophie was invited to Pall Mall and the three of them played at families. The child was biddable. For the price of a yard of ribbon she called Pauline 'Mama' and was petted for it. It was all extremely amusing. A grand affair. In his dreams he hauled coal sacks on his back but dreams were forgotten by breakfast-time. Why should he not be happy? His Portuguese was an angel, perfect in every respect, though it was true she had the most exasperating way of chewing her food. She ate a peach as though it were the Host. She would not undress in front of him. She was worried about the servants. 'Monsieur,' said the Chevalier, mimicking her speech in the mirror, 'even love has its rules of decency.'

By the time they attended Mass together in Warwick Street for the second time, he had forgotten her story. It had collapsed in his head, quite suddenly, like a house of cards, so that when, during their afternoon amours, the sun creeping away from their bed like an aged servant, she mentioned her grandfather or a certain Brazilian princess or the Marchioness X, he solemnly nodded without the least recollection of who they were, nor could he quite be bothered to ask. Sometimes he thought he would prefer it if her life had been farcical. Her pale smiles, the smugness of her suffering, began to exasperate him. Who would console him? Had he not also suffered? Did she think it was easy being Casanova? He would have given a hundred guineas for a really good Venetian joke. He had not laughed in weeks.

It ended in August. A letter arrived from one of the personae of her interminable story with a cheque for twenty million Portuguese reis and an assurance that she would be free to marry Count A upon her return to Lisbon. Martinelli, using one of those useful English newspapers that offered such things, helped her to choose a good second-hand carriage, and the Chevalier accompanied her as far as Calais, genuinely fond of her now that she was leaving. In the Place d'Armes, sheltering from a sharp salt rain that lent them all the tears they needed, he kissed her one last time, technically excellent, and waved adieu with his handkerchief.

He had expected to feel a certain relief. Instead, almost immediately, he missed her, missed the distraction of not liking her much. It had been an occupation of sorts and now he was back to before, sitting with his make-up smudged, waiting for the next performance.

In an inn on the harbour front he drank for an hour and then took ship on the night tide for Dover. On this voyage, for the payment of five sols, he danced the blanket hornpipe with the captain's daughter. She said she was fifteen years old and that she was already tired of the sea.

'So the letters, signore, those you could not burn, were not from your Portuguese.'

He shook his head. Whatever part of the human mechanism it was that registered the passing of time, it had ceased in his own brain to function. Had he been asleep? His visitor was sitting in the chair opposite him so that when he looked at her he saw the table, the door, the fireplace, the window. Then, of course, he realised that he must have been asleep for there was a fire now, not of paper but of logs, and on the table – which had at last been swept of its clutter – a candle the length and thickness of a baby's arm filled the room with the expensive, ecclesiastic scent of good wax.

'Signora, you will excuse an old man . . .'

Had she told him her name? Did he know her? The style of her dress seemed somewhat old-fashioned and the veil she was wearing, with its fringe just below the line of her eyes, was a genuine Venetain *zendale*. Perhaps she was a fellow citizen, an exile like himself. He tried to guess her age: twenty-five? Forty? No ordinary woman, that much was certain. Could she be the princess who had given Finette to him when poor Melampyge died?

'The authoress of these letters, signora, was a woman who had taken in a hatred of the male sex with her mother's milk. The day I first met her – he smiled – 'was the unluckiest day of my life. It was September, signora. The first cold evenings had come. Jarba lit the fires. Without Pauline I was content to let time pass idly and hardly went outside my door other than to take the air in the park or drink chocolate with Martinelli. If a man could content himself with such a life, what trouble he might avoid! But soon, like a bored child, I was casting about for some diversion, some adventure, and in that mood I was stopped in the street by a certain Malingan, a Flemish officer I had once helped in Aix-la-Chapelle. I am sure, signora, you have noticed how all attachments are stronger upon one side than upon the other, all relations unequal. I did not care for this Malingan yet he appeared to think well of me. Already, on several occasions, he had asked me to dine with him but I had always found some excuse to refuse. Now, sickening again of my own company, I accepted, and on the following evening I visited his house. The other guests, foreigners like myself for the most part, all of them with some complaint against the world, were not brilliant people, they could not dazzle. As soon as we had eaten I decided to take my leave, but as I stood up from the table I saw Malingan by the door talking with a young woman who, feeling my eyes upon her, turned to me and smiled. Signora, there are not many such smiles in the world, and I knew I could not leave that house without discovering this beauty's name, but as I walked towards her, I was certain that we had met before . . .'

5

'Allow me to present,' said Malingan, 'Monsieur Cas . . .'

'Seingalt,' interrupted Casanova, 'the Chevalier de Seingalt. But there is no need to introduce us as we have already met. Is that not so, mam'zel?'

'Indeed, monsieur. In Paris. You sat me on your knee and were good enough to kiss me.'

'You were a child then, or I should not have dared be so familiar.'

'I was thirteen.'

'And now?'

'I am eighteen.'

'No longer a child.'

'No, monsieur.'

'I am flattered, mam'zel, that you have remembered me.'

She laughed. How could she forget the famous— 'What name is it you use now, monsieur?'

'Seingalt. A man may have more names than one, mam'zel.'

'A woman likewise,' said the Charpillon, the wing of her fan unfurling stickily.

'I recall,' said Casanova, 'that you were Boulainvilliers in Paris. Or was it Augspurgher?'

'Augspurgher is my mother's name.'

'She is in London with you? She is well?'

'She is well, monsieur.'

'And your aunts?'

'They too.'

'May I ask where you are living?'

'We have a house in Denmark Street, near to the church of St Giles. Is the Chevalier thinking of visiting?'

'Is mam'zel inviting me to?'

Malingan had left them together. Casanova bathed the girl in the hazel lustre of his gaze.

'I have heard,' said the Charpillon, 'that you were the gentleman who placed a certain notice in his window.'

'I am not ashamed of it.'

'They say the joke cost you dearly.'

'They are wrong.'

'The rooms are now free? I should like to take them for myself.'

'Your mother would approve?'

'No, monsieur, she would not. But I would like to punish the author of such a notice.'

'He committed no crime.'

'He offended against my sex, monsieur. He was laughing at us.'

'Mam'zel, I assure you I was innocent of any such intent. And you must remember that I was a stranger here. A condition I was concerned to prolong for as long as possible. Tell me, though, how would you punish . . . this unfortunate author?'

'By making him fall in love with me, and then torturing him.'

'Your plan is monstrous, mam'zel! But are you so convinced of your charms?'

'You know the saying, monsieur: "Some dogs like to be bitten"?'

'I have heard it, though not from a mouth as young or as pretty as yours. For the honour of my kind I should like to prove you wrong.'

'What is your "kind", monsieur?'

'What is yours, mam'zel?'

She laughed. 'You may find that for yourself, if you know how to look.'

They were both smiling now, tightly, like strangers on the brink of an intimacy or friends on the verge of some unpleasantness. Casanova took the rose from the lapel of his coat, a blood-red rose which he had cut that morning in his garden at Pall Mall.

'Beauty,' he said, carefully snapping off the thorns, 'is the natural compliment of beauty. Please . . .'

She took the flower, turned it in her gloved fingers. 'Monsieur,' she said, 'I feel I have known you all my life.'

6

'Augspurgher!'

He spoke the name aloud as he journeyed home and chuckled to himself so that a whelk-seller and a baker's boy in conversation on the edge of Great Sheer Lane looked round at him and scowled. What did it matter? Had he not just met a ravishing young woman, a beauty with an edge of wildness to her? And had they not already talked almost like lovers? And did the girl's mother not owe him six thousand francs?

Immediately he was home he rifled through the papers he kept in a large green leather attaché case and after a few minutes of searching uncovered the bills of exchange, scrolled documents threaded with the deadly Latin of the law and stamped with a seal as thick as a man's boot-sole. The debt had been incurred four years ago in Paris: a matter involving some jewellery and a crooked Genevan named Bolome. He would only need to swear before a magistrate to the bills' authenticity to have the whole family flung into a sponging house!

Knowing that the Augspurghers of the world always kept one case packed and ready for hasty departures, he set out on his visit the following afternoon, not wanting to find the house empty, or perhaps already inhabited by some quite different, more innocent family. It was not far from Pall Mall but twice he became lost in the tangle of courts and alleys around Soho Square and found himself unexpectedly re-entering the square from a different direction. He reached the house at five o'clock, the short narrow street half in shadow, half in sun.

In the front room he kissed the air above Madame Augspurgher's hand.

'Such a small world, monsieur . . . Chevalier.'

'Indeed, madame, no bigger than a marble.'

They sat, they spoke in French, the kettle twitched on the fire. The Charpillon's two aunts were present; thin, long-skulled women, side by side at the table like twin guardians of the door of death in an Egyptian funerary mural. One of them took a key from around her neck and unlocked the tea caddy. Their servant, a child still, graceless and mad-looking, brought in the tea dishes and sugar. The evening leaned against the window panes. There was a wasp in the room. They can smell the sugar, said the mother. How does Monsieur like London? Is it not very smoky? How long does Monsieur intend to stay? As long as that? Then we hope he shall not be a stranger.

Casanova stroked the sleeve of his coat. It was the cream coat with the twining silver vine leaves. He plucked a thread, and while he chattered with the women, now answering an aunt, now the mother, now, for form's sake, addressing a remark to the grandmother who had been led in by the servant girl and deposited on a chair from which her feet dangled several inches above the carpet, he took in the fragile economy of this house of women; the care with which Aunt One measured the tea into the pot, the way Aunt Two counted the nuggets of coal the maid dropped with tongs on to the fire; the genteel but pared-down appearance of things, of the women themselves, for the older women looked the types who now and then starved for a week to secure some luxury for the young nymph in their care.

The cards came out. They played whist. Casanova, sitting with his back to the door, lost gracefully. Indeed he was prepared to lose heavily – though naturally they were playing for trifles, small change – in order to sit across the table from the Charpillon and watch the sea-swell of her bosom, the candlelight catching the gloss of her eyes; but as they finished the last rubber and the pennies and shillings were divided between the winning players, he was alerted by an interplay of glances at the table and turned to see three men, all of them armed, lolling in at the doorway.

One he recognised instantly: Ange Goudar, a professional gambler sometimes known as 'The Chinese Spy', a name under which he wrote scandal for the papers. The other men, who looked like brawlers, like paid witnesses, were introduced as Rostaing and Cauman.

Casanova stood up slowly, bowed. How long had they been there, entertaining themselves with their eavesdropping? Their presence was no accident. Doubtless they had been summoned by the Charpillon's mother as soon as she had known her old creditor was at her heels. He sat again, sniffed, feigned indifference, though he could feel his face flushed with anger. How dare these spindle-flies, these gutter-eels, try to frighten him? And anger with himself for letting his guard down. Had he learnt nothing in all his adventures? Did he not already have the clearest proof of what manner of people the Augspurghers were? He filled his cold tea with expensive sugar, swallowed it and shuffled the cards.

'A hand of piquet? Perhaps your friends would care to join us?'

The Charpillon alone had the grace to look embarrassed.

7

He did not go straight home but walked at thinking pace past lamplit shops and taverns. The whole visit had unsettled him. He had the feeling that he, who should have had the upper hand, had been, in these opening moves, thoroughly bested. It was very . . . something. He wished Martinelli were with him, or Jarba.

He paused, watching a cortège go past, the hearse dressed and plumed in white to denote that the corpse it carried was a maid. A woman walking behind the draped coffin suddenly glared at him so fiercely he was afraid she would shout some denunciation, but then he saw that she looked at everyone with the same wild stare and that her grief had unhinged her. He would have liked to comfort her but the procession, which left in its wake little ripples of disquiet and relief, shuffled down one of the side streets, its slowness a last gift of luxury for the sleeper in their midst.

Looking round, he found himself by the church of St Anne's and he went in, kneeling in a pew at the back and mumbling a rapid paternoster. Heaven, hell; the universal smell of churches. Heaven he could not imagine at all, only that he was unlikely to know anybody there. As for hell, where would Dante have placed him? In the second circle where those who have committed the sins of the leopard are tossed for ever upon a howling wind like starlings in winter? Or would he sink deeper, into that basal region below the wood of suicides inhabited by panderers, seducers, sorcerers and hypocrites, all of which he had been at one time or another? Sometimes he envisaged a hell tailor-made, as all hells should be, in which he rattled from city to city, from lodging house to palace, living out of cases, pursuing women, pursuing money; never at peace, never still, never able to put his feet under the table and say 'This is Home'. An eternity of faro games and lewd outings, of lecherous old ladies, jealous husbands, of vermin and insatiable sisters.

He rested his brow against the sour, prayed-into wood. He was not used to London yet. The city was always surprising him, making him walk with his head turned, startling at some novelty. The dogs, even the pigeons, seemed to know that he did not belong. The rules here – as Martinelli had warned him – were unlike those anywhere else in the world, so that one must constantly be on one's guard and grin like a halfwit. If a nation were measured by its contradictions then the minister must be warned – England was vast! Only yesterday, on his way to Malingan's, he had come upon a group of men, well dressed, standing around a fallen boxer whose face had been reduced to stewing steak, scrag-end. No one had been permitted to help this wretch as two of those who stood about – breezily in their good coats – had a bet on the fellow's survival and would brook no interference that might affect the outcome. Yet if a man thrashed his horse in the street he was condemned by all and called un-Christian. Every man felt free to criticise the government in terms that would ensure his arrest in Venice, and yet the great lords here had more power than any in Europe. Foreigners were hated and Jew-baiting worse even than in the territories of Germany, but London was full of exiles who thrived in all manner of business. He himself had made the acquaintance of a score of Englishmen, had been charmed by them, yet did not know what one of them thought of him in their hearts, nor what they said of him at their dinner tables.

He looked up. An old priest was shuffling down the nave towards him, his white head seeming to float above the black of his coat. Casanova crossed himself, rose from his knees and walked heavily into the night.

8

In his chamber he unlatched the shutters and looked out. A gentleman and his lady, somebody's lady, were coming from the direction of the Royal Opera House on the corner of the Haymarket. A boy with a flaming torch walked ahead of them. It was too early for the night-soil men.

Softly, the Chevalier whistled tunes between his teeth. Folk songs, ditties learnt in boyhood from his mother or perhaps – for Zanetta's visits had been like snow in Salerno – he had learnt them from someone else, possibly Bettina, Dr Gozzi's younger sister, who had liked to sing to him and who, at Padua, when he was eleven years of age, had woken the old Adam in him at bath-time, and later, as a kind of love token, had passed to him the smallpox so that for a week his face had bubbled like milk in a pan. He still possessed the marks, the physical memory; shallow grey scars which he dusted with powder but could never quite conceal.

He stripped off, pulled on his nightshirt, night-socks, nightcap, puffed the candle out, pulled up the sheets.

The Charpillon appeared like smoke in the dense black above the bed. Her chestnut hair, astonishingly long and thick, her blue eyes languorous and brilliant, her hands white and biteably plump. Her skin was slightly flushed as if she spent her nights naked in a pit of rose petals like a Carthaginian princess. And those earlobes! Little satchels of pink and silver . . . For a moment her hair seemed to pulse around her head as though she were lying face down in the water and he saw her from below. He teetered at the edge of sleep, the mirage faded. Then suddenly he was alert again, leaning on an elbow, his ear cocked to the night.

From the other side of the street he heard the sound of a window being slid open on its sashes and then a man's voice calling clearly – though for Casanova, incomprehensibly – a single short refrain that rang out in the suttled night-time of the town like coins falling on to paving stones. He waited, wondering if there would be some answering call, but none came, and after a while he heard the window close again.

She was there when he woke, no apparition now but flesh and bustle and laughter. Jarba was standing at the door with eyes a hundred years old.

'I have come for breakfast,' she said, 'with my aunt. We have a business matter to discuss. Are you awake, monsieur?' She blew on his face, a breath of coffee and youth.

'I believe,' replied Casanova, 'that I may still be dreaming.'

He caught her wrist, pulled her down. Why not get it over with now? Jarba could watch, indeed, he could join them if he wished, but the Charpillon, still smiling, and showing in her movement the skill and timing of a fencing master, struck the Chevalier across the bridge of his nose with the blade of her fan, not hard enough to break either nose or fan, yet with enough force to flood his eyes with tears.

'*Malora!* Are you mad?'

'Only with hunger, monsieur. Do you have eggs? Cold meats? Fruit?'

Jarba brought a clean handkerchief from the handkerchief drawer and Casanova wiped his eyes.

'Take care of our visitor, Jarba. Anything she wants. Turtle eggs, wild boar, stewed pomegranates. What is the point of having wealth if one cannot give a young lady what she wishes for her breakfast?'

The Charpillon went out with Jarba. Casanova called after them: 'What is this business matter?' then clambered from his bed and padded to the washstand, saying: 'As if I did not know.' His hands, ringless at this hour, mute, drew up the steaming water to his face.

The table was laid for breakfast. Good things were brought in. The women seemed genuinely hungry and the toasting fork began to glow. Still dishabille – for what gentleman dressed before breakfast, before noon? – Casanova admired the Charpillon's buttery fingertips, the way she licked the crumbs from her lips, and when at last they were done he leaned forward with his napkin and wiped a spot of grease from her chin. She offered her face, very prettily.

'Now,' he said, 'we may talk. Be quite frank, I beg you.'

'My dear Chevalier de Seingalt,' began Aunt One 'I wish to discuss with you – seeing how we are already friends, and old friends too, is that not so, Marie? – a remarkable elixir which we call the Balm of Life. Monsieur may even have heard of it. I assure you that everywhere it is known it is spoken of as a wonder. My sisters and I learnt the recipe many years ago and we lived very well by it in Franche-Comté. It has such a delicate flavour and such power to restore even those the physicians have despaired of that one cannot make enough of it.'

She stopped and smiled at him. He waved his hand for her to continue.

'The only difficulty, monsieur, is that one needs to purchase many ingredients – rose jelly, saffron, powdered horn, seahorses – the Chevalier has no idea how many things. Then there are the bottles, the corks, the labels . . . A considerable outlay, monsieur.'

'Madame, I comprehend it exactly. What is the extent of this outlay, in round figures?'

'Monsieur's directness does us honour, I am sure, does it not, Marie? But you must not expect a woman to be a sensible judge of such matters. However, I am advised that an investment of one hundred guineas would meet every expense.'

'Pray, madame, who is your kindly adviser?'

'He is a gentleman monsieur is well acquainted with: the Chevalier Goudar.'

'Goudar? Of course. One's affairs are always in safe hands with Goudar. And if I made such an investment and the balm – your elixir – were manufactured, doubtless we would all be rich beyond our dreams. Is that it, madame?'

The aunt tugged gently on her lappets. She had an odd, coy, girlish expression on her face.

'I shall give my decision this evening,' said Casanova. He turned to the Charpillon. 'Your niece shall hear it when she visits me.'

The aunt smiled. 'I shall send her, monsieur. After all, it is her future I am thinking of.'

'I too, madame.'

The company stood.

9

The Charpillon returned after dark. Casanova watched her pay off the chairmen, the top of her head only reaching to the middle of their chests. Though they had not come far and their burden had been a light one the men were steaming like cattle. She put coins into the palms of their hands then turned towards the house and the cardano lamp Jarba had hung outside the front door. As she mounted the steps she glanced to the window and the Chevalier stepped back into the room. Behind him, at a table in the middle of the parlour, four men were playing cards, familiars of the international demi-monde from whom, even in London, Casanova could not entirely escape. Men with whom he had attended bacchanalias or shared a prison cell or taken money from at the faro table. Eaters of other mens' suppers. These, and a hundred like them from here to Tashkent, were the remnants of those sharps and charming pranksters he had run with in his youth. It was hard to recognise them now: lean, cynical men with bad skin, loyal as snakes. Their sole virtue a certain grim bravado.

Jarba announced the Charpillon. When she entered the room the men suspended their game. They pushed back their seats, stood, bowed amorously. She was wearing a dress of shot silk, a cap with a white feather, and a long red cloak of the kind called 'Capuchin' on account of its deep hood. The men cruised her with their gaze: Casanova wanted to stamp his feet, to throw the china figurines at them, but he knew they could not help themselves. Her nature drew nature after it. Just the kind of girl, the kind of beauty, a god would hide himself in a swan for.

'My dear Marie.'

'Chevalier.'

He took her hand, kissing it, touching it quickly with the point of his tongue.

'Come with me into the next room. We shall discuss your aunt's business. Everything is prepared.'

As he closed the door behind them he heard one of the card players say: 'Aunt's business'! I have not heard it called that before.'

When they were alone, standing together in the mouth of the room, he surveyed, with an inward nod of satisfaction, the scene he had that afternoon created. The only light came from the fire and a two-branched candelabrum on the mantelpiece. The shutters were shut, the little garden hidden from sight. On one of those delicate English tables with legs like a greyhound stood a bottle of champagne and two flutes of greeny glass. The cork softly punched the palm of his hand (he recalled his first time, the cork striking his intended between the eyes like a bullet), the wine gasped, a rope of silver bubbles turned to gold in the glasses. They sipped, she simpered. A sticky, venerous dew was forming on his fingertips.

On the table beside the bottle were some papers, an impressive-looking quill, a horn of ink and a stick of crimson sealing wax. On the top sheet of paper he had written:

THE BALM OF LIFE

in the neat script he had learned as a youth in the law offices of Giovanni Manzoni in Venice. Beneath were several paragraphs from yesterday's *Whitehall Evening Post* which had, to his uncomprehending eye, a sufficiently proper look to them but which, for all he knew, could be some scandalous story, or even editorial guidance on how to avoid the Influenza, the new disease from Italy. He believed that the Charpillon would be as little able to read it, this marriage of cook's Latin and low German, as he was himself, and the dimness of the room did not invite scrutiny. He tidied the papers, let her have a glimpse of them, of his signature in large letters on the bottom of the last page, then led her by her wrists down into the nest of cushions on the settle. He hardly knew where to start with her. He reached for her hand, guiding it – not too suddenly – from her lap into his own, then, leaning forward, he kissed the tenderness where her jaw and neck met in the delta beneath her ear.

She bore it a moment, then shrugged him off and walked to the fire, her face darkened by a blush he could not read. Modesty? Anger? Desire? For half a minute neither of them spoke. She had struck an attitude; it was his duty now to regard it. In the silence he could hear the faint flick, flick of the cards in the adjoining room.

She said: 'I hope, monsieur, you will be able to satisfy my aunt.'

'I was hoping, Marie' – what else could he say? – 'we might satisfy each other first.'

'Monsieur?'

'You will not find it tedious, my dear.' He reached out a hand to her but she did not move.

'I am afraid, monsieur . . .'

'Afraid?'

'That there has been a misunderstanding.'

'I promise you, Marie, your aunt understood perfectly.'

'Monsieur, a niece may be innocent of the understanding of her aunts.'

'It would be charming, my dear, to think so.'

'Aunts are such worldly women, monsieur.'

'And yours in particular, Marie. I am sure you are aware that they – and your mother – owe me a sum of money. Six thousand francs, to be precise. Two hundred and fifty pounds in sterling. I have the bills with their signatures upstairs.'

She was gazing into the fire, one hand resting on the mantel-piece, one finger describing little circles on the wood. She said: 'Monsieur, you are not talking to the point.'

'The "point"?'

'The money is for the Balm, monsieur.'

'The money, Marie, the guineas that your aunt requires, they are for you. They are . . .'

'A present?'

'Precisely. In return for certain favours, of course.'

'But a present is surely given freely or not at all.'

'Marie, one gives to those who have made one happy.'

'And I have made you happy? It does you honour that you are made happy by the opportunity to help a family of poor women.'

In the fire's glow she looked almost noble; Joan of Arc defying the English at Rouen. Had he misjudged her? After all, he knew almost nothing about her save that she was young, disturbingly pretty, and that her mother owed him money. Was this resistance of hers, this verbosity, this refusal to play along, to own the part that circumstance had clearly ascribed to her, was it the art of a coquette or the modesty of a young woman who found herself in receipt of unwelcome attentions? He dropped his posture for a moment and massaged his temples. He would have liked to have taken off his wig and given his scalp a good hard scratch. Something in his plans, his calculations, had apparently gone wrong. Something small but crucial had been overlooked.

'My dear . . .'

'Chevalier?'

'I . . .'

He knew that he must talk to her, caress her mind before he could engage her body, but for once the words did not come. He heard them yet could not bring himself to speak them. Dainty phrases, blandishments, witticisms. He felt that what he was hearing within the walls of his own head was all that in the future he would ever have to say: his diminishing reservoir of language which, when he had used up the last 'I adore you', the last 'sit here, my dear', the last 'forgive me', would leave only silence, the impotence of the tongue, death. Peace? He breathed out like a swimmer. If spending words brought one nearer to the grave, so be it. He talked to her, just opened his mouth and spoke, half his brain thinking tactics, the other half looking down from space and seeing a hundred Casanovas riding the wheel of their lives, each day another pig-white hair to pluck from nose or eyebrow, and in their hearts the knowledge that the vertex had already passed, that there was nothing now but twenty, thirty more years of being Casanova; a tedious, more grudging re-enactment of the done.

He stood up from the settle, his knees creaking like pigeon wings, and walked towards her. When he was close beside her she turned to him, but her face, which he had hoped might resolve this idiotic mood, seemed shockingly void of any distinction, the mere white template of all their faces – Bettina, Henriette, Morphy, Theresa, Mamon, Zoe, Victoire, Etsuko, Milagros, Ludwig, Augusta, Pauline, Catarina, Pascal, Juliette ... Was this a failing of age, this slide of the world into anonymity? It was like a creeping blindness. Something far within him began to panic.

She said, gazing at him queerly: 'The money, monsieur?'

He waved a hand as though fending off her words, as though her words were a cloud of insects. 'We shall talk of it another time. Next week perhaps, or the one after ...'

He exited by the door into the passageway and pressed his forehead against the banisters in the hall. After a few moments, Jarba appeared, Ariel-like at his side.

'See them out, Jarba. All of them. Then bring wine into the parlour.'

'Signore?'

'Do not ask me, Jarba. Do not ask.'

10

Everyone had gone, home to whatever homes they had. Casanova turned over the cards on the table: knave of hearts, queen of spades, king of clubs. The room was close. He drew up the window. A fog was forming, creeping up from the river, threading its lacy fingers through the London streets, weaving around the wooden posts at the pavement edge, tangling in the chimneys. The Chevalier sighed. He was too restless for bed and he did not wish to drink more wine. Since the Charpillon had left he had finished the champagne and drunk two bottles of Lafite (the English had more than their fair share of the good Bordeaux). He knew the wine was in him, he felt it filtering into his blood, but of the grape's cargo of joy, of lightness, there was nothing. He closed the window, closed the shutters . . .

In the park, in sheets of silvery fog, men and women were copulating more or less openly: the men ploughing, the women ooohing and aaahing politely. The trouble with sex, mused Casanova, was that everyone thought they could do it. Nobody believed this about poetry or glass-blowing. He would have minded less were he not convinced that many men, and women too, performed the act out of some misguided idea that it was expected of them. They had no real interest in it, still less any calling. He himself, who, on a good day, could enter a woman's mind as he entered her body, who knew anatomy as well as any sculptor, who had studied the maps that chart the nerve forests, the blood lakes, the undulating savannahs of the skin, who understood how to tease from the shyest creature the full gross banquet of her secret desires, even he could not consider himself much more than a beginner. Only one pair impressed him, young Dionysians, almost children, writhing in the milky air and setting their teeth chattering with joy. He stopped to observe them and was startled by a cow that had wandered away from the lactarium, its hooves slippered by the early dew. Owls hooted, a fox slid past. Were there wolves here? Bears?

From the park he emerged into Horse Guards Parade. A half-dozen lights showed from the houses, lights seeping through bandages of fog. A few late-night walkers were making their way home, coats buttoned, though at this hour with their swords worn on the outside or with stout oak staffs in their hands. He passed the Plantation Office, walked beside the tall brick wall of the privy gardens and came to Whitehall Stairs. At the bottom of the steps a single boat, a sculler, rode the flood, but before he could summon the boatman's attention a great man-shadow pushed past him, strode to the water's edge, and was on the point of manoeuvring himself into the craft when Casanova called to him:

'Monsieur! I should also like to take this boat. Where we are bound is of little importance to me.'

The boatman stared; the man-shadow turned. For several seconds they were faced off as though about to sing a three-hander from Galuppi's *Il mondo della luna*. Then the man-shadow, having apparently reassured the boatman that the foreigner was not a threat to their lives, addressed Casanova in a respectable French, though with an Englishman's disdain of any accent other than his native one.

'I take this boat as far as Temple Stairs. If that is convenient, then I should not object to your company.'

The Chevalier bowed. Throughout the world, thank God, there was still the great Republic of Gentlemen. When it fell there would only be barbarians and women. He said:

'Monsieur, you are very gracious to give consideration to a stranger. I do not know where the Temple Stairs are. I am sure that wherever they are they will be delightful. My intention is to while away some tedious hours of the night. My mood is curious.'

It was colder on the river. To warm himself the man-shadow took the oar from the boatman and, showing both strength and skill, sculled them past the banks of old London, the rotting timbers, the moored ships with their masts lost in the fog. Behind them the lamps of Westminster Bridge dropped their light feebly upon the waters. Casanova, in the bows of the boat, drew up his legs, closed his eyes and listened to the language of the river, which in its gurglings, its patter, its long liquid sibilants, was not unlike the chatter of Venetian canals, though the canals' intimate echo was missing. Would he ever see his boyhood home again? Would the Inquisitors – old men whose only passion was the State – ever see fit to lift from him the doom of exile? He imagined sometimes that he might slip quietly into the old city, live quietly, draw no attention to himself . . . But every procuress and *confidente* would know of his arrival within three hours. An hour after that he would be arrested. Whatever he did now, however he might change, there would always be an indelible mark set against his name in the secret ledgers. He had not forgotten the garrotting stool he had seen when the jailer, Cavalli, had led him up the stairs to the cells under the roof of the Doge's Palace in '55. He had escaped from there once. It was unlikely they would give him a second opportunity.

At Temple Stairs, intending to unbend his mind in the mysterious thoroughfares of the town, Casanova excused himself, but the man-shadow detained him and enquired if he would care to pass an hour in some local hostelry, the Black Lion perhaps, which could be easily reached by cutting through the Temple. Reluctant to repay the other's kindness with a refusal and curious to see what might come of this acquaintance, the Chevalier accepted, and the two men, of a build to make any footpad cautious, strode through unlit alleys, the man-shadow never faltering so that it was evident he could have made the journey in a blindfold.

At the Lion a few late drinkers sat with their pipes and glasses, the air warmed by an excellent fire near which a three-legged hound lolled and scratched and cast a wary eye on the new arrivals. A boy showed them to a corner table and Casanova, grateful for this unexpected intercession in what had promised to be another night of talking himself down from the high ledge of his unhappiness, was inspired to order a glass of ale, a drink he could not abide. The man-shadow, now divested of his shadows and suddenly as substantial as a mallet, an outhouse, asked in a tremendous voice for lemonade.

'I take nothing stronger, monsieur. Nothing stronger than tea. I drank enough in my youth for two men. There were few who could match me then, glass for glass, bottle for bottle.'

'Indeed, monsieur?'

The Chevalier scrutinised his new companion, a man perhaps twenty years older than himself, dressed in a brown suit, the material of which, though frayed in places, chewed even, looked as thick as sailcloth. His wig likewise, despite being singed at its wings – no doubt from holding a candle too close whilst reading – had about it an air of indestructibility. He sat, this remarkable stranger, rocking on the back legs of his chair, now and then giving a half-whistle, or clucking with his tongue against the roof of his mouth, his gaze roving about the room like a prizefighter's.

Having made their introductions, the two men settled to the

business of TALK. Both produced an epigram, a pun, a quote from Horace. The Chevalier held his own, just, though most of his reading had been done rattling in a coach, too hot or much too cold, through one or other part of Europe. Or sprawled on the day-bed in a palazzo, flicking through Homer or Montesquieu, limbs languid after hours of carnal wrestling with the mistress of the house. He had learnt more by talking and liked to think that there were few men who had talked more to more people than he had. Much of it – most of it – stuff without value, but his mind was a threshing-barn and the wisdom-corn of a million conversations amounted to something.

Theology, history, Euclidean geometry, Palladian architecture. Poetry, pensions, politics. This was no épée in his companion's hand but a mace, a pikestaff. Casanova's brain was humming, he was sweating inside his shirt. The fellow across the table from him had the kind of nose that sniffed out brags, lies, bunkum. Apparently he really did know everything, and Casanova, who had been considering using his old childhood trick of inducing in himself a spectacular nosebleed, was only saved from exposure (as a what? A what?) by the older man's bladder. They quit the inn and voided themselves against a wall in Water Lane.

'These days,' said the man-shadow, who a moment earlier had been confuting idealist philosophers and lamenting a decline in the standards of sermon-writing, 'these days I piss like a horse. My friend Dr Levett says it is the kidneys.'

'If you will permit me,' said the Chevalier, whose own jet of ale seemed a mere streamlet by comparison, 'I will bring you a remedy that I have never known to fail.'

He had no such thing, of course, but he intended to cultivate this chance acquaintance. He had not entirely lost his faith in providence, in the gift – whether heaven was its source or it were merely the happy junction of purely human circumstances – of unexpected good fortune. Might he not, in providing a remedy for the other, have a remedy for himself? Might not something of this man's substantiality rub off on him? And when one claims to have a potion, one must always declare it is infallible.

Arm in arm they returned between high, dripping walls, hearing sometimes, behind or ahead of them, shuffling footsteps or the growl of a dog. The boatman answered the man-shadow's call and Casanova stepped nimbly down into the boat and stood with his arm raised in salute, watching his new friend until, as the fog thickened between them, they were lost to each other's sight.

In Pall Mall, before retiring, Casanova took his quill and wrote:

'Met this night, the last day of September 1763, Mr Samiwell Johnison, who has chambers at No. 1 Inner Temple Lane and who is an ornament to his country.'

With wetted fingertips he extinguished his candle and lay back against the pillow with a sigh. He was almost asleep, the day's adventures reduced to a cloud of stray thoughts, half-dreams, when he heard again the mysterious calling of his neighbour. Why was he never answered? It was a call as lonely as a curlew's. Poor devil. Jarba would know what it was. Dear Jarba . . .

The Chevalier was behind the screen – an old thing of ragged wood and rotten silk – sat upon a large pot. He was forced now to sit like a woman even for the lesser inconvenience, and some obstruction in the coils of his bladder had turned the once pleasant act of micturition into a torture not even the Inquisition could have devised. He peered down at the shrivelled purple gourd of his manhood. His manhood! The object between his thighs reminded him of the piece of gut little Angela Calori had gummed over her honeypot all those years ago in Milan so that she could work the theatres and fool the old priest who inspected the actors. She had not fooled Casanova, though. Dear girl . . . dead girl. Extraordinary how one could remember things from fifty years ago yet could not recall who one had spoken to yesterday.

He called: 'Forgive me, signora, I shall not keep you long . . .'

'Tell me, Chevalier, was the Charpillon more beautiful than your Portuguese friend? More beautiful than Henriette, or Manon?'

'I have told you of Henriette?'

'Of course.'

'When Henriette left me at the hotel in Geneva she scratched with her ring on the window glass . . .'

'"*Tu oublieras aussi Henriette.*"'

'Then indeed, I have told you. But it was not true. I never forgot her. She played the cello, wore her hair short. I worshipped her, though she made me swear never to look for her, and that should I ever see her I was to pass her by as if we were strangers. No man would dare to make such a demand, signora. I was astonished. Terrified.'

He clenched his gums, forced a thread of pink water from his big, sagging body. He yelped; he could not help it. Finette put her head around the screen. He nodded to her, smiled, smiling to think that his last affair was with a bitch terrier.

'As for the Charpillon,' he said, catching his breath, 'how does it go in the Song of Solomon? "Clear as the Moon, lovely as the Sun, terrible as an army with banners."'

'Then,' said his visitor, 'I pity her. To be so lovely and so young – for she might have been your daughter, signore – is to carry a great burden.'

'Pah! She revelled in her power to turn men's heads. Old men who slept with their prayer books could not help but stare at her. Street dogs trailed her like suitors. And you should save your pity, for she had no more compassion than St Just or Tallien.'

'And yet you could not burn her letters.'

He eased himself once more into the armchair. Finette had temporarily deserted him for the fire, and his visitor, sitting demurely on a seat an arm's length from his own, was smiling at him with her narrow lips. He knew then, looking at the bone-white shadow of her face beneath the veil, that were he to touch her skin it would be as cold as morning grass, as cold even as the earth beneath it.

'I feel certain, signore, that you shortly received another visit from your young friend.'

Was this one more story or was this the last? He glanced towards the candle, the flame burrowing into the wick.

'No, signora, it was not the Charpillon who came, but her ambassador . . .'

11

In his dressing gown and velvet tarboosh the Chevalier was sitting by the fire in Pall Mall, a cup of chocolate on the table beside him. On his lap he had Volume One of Johnson's celebrated dictionary, which Jarba had fetched the day before from Mr Payne's bookshop on Paternoster Row. What beautiful words it had! And even if one did not understand them one could speak them into the friendly air of one's room, an alien music that entertained the ear and stimulated the imagination.

He was disturbed by the ringing of the doorbell and was trying to decide whether or not he was at home when he heard a woman's voice, polite yet anguineous, which he immediately recognised as the Charpillon's favourite aunt. She entered the room bobbing her head and smiling like an abbess he once knew who took in rich girls for abortions.

'Madame . . .'

Casanova stood, briefly took her hand and waved her to the chair on the other side of the fireplace. He sent Mrs Feaver for another dish of chocolate. The aunt sniffed and dabbed at her nose. She had a cold and when she sneezed her bones rattled like dice in a leather cup.

Until the chocolate arrived they talked about the weather, how it had become slightly colder, slightly wetter and, well, monsieur, almost like winter already; such a damp season in this country. For her health the Chevalier recommended a glass of sherry to be taken each morning with half a nutmeg, and that she might grate the nutmeg and smoke it in a pipe if she preferred.

'How kind monsieur is, how clever.' She promised she would send the maid out for nutmegs the moment she returned home, though the Chevalier should know that the wretched girl was constantly stealing. Worse than that, she had an admirer, a hairdresser if you please, a very young and foolish person, though monsieur must agree that it was only natural that a girl, even an ugly and not very clean one, should have an admirer. We cannot go against nature, *n'est-ce pas?*'

Mrs Feaver came in with the chocolate, made the way Casanova insisted upon, so rich and thick one could plant roses in it. He waited politely while the aunt mouthed the steaming rim of her cup. When she had taken in a little of the drink she said: 'You have not asked after Marie, monsieur.' Her voice was different; brisk, flirtatious.

'Why, madame, should I ask after your niece? We are barely acquainted.'

The aunt waggled her fan at him and laughed, holding a hand over her mouth to conceal the grey baby-stumps of her teeth.

'My dear Chevalier, if she has offended you then . . .'

'I assure you she has not offended me. How might she offend me? She has not offended me in the least.'

'Monsieur, I cannot tell you how relieved I am to hear it. Marie is so very young and young people do not always know what is best for them. But she is an obedient girl, she is guided by me. I am privy to her most secret thoughts. There is a certain gentleman who is often among them.'

Casanova examined the backs of his hands. He was aware that his pulse had quickened but he was determined not to betray the slightest enthusiasm. Years at the gaming table had taught him how to do this. He said:

'If she chooses, she may visit me. My door is not barred to callers, as you yourself have just demonstrated.'

'Would that be quite proper, monsieur? These are such cynical times.'

'What is your suggestion?'

'Perhaps if the Chevalier were to come to Denmark Street? Indeed, why not come this very afternoon? I shall see to it she is at home.'

'She will welcome me?'

'I am sure of it.'

'And what of our little business venture?'

'I have made up a bottle of the Balm for monsieur to sample.'

'Perhaps I shall not need it.'

She shrugged, complacent now, as if she knew she had him, had known it all along. 'The Balm has so many excellent properties, monsieur is sure to find some purpose for it.'

'Then no doubt we shall reach an understanding, madame. An accommodation.'

'I shall look for you this afternoon, monsieur. At four o'clock?'

12

When she had gone, when the odour of her had drizzled out of the air, Casanova sat for an hour in a glow of wondrous expectation. He ordered a lunch of soup and tongue and eggs, and had Jarba draw the water for a bath. Out of the bath, glowing like a giant langoustine, he rubbed bergamot into the matting of his chest, then put on a robe and waited for Cosimo the barber, who arrived, ten minutes late from his last appointment in St James's Square, running up the stairs and entering the chamber, breathless but somehow already chattering, already pulling out his towels and strops and jars of unguent. Tying on his apron, he shaved the Chevalier's face, unfolding the creases, the little bags, the small slippages, tickling out every last hair and dispatching it with a flick of the razor's tongue, then setting about the wig, rushing it with grease and powder and hot tongs. The man was an artist: the wig on its leather head seemed to breath like a fabulous, flightless bird.

The Chevalier dressed. He put on a shirt with plenty of lace at the cuffs, a double-breasted waistcoat lined with pink silk and edged with pink cord, tight-fitting buff silk breeches and a dark blue frock-coat with a high collar. He had a chain for his watch, a chain for his wax seals. Italian shoes from the Piovasco brothers in Rome set with semi-precious stones. Jarba handed him his sword hanger. He slipped it over his head, put on the wig with its tail of poor-man's hair and inspected himself in the mirror. How many men in all of London could hope to see such a figure in their looking-glass? He stepped closer, touched the cool fingertips of his left-handed brother. Surely he was more irresistible now than he had been at twenty-five, at thirty, yet he did not care to meet his eyes too long for they sparkled equally with desire and with misgiving. Was Venus his guide, or Momus, god of mockery?

At Denmark Street on the stroke of four Aunt One greeted him, put a finger to her lips, took his arm and hurried him past the open parlour door. The other women – with the exception of the Charpillon – were sat in a row working on a tapestry: grandmother, mother, Aunt Two and even the servant girl. They looked up at him briefly, coloured thread between their teeth, thimbles on their fingers, as though he, or someone, always called at this hour. They said nothing; they went on with their sewing.

Aunt One chivvied him up the stairs, entreating him in a whisper not to raise his voice, not to tread so heavily, not to let his scabbard play arpeggios on the banisters.

'You are certain she knows I am coming?' he asked. He was not put out by the aunt's behaviour. He had seen girls given up in every imaginable way, but he would have liked to have been more certain of the rules here.

The aunt waved her hand at him as though the question were trivial, then once more put a finger to her lips. They were stood outside a door on the landing of the second floor. She opened it, just wide enough, and pushed him gently but firmly inside, closing the door behind him.

He appeared to be in the Charpillon's boudoir – no, it was certain. There was the cloak she had worn to Pall Mall; there, hanging from the edge of the dressing-table mirror, the French beads she had been wearing the day he met her at Malingan's; and there, one standing and one on its side at the end of the bed, her little shoes, braided with blue satin. He stooped and picked them up, examined the wear on the heels, the shallow moulding of her feet on the inner sole, the scuff on the fabric of the left shoe as if perhaps she had caught it on the step of a carriage, or some clumsy partner had stood on her foot during a country dance. He sniffed them; he would have liked to have worn them himself had his feet not been twice the size of hers.

He pulled back a corner of the bedcover, palped the bolster, peeled off a hair and held it up to the light, turning it so that it gleamed and curled like a live thing. On the dressing table he investigated a little ball of wool stained with crimson grease which she must have used, this morning or last night, to wipe her lips. He slipped it into his coat pocket, then opened the drawers and delved delicately among the pins and ribbons, the boxes of beads and cheap rings and seashells. There was nothing indiscreet here, no leather consoler or suspicious-looking bonbons. No secret diary, no love letters or proscribed reading. Indeed, the only book in the room – nestling in the petalled softness of her small-clothes – was a novel, and the Chevalier had just sat down with it to await the Charpillon's arrival when he heard a sound, a snatch of dreamy singing, coming from – there! – the far side of a door he had assumed led into a dressing room or walk-in wardrobe. He set down the book, went to the door, put his ear to it, and was about to knock when his hand dropped to the moulded brass of the handle; wraith-like, he slid inside.

At first, nothing at all could be discerned. He was standing in a warm, odoriferous cloud from the heart of which, this creamy half-world, came the sound of stirred and pooling water. A voice drawled:

'Pass me my towel, Auntie dear . . .'

He tiptoed towards her. It was her hair he saw first, the only thing of colour in the world other than his own blue presence. She had her back to him, lying in the bath, her head pillowed on a mass of chestnut curls. Candles, fixed by their wax to the wooden rim of the bath, illuminated the goddess. Her breasts swayed like lilies in the currents of gold-flecked water. One milky knee and thigh protruded, steam swirling from the skin. She arched her back, stroked her throat, sighed exquisitely.

'Auntie, where is my towel?'

He was tempted to try an impersonation of the aunt in order to let the game continue. He would hold up an invisible towel, she would pretend to have soap in her eyes . . . Ah! there was something about bath time amours which had always delighted him. The steam and splashiness, the sensual heat, the radiant limbs, the slide of the water. It was Bettina Gozzi's fault no doubt, but what agreeable, what toothsome memories . . .

'SPY!'

She sprang up, not like a goddess now but like an animal startled at a water hole. She stepped hurriedly, awkwardly out of the bath, knocking over a candle and extinguishing the others – all but one – with the droplets that span from her skin.

'Marie?'

'Is this your Italian chivalry? This?' She had half turned her back to him, spitting the words over her shoulder like cherry stones.

'I am not Italian, Marie. I am Venetian. And why are you now hiding those charms you so recently displayed for me?'

'You are mad! Mad and wicked! I demand that you leave immediately.'

'Ha! My little Charpillon, what a very passable actress you are. Such modesty, though somewhat belated, does you credit, but do not overplay it. I shall dry you before you take a chill. Look, you are trembling.'

She backed away from him, keeping the bathtub between them.

'Another step, monsieur, and I shall scream until the whole street is at the door! They warned me that you were a dangerous man. I should have listened.'

'My dear, it was your aunt, your favourite aunt, who brought me here.'

'A lie!'

She looked authentically scared, outraged even. The Chevalier paused. The loveliness of the girl before him was almost unendurable and yet even while his senses were flooded with her beauty he had a fleeting vision of himself sat at Pall Mall, reading or just pretending to read, his stockinged feet warming at the fire. He looked round as though he had decided to leave, then knelt at the edge of the bath.

'This is what you wish for? Very well . . . I am your humble supplicant. Come, I shall kiss your toes. I shall be your slave.'

'Why do you hate me, monsieur?' She had the towel now and clutched it with both hands just below her chin. It was not a very large towel.

'Hate you? Marie, I cannot eat for thinking of you. I am your creature, your . . .'

'More lies!' She stamped on the floorboards like a child. 'A gentleman does not treat a woman he respects in such a way. Creeping up behind her, insulting her. If you have come here to rape me then go ahead. I only ask that you kill me afterwards.'

'Rape? What manner of monster do you take me for? Do you know who you are speaking to? You think I rape women?'

Lukewarm water was seeping through the silk of his breeches. He was beginning to feel ridiculous. More ridiculous.

'Monsieur,' she said, shuffling back to the refuge of the shadows in the corner of the room, 'I do not know what to think. I am too frightened to think.'

Was this a trap? Were those widow-makers Rostaing and Cauman downstairs waiting for the signal to rush in with the watch? Could no one be trusted? Her eyes were glistening, though whether with tears or bath-water he could not say. It was the moment for some decisive action, but when he reached inside there was nothing but petulance, wheedling.

'Why do you think I was brought here?' he began, the pitch of his voice weirdly high. 'Do you deny that you knew I was coming here this afternoon? Do you mean to tell me that you did not know I was in the room, that you did not deliberately inflame me with your nakedness?'

'Monsieur,' she answered, 'you have spent too long among depraved company. It has coloured all your thinking.'

Why was he not angrier with her? Why was he not homicidally enraged? If he could only be more certain that this was indeed the cosy farce, the cozening he suspected, then it would be the simplest matter in the world to overwhelm her. He could gag her with the towel then afterwards silence her with money, or even give her skull a couple of good cracks on the floor. No

69

reasonable person could find fault with such behaviour. Why then was he still kneeling? This – twisting the diamond on his finger – this was the latest flower of those black buds that had been growing in him since Munich.

Between gritted teeth, more to himself than to the girl, he hissed: 'This should not be happening.'

'Out, monsieur!'

There was a stillness between them, as if the cogs of Time had rusted in the humidity of the room and left them stranded. Stillness; but not quite, for he had the strong impression that he was melting, that if he were to remain there long enough he would be nothing but a slick of brilliant oily blue on the bathroom floor.

Half in, half out of the door, he looked back at her, his eyes zesty with a malevolence that made them glow through the steam. 'Next time I see you . . .' he began, 'next time, I . . .' But she stared him down, the light in his eyes dimmed and the threat stuck in his throat, like a ball of auburn hair. If he stayed another minute he would begin to retch.

Aunt One was waiting for him at the bottom of the stairs.

'Tea, monsieur? A glass of wine? No? You are quite sure? Here, then, is the Balm.'

She put into his hand a small stoppered bottle. He took it, gaped at it stupidly for a moment, then extracted from his pocket-book a note for a hundred pounds. Daringly, she waited for the shillings; he found them for her, a little crush of silver coins some of which fell, ringing, on to the worn tiles of the hall. If she demanded his shoes now he would take them off and give them to her. He blundered past, the material of his breeches sticking to his knees in dark ovoids. In the parlour the women went on with their work.

13

All night – not daring to enter the vast fur-lined wardrobe of sleep, to have dreams come at him like wolves – he sat up at the dining-room table sipping coffee and solving problems in Probability. As dawn came, showing one by one, like an auctioneer, the things, objects, mysterious surfaces of the world, Casanova, ashy white, stood up from his calculations and went to the window. He knew that a man did not age evenly – so much an hour, so much a day – but rather in fits, and that during the night he had suffered such a fit and had been edged – shoved – a little closer to the company of his ancestors, that rabble. Later, hollow with fatigue, he tried to laugh at it all, to lecture himself on the way of the world, to lecture Jarba, the walls, the crackling fire. One always had to take the big view. Why make a fuss? Why grizzle like a man with toothache? Why entertain sudden thoughts of poisoning oneself?

Pah!

Frankly, one saw comelier girls in the park every day. Nice girls. Respectful. Not tramps. He would start again. One could, in all probability, start again. It should not be difficult in a city like London to avoid her. He felt suddenly absurdly pleased with himself, full of admiration for the virility of his will, and after this, the renunciation, the day went surprisingly well, though at some point in the afternoon, about the hour when the English indulged in the heartless ceremony of tea-drinking, he found himself in a street he had never seen before, shaking like a drunk.

It passed.

The next day was easier. A week passed. Then two. The world became suspiciously normal, a little season of ambiguous calm like a truce each camp employs to renew itself for the inevitable.

'My name,' he said, to whatever surface would throw back his reflection, 'my name is Casanova!' But the invocation did not work as it once had. The power of the spell was diminished.

14

This time they were going up the river: Dictionary Johnson, Casanova, Jarba, and Francis Barber, Johnson's servant, a boy of eighteen, son of a Jamaican plantation slave, given to the lexicographer as a present by Mr Richard Bathhurst in 1752. It was a perfect evening, cold but lovely, the boat drifting through the long silver room of the day's last light. The conversation had been refined and they had been down as far as Wapping dock where the Chevalier had been able to observe the shipping – which was prodigious – and to memorise the names of some of the vessels so that he would have more to report to the minister than mere impressions of English life and manners.

They disembarked at Vauxhall, paid their entrances to the pleasure gardens and set off under the trees whose branches were hung with paper lanterns, the path strewn with ragged geometries of coloured light. In the shadows, men and women, some with masks, sported and chattered and pursued one another like the happy ghosts of Elysium. Music was everywhere, it tugged at their feet like an undertow, and by the Chinese pavilion Casanova joined in the dancing, the man-shadow waving him on good-naturedly, calling out that he himself was too old for such things now, though in his youth – God's truth, monsieur! – he had worn out two pairs of pumps in a single night.

A minuet, a polonaise, then country dances; the men flinging themselves about like pantomime horses, the women scattering like leaves. When the music stopped the musicians bowed in their seats and the dancers held their sides, panting, looking down at their hands and shoes as though to confirm their identities. There was a fountain near by, gurgling by the base of a poplar tree. Casanova leaned to it, cupped the water in his hands and drank. Then, as he wiped the droplets from his lips, he saw her, the Charpillon, walking arm in arm with Ange Goudar. There was no hope of avoiding them, of slinking back into one of the avenues. She came directly towards him, smiling sweetly, all composure and girlish good manners. His hand slipped into his pocket, touched the cool of his little Venetian bloodletter. But this was not a tragedy; it was a puppet show, it was the commedia.

'Chevalier! What a pleasant surprise.'

'Mam'zel. Goudar.'

'It seems an age, monsieur, since we saw you last.'

'And yet to me, mam'zel, it seems barely an hour.' He was braced on the gravel, ready to spat with her, to come, as soon as possible, to the name-calling. But she would not fight. Instead she teased him, though with such apparent fondness there was no opportunity to take offence. She called him a bear, a handsome bear, the most handsome bear in the world. Then she turned to the man-shadow. Would Monsieur Bear not introduce her to his friend?

Because he dared not look her in the eye he talked to the end of her nose, or to her chin or to one of her ears, but each of these alone was enough to send flights of moths through his bowels. And when the great logophile nuzzled her hand like an ox sniffing a flushed white rose, lingered over it, grazed upon it with such naïve and idiotic lechery, Casanova turned away, furious and embarrassed, and stared at the bandstand.

'I am quite starved!' declared the Charpillon, who possessed that treasure of youth, an appetite indifferent to all circumstances.

'We were about to leave,' answered Casanova.

'We have barely arrived!' said Johnson, loudly enough for most of the garden to hear him. 'Sure you would not have us cross the river again with nothing in our bellies but air?'

They walked through the colonnades – Goudar grinning delightedly as though he were watching a scene from Goldini – and took a private supper room that smelled as if it had been recently used for something more than supper. The old dog-bitch scent, the venereal musk, even the cello print of a woman's back on the tablecloth. Casanova, a few steps ahead of the party, quickly smoothed the linen as though it had been the surface of his own troubled mind, but with that caress infected himself with a stranger's pleasure. As they settled at the table he felt the change gather pace; the hooves hardening inside his shoes, the coarse-haired beard oozing from his chin, the blackening of his eyes. Why is it men say, 'It was only lust', as if lust were not an all-consuming fever, a thirst of such urgency the mind is instantly rid of all extraneous considerations, all tender resolutions ... *Cospetto!* There would be time for philosophy, for pure and beautiful thoughts, when his teeth were gone and the breath rattled in his lungs like water in a kettle. He must have this girl. Must! He did not care what it cost him, what money, what drenchings of self-disgust. He reached under the table. The Charpillon was watching Jarba make his shadow-beasts on the supper-room wall. The Chevalier's hand scuttled up her leg, gathering the layers of material – apron, gown, petticoats, shift. Then

a stocking,

a bow,

skin, hot as the brow of a child with fever, cool as silver in a drawer.

The waiters came in, shifty, boiled-down men carrying bottles and glasses, juggling with knives and plates, setting the table with insolent dexterity. The Charpillon clapped her knees on the knuckles of the Chevalier's hand. There was a distinct cracking sound. His face turned white. The blood drained from his teeth and his fingers slid limply from the mouth of her skirts. If only it had been his other hand – she would have impaled herself on his diamond!

Food arrived: plates of oysters, wafer-thin slices of ham, pastries. The Charpillon effortlessly avoided his eyes. She was asking Johnson to examine a little bruise on her shoulder, and this man who had seemed so rooted, whom Casanova had admired for appearing to be the kind of man who was not blown along life's gutter by every breeze, was carrying on like someone else entirely – a Don Juan, a Casanova!

'Circe . . .' said the Chevalier, unable to stop himself and louder than he had intended.

'You spoke, monsieur?' asked Goudar.

'I said nothing. You will excuse me. I am indisposed.'

He left the room, the antic shadows. The night was colder now. He examined his hand, massaging the knuckles and stalking about in front of the colonnades, unable either to stay or to leave. Eventually she came out. He did not need to turn around. He could recognise her walk as surely as he could recognise her voice.

'The Chevalier is unwell?'

He waited a while, silent, staring out into the heart of this tawdry playground as though he might see himself emerge from the bushes, a fellow of infinite poise who knew exactly how to handle difficult girls. Who was it – Bragadin? – had told him once, years before, that every thought contained within itself the seed of its opposite, that all human passion was paradox. His feelings for the Charpillon were so riven, so starkly opposed, as to be almost lunatic. What exactly did he want of her? *That*, of course, but what else? To help him to forget? To help him to remember? He imagined that there were parallel worlds where he simply walked away from her, a slow triumphant stroll to the river. He knew, however, in this one, for better or for worse, that he would stay. He turned to her, stood close, and begged her in plain French to come with him, to come now into some lanternless corner of the garden and to show him her pity. He implored her: Make me happy, Marie. Be merciful. Be . . .

'I will make you happy, monsieur. You are assured of it.'

For a moment he did not understand what she had said. The trees seemed to be listening, leaning closer.

'I am?'

'Certainly. But not here. Not like this. We are not criminals, monsieur. We have nothing to hide.'

'Tell me,' he whispered, squeezing the words from the tightness of his throat. 'When? How?'

'I will make your happiness when you have made mine. Is that not how it should be? You must visit me. You must be kind.'

'Promise me, Marie, that this is not a game.'

'It is not a game.'

'It is certain?'

'Quite certain.'

'Then, to show that we are agreed . . .' He reached for her, eyes shut, the kind of adolescent lunge he had not made since the days of Nanetta and Marta Savorgnan when perhaps it had appeared charming, but his arms gathered only air, his lips pressing against a faintly perfumed absence.

On the journey home, Johnson was holding forth about a recent translation of Tasso for which he had provided the preface and which had been presented to the Queen. It was only with some difficulty that Casanova did not send him tumbling into the river, as though that voice were a flame to be extinguished by the water. But they parted as friends, shaking hands, glad of the darkness.

'Visit me!' called the man-shadow as his boat pulled away from Westminster Stairs.

The Chevalier smiled his weariest smile, waved, then hurried home through the park with Jarba. Really, this business, it was enough to give a man religion.

15

'The Chevalier Goudar is here to see you, monsieur.'

Casanova opened his eyes, blinked at the light. Apparently it had happened again: the unasked-for miracle of morning.

'Does he say what he wants?'

'Only that he will not detain you long.'

'Ha!'

He washed, dabbed his face with powder and spent his customary interval at the mirror. Surely, he thought, arranging his tarboosh on his head, a man should become more accustomed to his own face, more familiar with it. Yet it seemed the reverse was true, and that the face that loomed in the glass during these solitary levees, the face of a saint, a child abductor, was increasingly strange to him, mysterious.

Downstairs, Goudar was working with the bellows at the fire, getting the flames to dance on the coals. They greeted each other, Goudar smirked, Casanova raised an eyebrow. Jarba brought in the toasting fork and the bread.

'England's contribution to world cuisine,' said Goudar, taking the fork and impaling the first slice of buttered bread.

They sat. They ate their toast. Goudar gave news of the town, gossip so fresh, so amusing, Casanova could not help betraying his interest. Nothing, it seemed, in the whole of this great metropolis, was hidden from Goudar's eye and ear, his reptilian intelligence. Eventually, inevitably – for it had plainly been Goudar's intention from the first – the talk came round to the Charpillon. Goudar asked: 'Do you love her?'

'Love!' Casanova made a small gesture of dismissal with his fingertips. 'How could one love a woman like that?'

Goudar, who this morning appeared to Casanova smaller and even more disturbingly immaculate than usual, flicked a crumb off the table. Casanova followed its trajectory, saw where it landed on the carpet and said – as if the action had silently contradicted him – 'Whatever it was I felt for her, I assure you I have come to my senses.'

'You no longer have any interest in her?'

'I despise her.'

'Then everything is well.'

'It is.'

'You do not wish to call on her, as I know she invited you to at Vauxhall?'

'I have called on her too often already.'

'And if she were to come to the door now you would send her away?'

'Assuredly.'

'So if I were to tell you she is outside, longing to see you . . .'

'Outside?' He leaned towards the window, biting his lip as he realised his mistake.

'I am afraid, dear friend,' said Goudar, touching for a moment the other man's thigh, 'you still have a little of your fever. If you will allow it I shall be your physician.'

'With you as my physician, Goudar, I do not think I should live very long.'

'You are unjust, monsieur, yet I wish to help you because I think we are alike. Do not look appalled. I know how you hold me. You do not care for me because we are of the same tribe, and you do not care to see yourself doubled. But monsieur, the world is big enough, there are enough amusing women and rich fools for the both of us. And who knows, one day you may need my help . . .'

'The day I need your help, Goudar, I shall be in desperate straits indeed.'

'None of us, dear Seingalt, can see how things will turn out. No man is so secure he cannot be brought down. Today you have all you desire – almost all – but how will things stand next year? In five, in twenty-five years? Were we born with silk on our backs? No, monsieur. We have risen by our wits. We succeed because we are not afraid to gamble, because we know how to give others what they wish for. Forgive me, but I know very well that you have paid for this charming house and your fine clothes with money you cozened from a deluded widow to whom you offered the gift of immortality. How was it to be achieved? Were you not to impregnate her in so marvellous a fashion she would be brought to bed of her own reincarnation? Who but you, Maestro, could have imagined such a scheme! How happily the lady must have parted with her fortune!'

'She still has funds enough to buy five Goudars,' said Casanova, softened by this recognition of his work.

'Well,' said Goudar, 'we shall not discuss Madame D'Urfe now. I meant only to make it clear that we say and do what is necessary. We are not afraid to get our hands dirty. We understand the game within the game. We know money better than any banker. We have style. We despise only boredom and cowardice . . .'

'And do we like ourselves?'

'Certainly.'

'And if we do not?'

Goudar picked up a silver teaspoon, polishing it with the ball of his thumb.

'If we do not like ourselves, monsieur, then we are lost, for a man who does not like himself is full of doubts. We survive, we exist, because we are credible. When the rope-walker doubts, she falls. When the swordsman doubts, he dies. We should fear doubt more than a stiletto.'

Casanova sat back in his seat; what excellent furniture the English made! He said: 'There may be some truth in this, Goudar. As for whether we are the same, suffice to say I play for bigger stakes and keep better company.'

'Though you are keeping mine now and quite enjoying it if I am not mistaken.'

'One must sometimes breakfast with the Devil, Goudar. But tell me, what is the true purpose of your visit?'

'As I have already said, monsieur. I have come to be your physician. To cure you of that troublesome girl.'

'You are certainly thick with her. But I have told you that my intention is to stay away from her.'

'My plan is a better one. Eat your fill of her. When you are sated, you will be free.'

'Merely coming to the table does not ensure that one may dine. If the matter were so simple . . .'

'But the matter is simplicity itself. You do not know her as I do. Are you aware that she was the mistress of Morosini, the Portuguese ambassador? It was I who arranged the whole affair.'

'You were the pimp?'

'I was the go-between.'

'And since Morosini?'

'She has been used by various gentlemen, but none has taken her as his titular mistress.'

'That I can understand.'

'The fact remains, monsieur, that you are rich and she is poor. What has she to sell? Nothing but her beauty. What has her mother to sell? Nothing but her daughter. The Charpillon is the family's sole commodity, and a good one too, though every year her value must decrease. An experienced woman who has preserved herself may command a good price for several years, and there is a time when a man wishes to talk with the women he has paid for and an older woman will have better conversation. But youth is the flower we love to have in our garden, youth and beauty allied in perfection. It is the loveliest bloom, but its time is brief. Madame Augspurgher knows this well and must choose her moment wisely. She must not sell the girl too cheaply but neither can they price her out of the market. We must deal with them in a businesslike manner. Empower me to take your offer and I will act for you as I acted for Morosini. The whole matter then was taken care of in three days . . .'

'Morosini paid you well? What was your commission?'

'This ...' He drew from the inside pocket of his coat a document and showed it to Casanova.

'You see, monsieur. It is signed by the mother and gives me the right to spend the night with the girl after His Excellency's departure.'

'Naturally they reneged?'

'They did. The girl is still a minor so I cannot take the matter to law.'

'In spite of this you continue to do business with them?'

'I should have insisted on my commission before passing her to the ambassador.'

'And what you failed to gain from Morosini you will gain from me? Thank you, but I do not think I would want her after she had been in your hands.'

'On this occasion I am prepared to forgo the commission.'

'I find that somewhat hard to believe.'

'Strange as it may seem, monsieur, I would like to be of service to you.'

'How suspicious you make me!'

'You may choose not to believe me, but how can I threaten you?'

'Very well. What price should I offer?'

'One hundred guineas will settle everything.'

'She could have had the money the first time she came to the house.'

'They are ambitious, and it is better to deal with the older women. With them one may speak man to man.'

'And you will deliver the offer?'

'I shall go the moment you agree.'

'Then go.'

A pause.

'Yes?'

'There is one more thing.' Goudar stood and signalled at the window. 'Something by way of insurance should she prove more stubborn . . .'

After a moment the door into the parlour was opened. Jarba came in and behind him Cauman and Rostaing, carrying between them some manner of chair. They set it down and grinned at each other like grave-robbers.

'This,' said Goudar, 'was made for a gentleman who did not like to pay at all.'

'I suspect,' answered Casanova, crossing the carpet to examine the thing and then tentatively stroking one of the leather armrests, 'something monstrous.'

'It will not hurt her,' said Goudar, 'but you have only to have her sit in this chair to be sure of her. Watch.'

Goudar sat. Instantly his hands and feet were pinioned by steel brackets springing from the wood so fast there would have been no chance of evading them. The clasps at his feet separated his legs and at the same moment a fifth spring pushed up the seat, thrusting his pelvis forward as if he were about to give birth.

'I was right,' said Casanova, as Rostaing released Goudar from the chair. 'And yet I must admit it is ingenious.'

'It is modelled,' said Goudar, 'on a device at the house of Madame Gourdan on the rue des Deux Portes. If you wish to have it you must tell me immediately, for there is a man in the next street who . . .'

'Naturally,' answered Casanova, 'and I think I may guess the price.'

Cauman laughed, tensing his neck, so that one could see in the shilling-coloured light the pale criss-cross of scars at his throat.

16

For the remainder of the morning Casanova attended to his affairs, raising money on a dozen black pearls, speculating on the international flower exchange, then crossing the town to Inner Temple Lane where, though it was long after midday, Dictionary Johnson was still in bed. Francis Barber showed the visitors through to the living room, the dining room, the all-purposes-and-occasions room, where a middle-aged man and woman, like a pair of automatons whose springs had unwound, were sat in straight-backed chairs at a table. The man, garbed in a dust-coloured coat, the threads of which protruded like the fur of an elderly rat, introduced himself as Dr Levett. He spoke French quite as fluently as Casanova, who immediately enquired where the doctor had learnt to speak it.

'Monsieur,' said Levett, 'I was in my youth employed as a waiter in a café near to the Hôtel Dieu in Paris. It was there I became acquainted with some surgeons of that great institution, who were kind enough to give me instruction in the art which I now practise in a most humble way amongst the poor of this town. This lady here is Miss Williams. Her father, Mr Zachariah Williams of Wales, did most important work towards establishing the means by which mariners may ascertain longitude at sea.'

'Madame,' said Casanova, sweeping the air with his hat, 'I am honoured to meet the daughter of so eminent a philospher.'

The woman turned towards his voice, his breeze, her blue eyes scummed with blindness. She seemed to be listening for something in the distance, like a door slamming on Fetter Lane.

Casanova sat down. Jarba walked to the window. Clouds the size of cathedrals, English-grey, were drifting towards the river. Dr Levett, who appeared to have slept in his clothes, to have slept in them for years, scraped patiently with his thumbnail at a stain on the thigh of his breeches. Apparently, neither he nor Miss Williams possessed any conversation beyond that which they had already ventured, and they had lapsed again into themselves as if there were no one else in the room.

The Chevalier wondered if he would ever be at ease among the English, who, despite their money and their men-of-war, were a grubby and melancholy race, infected by the rain, by their stark religion, by lack of soup perhaps. More cunning than the French, less likable but more interesting than the Dutch, more vicious than the Spanish, more stubborn than the Germans, more political than the Italians . . . What was one to make of such people?

There were creakings overhead. A minute later, Johnson appeared, large as a wherry boat, a little turd-brown wig on his head. Dr Levett came suddenly to life, shifting industriously about his patron and filling the teapot from the kettle that for some time had been steaming on the iron swing-back above the trivet. Johnson greeted his guest then sat heavily, tasting his own mouth while Levett passed the pot to Miss Williams, who poured the tea, much of it on to the table, then dipped her fingers into the cups to tell if they were full. At length, the tea reached Johnson, the oily liquor cool enough now to be gulped, which he did, bracing the china between his lips, before shuddering and handing the cup back to Miss Williams, who set about the painful business of refilling it.

Casanova and Jarba had brought queen-cakes, macaroons in coloured papers, Spanish oranges. Dr Levett looked at the food with undisguised interest. Jarba divided up the cakes. More tea? Yes, more tea was needed to wash them down until – one o'clock sounding at intervals across the city – the constitution of the great logophile was revived and the tide of sense, having receded through half the night and half the day, was on the flood again. He knuckled the table and blew out large, loosely wrapped parcels of air.

'Why, sir,' he began, scouring the pith from the orange peel and then cutting the rind into small squares with an instrument not unlike the one the Chevalier had in his pocket,

'I love the university of Salamancha . . .'

and

'I used once to be sadly plagued by a man who wrote verses . . .'

and later

'Sir, to leave things out of a book, merely because people tell you they will not be believed, is meanness . . .'

Comforted by the lexicographer's emphatic tone, sipping it like a tonic, Casanova allowed himself to hope that the world was indeed solid and he himself in no danger of disappearing like a morning fog or an unsound proposition. The shimmering of the world which he had so often experienced since Munich was merely a weariness – a profound one to be sure – but no more than he should expect after lying for weeks in the foul air of his own distress, disease combing the blood and the doctors probing him as if he had been a piece of spoiled meat. As a man got older he naturally took longer to recover. And now, when he should have been resting, convalescing at some suitable retreat in the country well away from the temptations of the city, he had got himself enmeshed in one of those affairs one could not quite let go of, even when, in one's heart, one knew that one should.

He looked down at his hands, turned up the palms and gazed at the lines. He had come here, to this little island, to be healed, saved, confirmed. But what was he trying to save? Some heirloom of the self, a fragment, a romance, a dream. Must he hold on to a name, a certain style? Somehow he would have to think his way out of this mess, bludgeon it with his intelligence. He was a citizen of the Age of Light, not a Sicilian peasant, cowering in a world crammed with omens. He closed his hands, shut them like books, then quickly, with a little flush of shame, crossed his fingers and touched the table for luck.

He was taking his leave – returning Dr Levett's bow, taking Miss Williams's blindly proffered hand – when the logolept, who had carefully pocketed the little squares of scraped peel, said:

'Seen that girl again, Chevalier? You might bring her for tea some time. Though I think not too often. Miss Williams here would not approve of it.'

There was that look again in his eyes, the one Casanova had seen at Vauxhall, though it was more guarded now in the sobriety of mid-afternoon.

'You admired her?' There was a trace of irritation in his voice, of disappointment, condescension . . .

'Ay, monsieur,' answered Johnson, bustling in his chair, 'I am not immune to female beauty, whatever you may think proper. My wife is dead eleven years, her fleshly parts resolved to earth, her spirit to sublimity. I, however, like all men, am as much dog as angel. The dog in me admired the girl at Vauxhall. I dare say the dog in you does not care to have a rival. Do not fear. I shall not steal her from you, though I have my arts.'

Outside, the Chevalier laughed a curled Venetian laugh the length of Fleet Street.

'Tell me, Jarba, what did he mean? What "arts" can he be speaking of? A magic powder to throw into their eyes so they do not run from him? Strange, mistaken fellow. He should keep to his books, his etymologies. Leave the *ars amatoria* to those who understand them. Was he serious? Does he imagine he could steal the Charpillon from me?'

'That,' said Jarba, 'would be impossible, as you do not yet possess her.'

'You are mistaken, friend. My money is speaking to her now.'

They walked down Ludgate Street, circumnavigated St Paul's, stopped for coffee at Child's and made their way – Casanova holding a scented handkerchief to his nose against the stink of the Fleet ditch – to Blackfriars to watch the work on the new bridge. Like Labelye's bridge at Westminster, it was being constructed from the middle of the river out towards the banks so that the newly completed hundred-foot elliptical sweep of the central arch stood in the water like a stranded mammoth, its grey back infested with human fleas. From his jacket pocket Jarba took the weathered cylinder of his telescope, drew it out to its full extension and passed it to Casanova who, after a momentary hesitation to wonder if the instrument might not have been tainted with the captain's luck, set the brass lip to his eye. Colours, sweating faces; blocks of Purbeck stone; ropes, tackle, oaken piles, rams; all manner of cunning engines. In the midst of a boil of labourers he saw Mylne, the young architect, sat at a table, his plans laid out like a tablecloth, his compass, dividers, pens and rulers like strange cutlery.

'See,' he said, handing the telescope to Jarba, 'the architect is dining on air. When the air is devoured, his bridge will be finished.'

How simple, he thought, as they turned away, the lives of these workmen must be! Work. Sleep. The simple dignity of labour. Did they know their good fortune?

17

They had been home for less than an hour, the Chevalier sitting in his favourite armchair quartering an apple, when the parlour door was rudely opened, Mrs Feaver was brushed aside, and the Charpillon entered into the room like a pocket Amazon. She fixed him with the green fire of her eyes and said:

'Is it a fact, monsieur, that you charged the Chevalier Goudar to tell my mother that you would pay a hundred guineas to pass the night with me?'

She had not come alone but was accompanied, as beautiful

girls like to be, by a friend who, though pretty, was a clear degree or too less lovely than the Charpillon.

'Good afternoon to you, Marie,' said Casanova, somewhat shaken. 'Perhaps Miss . . . ?'

'Lorenzi,' answered Miss Lorenzi with a smirk.

'Lorenzi. Charmed, my dear. I think I knew your mother. Perhaps Miss Lorenzi would like to wait in the other room where Mrs Feaver will bring her the nicest things to eat and drink. Then you and I, my little spitfire, may talk as freely as an old married couple.'

'Married!' cried the Charpillon, looking round at her friend. 'I would rather be married to my hairdresser.'

Casanova signalled to Jarba. Miss Lorenzi, with obvious reluctance, allowed herself to be led from the room.

'Now, Marie, let us be civilised. Will you not sit down?'

She was outlined against the window and seemed to pulse in and out of the afternoon light. She hesitated, then perched on one of the chairs beside the card table.

'May I say, my sweet, what a delicious surprise it is to . . .'

'Do you think, monsieur, that I shall bear these insults?'

'Insults again? Come, come. Let us not excite ourselves. The Chevalier Goudar is your friend. He has arranged these matters for you before, has he not?'

'Tch!' She expelled Goudar from the conversation as though he were a fly in a mouthful of wine. It was quite a display. The Chevalier could hardly remember having seen anybody look so furious. He was not discouraged this time. If her anger was genuine then it was a passion he could turn to his advantage. He said:

'Was the offer not enough? I would be willing to increase it by, say, another twenty-five guineas.'

'I would rather starve.'

'A hundred and fifty, then, which is my final offer.'

'You think you may haggle with me?'

'Half the money in advance. Half afterwards. Does that not seem perfectly fair?'

She looked around for something to throw, found only a pack of cards and hurled them at him with such force they scattered in a shimmering cloud in front of him like pigeons panicked into the air by the midday gun at San Maggiore. Tears started from her eyes. She walked to the window, fists clenched at her sides. Casanova picked the cards from his lap. In a different voice, softer, he said:

'Marie, if you think yourself insulted then I must apologise. I meant only to put things on a business footing.'

'Is that your word for love, monsieur? Business? Is this how you have earned your reputation? The great Casanova, whose charm is only in his purse!'

'And what of your reputation, Marie? How is Ambassador Morosini, by the way? I do not think he is the kind of man to sigh for long at a girl's feet.'

'Morosini,' she said, measuring her words, 'was a gentleman.'

'You were sold to him by your own mother.'

'He was a man of honour.'

'You were his toy.'

'Monsieur, I was happy to be the toy of such a man.'

'What, then, was his secret?'

'You who think only of money, you would not understand.'

'You are so rich you can despise my money?'

'I am not for sale, monsieur, to you or to anyone.'

'We are all for sale, Marie. Kings and empresses are for sale to the right bidder.'

'Who buys you? And what exactly would it cost?'

'I am older than you. My price is correspondingly higher.'

'If price is to increase with age then I assume you would pay two hundred guineas to sit on the sofa with my mother. Perhaps a thousand for my grandmother?'

'Now you are being ridiculous.'

What the devil, he wondered, observing her trembling shoulders, is she making such a fuss about? Business *is* another word for 'love'. No man ever extended his hand towards a woman – not in this eighteenth century – without there being, however subtle, some pertinent fiscal consideration. Who should know that better than the Charpillon, growing up in such a family? However, he did not care to be cast as a man who must always bluntly pay for a woman's affection. Once, there were women who had paid for him! Left purses under the pillow and taken pleasure in dressing him up in clothes he could not possibly have afforded for himself. They had shown him off like a prize, and indeed, then, he had been a prize, a young man with a limitless, uncomplicated appetite for living. As for Morosini, it was well known that he looked like a toad. It was impossible he could possess any fascination the Chevalier did not have in spades.

He rose, crossed over to her, stood behind her, not quite touching her. He could not see her hands and had the sudden thought that were she to turn around now with a hatpin or a pair of scissors and plunge it into his heart, would he mind so much? These scenes which he had played in a thousand times by a thousand windows with a thousand girls . . . He would have liked to have held up crossed fingers as a child does and say 'Pax'.

His hands settled on her shoulders. She did not flinch. He felt the warmth of her wrap, and for several seconds they rested together in this comfortable pose, almost anonymous, an older man and a younger woman. Anyone looking in might have imagined them as friends, an uncle and his niece even, gazing out without any great purpose at the afternoon traffic.

Finally, with a heave of breath, she turned, her eyes having resumed their customary colour, blue as the water in a tarn.

'Monsieur, if you only knew. If you only knew . . .'

'Knew what, my dove?'

She blushed, looked from his face to his throat. 'Knew that I adore you. That I have done so from the moment I first saw you when I was a little girl in Paris with no beauty to turn your head.'

'Ah, Marie, you were beautiful even then.'

'You will not believe it but you are the first man who has seen me weep.'

He did not believe it but was nonetheless delighted. 'My little gamba, why have you given me no proof of your feelings? You had almost convinced me that you despised me.'

'Because I hoped . . .'

'Yes?' Her voice was so small now.

'I hoped you would court me properly.'

'Properly?'

'Properly, monsieur. I do not want your money.'

'It was Goudar, Marie, who . . .'

'Goudar knows nothing about love, monsieur.'

'That is true. He is an insect.'

'He is my mother's friend. I hardly speak to him.'

'Of course.'

'If you had visited me every day, even for a fortnight, taken me to the opera, or to the gardens or for rides in the country, to Richmond, for example, then I should have given myself to you freely. For love.'

'You love me, Marie?'

'You still doubt me, monsieur?'

'No, my sweet, only myself for being such a fool. I . . .' He could not believe what he was saying, or that he was saying it at all, yet the moment was too precious to break up with quibbles about the truth. He doubted her profoundly but hot tongs would not have made him say so now. She was looking up at him, sweet and limpid as a Perugino Madonna.

She whispered: 'You will come, then? You will court me properly?'

'As Hippomenes courted Atlanta.'

'And no more talk of money?'

'Money, my dear?' There was a smell of fresh coffee wafting under the door. His cook made it, cold-pressed, according to a secret method of his own devising, with beans newly unloaded from ships of the East India Company. He was suddenly impatient to bring things to a close and have the room to himself again, to sit in his favourite chair, sip the black gold and dream of . . .

'Will you stay for some refreshment?'

'No, monsieur. I am still too agitated.'

'Of course. Well, then . . .'

'Yes . . .'

'Until . . .'

They had no more to say to each other. From the window he watched her go with Miss Lorenzi, arm in arm past the Painted Balcony Inn. A man in a red coat, a soldier perhaps, took off his hat to them, said something. The girls strolled by, laughing. When Casanova turned, Jarba was collecting the cards from the floor.

18

Such was the routine: every morning, Casanova and Jarba went to the Strand or to Ludgate Hill to buy presents, both of them armed against the gangs of desperate boys who would strip a rich man of his buckles or even of his life if it might be done without risk to their own. Then back to Pall Mall where the presents were unloaded onto the dining table and the Chevalier ran upstairs to change his coat while Mrs Feaver cracked a fresh goose's egg into a crystal goblet, Cosimo the barber called and Jarba whistled up a sedan chair. Shortly after two, Casanova would emerge again from his house, fragrant and refreshed, step into the grubby box of spongy leather – which always smelt as if the last fare had done nothing but belch all the way from Pickle Herring Street to the park – and float over the London cobbles to Denmark Street, where the Augspurghers, each day contriving a little farce of surprise at his coming, relieved him of his gift, sat him by the little fire and flattered him in measured strokes.

The afternoons were for outings. They went to Greenwich

to view the hospital; to the Old Bailey to see the trial of a woman accused of shop-lifting (and sentenced to die, for the goods were valued at more than five shillings); to the playhouse in Covent Garden to sit through *Artaxerxes*, this time in the company of Dictionary Johnson and his excitable friend, a young Scotsman with a face like a tulip bulb who attempted, during the pantomime, to pass a note to the Charpillon. To the cockpit behind Gray's Inn where Lord Pembroke was in attendance with his armoured birds; and to St Paul's to see a fashionable preacher and pay a shilling for a guide who whispered to them the titles and fortunes of the Quality. To Richmond, the palace of St James, Newgate gaol . . .

Two weeks of tearing about the town, spending money, amusing themselves as though the plague were coming. Even Grandmother Augspurgher, despite having been struck by an apple core thrown from the gloom of the two-shilling gallery at Covent Garden, seemed to have been loaned to the world once more, blenching her face and insisting on wearing her wooden teeth which, when she ate, galloped in her mouth like castanets. But despite the brooches, the breakfast sets, the bolts of Spanish indigo, the sheer machismo of the Chevalier's spending, his only reward had been the Charpillon's entire repertoire of smiles, and now and then, with the entire family looking on, he had been permitted to kiss her hand.

Such was the state of this confusing game when, taking his leave one evening from Denmark Street, afraid that another day of theatre touts and foreigner-hating shopkeepers and he would run amok with his little Venetian nose-slitter, he had asked Madame Augspurgher, in the presence of her daughter, when it should be

– when madame, specifically, the night of bliss – and after much hesitation, some feigned embarrassment and some tittering, he had been invited to supper the following evening, after which – should it so please him – he would be the Augspurgher's guest for the night.

On the appointed day he woke out of a nap in the drawing room at Pall Mall. He could not say what had woken him, a gust of dead leaves at the window perhaps, but as he opened his eyes five o'clock was striking from the cabinet clock in the hall and more faintly from the clock in the wall of the Smyrna coffee house. He roused himself, rubbed his face and went to the window. An evening of smoke and night clouds was spreading quickly from the east, while to the west the very last of the sun squinted between the houses on the park side and lay in dusty golden bars across the street. There was no sign of Jarba, no sound of life in the house at all, so Casanova lit the lamps himself and took one of them up the stairs to his room. All his thoughts now were on how he could derive the greatest pleasure from the Charpillon, how to make their flesh chime with that ecstasy which seemed with the years to have become increasingly elusive. From a drawer in the bedside cabinet he pulled out his travel-stained copy of Aretino's *Postures*, illustrated by Giulio Romano and with copious marginalia in Casanova's own writing. Then, settling himself by the window, lamp in one hand, book in the other, he selected and mentally reviewed his old favourites. 'The Siege of Troy', 'Monkey on the Lion's Back', 'King Solomon's Mines', 'Full House', 'Diamond in the Well'. For his entrée he chose 'The Dancing Swans', combining it for the sake of virtuosity with 'The Walls of Jericho', or 'Two Men go into the House, One comes out', or even – the girl was young and in good health – 'Odysseus outwitting the Cyclops'.

He pushed the book back into the cabinet and hunted around for his 'London overcoats', sheaths of top-quality lamb's gut, dried and oiled, the last of that consignment he had bought in Marseilles at three francs a piece. There was no doubt that they dulled a man's enjoyment and in the heat of the act gave off a disturbing odour of roast lamb, but after La Renaud – had that been his fifth, his sixth infection? – he had sworn to be more careful. Another attack like the last and he would be done for. Nor did he wish for another little Sophie, fond as he had become of the girl. Thinking of her he felt obscurely ashamed, as if she were there in a corner of the room watching him, her big eyes still blatant with innocence but already growing used to the world, the thinly concealed corruption of her elders; what would she think of him, her papa as a large overdressed doll rummaging in a drawer for . . . Ah, there they were. He slipped two of the small greased envelopes into the pocket of his waistcoat, blew out the lamp and left the room. It was too early for the Augspurghers'. He would have to walk in the park for an hour. No; a child could not possibly be expected to understand.

By the time he reached Denmark Street most of the other guests had already arrived, among them Rostaing and Cauman, and Ange Goudar who, as usual, appeared to be under the sway of a complicated private joke. The Charpillon, her loveliness subdued in a simple dress, no beauty spots – those tiny banners of seduction – and barely a hint of rouge, greeted Casanova in the hall. A bell was rung to bring them to the table. The Augspurghers' cook was mean and talentless but tonight the Chevalier dined as though he were in the château of the Marquis de Carraccioli. He was delighted to see the Charpillon filling her mouth with such enthusiasm. He had never seen a girl eat fish cheeks with such verve. The older women chattered like turtles, like sly guinea fowl, like ravens, keeping Casanova's glass topped up with their watered-down wine. Goudar seemed to be handling one of the aunts under the table, for the woman was growing a moustache of pleasure. The sweet came in, something grey with the texture of feet. The little servant girl did not trim the candles. She was standing against the dresser, eyes open but evidently asleep.

At midnight, the first guests stood up to take their leave. The Charpillon's mother, under the guise of replenishing his coffee cup, whispered into Casanova's ear. She wondered if, for the sake of form, he would be so complacent as to leave with the others and return when the house was quiet again. He nodded. It was to the woman's credit that she had not abandoned all propriety, and it would be more charming to sneak back in. Such adventures should always be surrounded by games, subterfuge, theatre.

He made his false goodbyes, went with Jarba as far as the church of St Giles-in-the-Fields, walked twice about the church then came back to the corner of Denmark Street to wait in the shadows. The clouds had departed and the moon, shrunk now to the size of a man's fingertip, stood high above the town.

Jarba said: 'You wish me to wait in the girl's house?'

Casanova shook his head, then leaned down and kissed his servant, warmly upon the lips.

'Leave the door unbolted, Jarba. Do not wait up for me. Wish me joy.'

They were still in the dining room, arranged in a light the colour of scorched butter, the serving girl clearing the table, an expression on her face of concocted idiocy, as if one should refuse to be intelligent in such a world. Casanova, the sap in his blood, winked at her, but she ignored him and snuffed one of the candles, slowly, with her fingers. He turned to the mother.

'Where is it to be, madam?'

She gestured minutely to the wall that separated the dining room from the parlour. The Charpillon was stood to one side, studying her nails and frowning.

'Monsieur,' said her mother, fidgeting with a piece of air and taking a step backwards, 'the Chevalier Goudar mentioned a certain sum. I thought . . . so we might put it from our minds . . . such a disagreeable thing . . . If you could . . . before retiring?'

The Charpillon stepped quickly between them. She glared at her mother, and taking Casanova by the flowing lace of his cuff as though he were infinitely delicate or not quite clean, she led him into the unlit passage and thence into the parlour where a single lamp burned upon the mantelpiece. The furniture had been pushed back to the walls and a bed made up on the floor. Why it should be here and not in her own room was a question that formed and then dissolved in his mouth. In this mood he would be content with the scullery, as indeed, several times in the past, he had been.

There was no fire. The room was chilly. He held out his arms to her. She smiled, pointed to the bed. He pulled off his clothes, all except his shirt which he kept on for the sake of warmth. He climbed into the bed. The sheets had not been aired. They were somewhat damp and ceporous. He stretched his limbs, mumbled something about the altar of bliss, then leaned upon his elbow to watch the Charpillon operate the secret strings, the unseen catches, the hidden buttons of her dress. Her clothes shivered on to the carpet until briefly she was naked, her body glowing like mascarpone, like the pulp of a freshly bitten apple. He had only a few seconds, however, to enjoy the sight of her, to let it pierce him, before she pulled on her nightgown, one that might have belonged to her grandmother so thoroughly did it swallow her, covering her from her throat to her toes, and which she took from a drawer in the chest between the windows, as if that were the natural place to keep such a garment.

She opened the little door of the lantern and blew out the candle within. The Chevalier protested. Were his eyes to be barred from the banquet?

'I cannot sleep in the light, monsieur.'

Sleep?

In the darkness he felt her slide into the bed. He waited a moment, listening to the seesaw of her breath, allowing the cloud of her warmth to reach him, then he wriggled closer, stretching out through the dark. A touch of blood-warm wool, the solid curve of a shoulder. How silent she was! How still! Like a child playing hide-and-seek.

He whispered her name. It was hard to be certain of how she was lying. He moved closer and felt her knees drawn up like fuzzy shields. Her arms were crossed in front of her breasts; her head was down, chin to chest. He smiled, assured himself it was delightful, yes, most delightful, this persistent teasing.

Touching her through the pelt of her nightdress, he ducked his head under the covers and his lips sought out some unprotected flesh to kiss. In his eagerness and the ebony black beneath the sheets he kissed his own shoulder, the smooth vinegary flesh giving him a thrill of solipsistic pleasure, but of the Charpillon all he could discover was the back of one hand, responsive as a clamshell. Gently, he tried to raise her head. Then less gently.

'Come now,' he said, careful to keep all trace of exasperation from his voice. 'To sharpen the appetite with hurdles is well and good. No man appreciates them more than I. There is a time, however . . .'

He stopped. Were it not for the evidence of his fingertips and the faint whiff of jessamine, he could easily have imagined himself to be alone in the room. He tried to turn her on to her back. He could not shift her. He tried to prise her hands away from her elbows but she gripped herself as though her life depended upon it. He lay back a moment, stared up through the speckled gloom and suffered an appalling premonition. What if . . . ? But that was impossible. Not even the Charpillon, not even the Charpillon's mother, was capable of such an imposture. More likely she was lying there waiting for him to utter some fond sentence, words like keys of honey to unlock her limbs. Or did she wish him to force her? Some liked a rougher game. Amazons and Spartans. The mating of tigers.

He sat up, shot off his shirt and began to work in earnest. One could hardly credit the strength she had. The moment he had pulled back one of her arms and left it to attend to the other, the first flew into place again so that for some minutes he was engaged in an odd Sisyphean game, labouring uselessly at the girl's body, beginning to sweat. He lifted her, dropped her, burrowed down to the bottom of the bed. If he could discover the hem of her nightgown he could work it up and peel her. Once she was naked his arts would inflame her beyond all further resistance.

He found her feet (and nothing was simple in this game). She had wrapped them in the nightdress, the ends of which she had managed to tuck and seal between her calves and the back of her thighs. He pulled, then, inspired by a little flash of rage, he seized a piece of the wool between his teeth and worried it, growling like a mastiff, almost uprooting his jaw, until the material suddenly giving way, he accelerated backwards from the bed, a square of sopping wool in his mouth. He spat it out, pounced on her, shook her, then experimented with a slap or two. She did not flinch. He shouted at her, leaned down close, his face pressed into the fine electricity of her hair. Bawled at her in French, in Italian, in prime Venetian. In desperation he tried words recalled at random from the man-shadow's dictionary.

'Windegg! Pointingstock! Lubber!'

Nothing.

He crawled out of the bed, crawled naked across the floor and involuntarily head-butted a chair. In the darkness it was easy to become hysterical. It seemed to him that he had been in the room for days. He thought: I must be calm. I must try to understand what is happening. I must have a plan . . . After a minute he crept back under the covers. He bade her goodnight, yawned, turned away from her. Let her stew! Let her own vanity ensnare her! For several minutes he feigned sleep, while the quietness, like a drift of black snow, gathered and pressed down upon him.

Were her eyes open? Was she watching him, waiting for him to turn to her? Stealthily he twisted around, holding his breath and peering at the uncertain coastline of the Charpillon. He sensed no answering stare. No arms opened to admit him. Incredibly, she appeared to be just as she had been when first he had reached out for her: head down, knees up, her arms belted across her chest. Despite himself he could not but feel some admiration for her. Such persistence, such perversity, was astonishing.

He nipped her with his teeth, her thigh in that tender region below the hip-bone. For the first time since she had come into the bed she made a noise, a whimper of pain, of fear too perhaps. Encouraged, he knelt over her, pinching and biting her, playing her as though she were some manner of complicated harp. He was afraid he would truly lose control, yet the sensation, a seductive vertigo, enticed him. Beneath his fingers he felt a faint trembling. Was it her, himself, or both of them? No longer could he begin to guess what was in her mind. She was as foreign to him as Bithynia. She was the perfectly kept secret of herself. She had beaten him. Why not admit it?

His hands circled her throat. His thumbs slid under her chin. He felt a kind of Olympian tenderness for her, having her life in his hands like a bird he was crushing. And through his hands, tightening around her neck, through the blood and flexed musculature of his arms, he did at last receive some slender knowledge of her, the tribulations of her hedged existence, the loneliness of beauty, the daily grind of wielding a power that was never quite powerful enough to free her. Yes, as she writhed beneath him, her hands clutching his wrists, nails gouging his skin, tearing at the glossy black hairs, he was discovering her, discovering . . .

GIACOMO!

He reared up from the bed, staggered back, collided with the table and launched something light and fragile into the air which smashed behind him on the floor. He heard her sputtering, dragging for breath, retching. How close had he come? Another minute? Half a minute? It had been closer than that. Casanova the woman-killer.

On hands and knees he fumbled for his clothes. He had to get out, dress, escape, but how vast the room seemed! Had his clothes been stolen? Anything was possible now. He wanted to shout 'Who's there?' but he was afraid he would be answered. Then his fingertips brushed against the material of his breeches. He clutched them, rolled on to his back and thrust in his feet, jamming them both into the same silken aperture. He struggled for a minute, more and more feebly, then lay still. He had passed into the eye of the storm and possessed, perhaps, half a minute before he would be deranged again by his unhappiness, half a minute of lucidity, of that preternatural calmness in which a man may save his life or else, with a coolness that so impresses the spectator, destroy himself.

He folded his arms across his chest like a defunct pharaoh. From the heart of the city came the peal of a bell, then the deeper note of the hour.

'Change or die,' he whispered. 'Change or die . . .'

PART TWO

1

Very early, a gang, more than a hundred strong, was waiting above Blackfriar's Steps to be hired for a day's work. Casanova, coming from the end of Water Lane, studied them, squinting through the half-light until he picked out two fellows, well made, who were standing at the back of the crowd, breakfasting on onions. He hailed them. The men looked at each other, looked at Casanova, pointed to themselves. Casanova nodded and smiled. The men approached, warily, for the rich do not usually hail the poor unless they wish to steal from them.

Fifteen minutes later, still clutching their onions, the former roustabouts wandered away towards the cathedral, pausing at every pane of glass to glimpse themselves, hatched from the morning's strange transaction, a pair of unlikely butterflies. A minute later, Jarba and Casanova, in short greasy jackets and hats that had obviously been used as lunch boxes, or worse, joined the back of a shuffling queue. Though the Chevalier had experimented with rending one of his older suits and having Mrs Feaver sew clumsy patches on, he had looked more like Harlequin than a man who earned his bread with his hands. There was a certain raggedness that could only be acquired over months and years, a certain gritty encrustation impossible to feign with a little soot in Pall Mall. The obvious solution had been to avail themselves of the genuine article. Now they were ready.

The foreman on his bench picked out those he fancied: the strong, the meek. Beside him, woollen scarf coiled about the lower half of his face, the clerk wrote down the names. There were lascars among this crowd, and silent, brass-eyed Chinese in quilted jackets. There were men blacker than Jarba and more incongruous than Casanova. There were women too, and children.

A north-east wind swirled the trash around their ankles, scattering the last of the night. Daylight, thought Casanova, taking in the full untidy majesty of the dawn, was never unambiguous. He slipped his hands into the pockets of his new coat, warming himself in the vestigial heat of another man's body.

'Name?' demanded the foreman.

'Jack Newhouse.'

'Hands!'

'Hans?'

Jarba held out his own salmon-pink palms; Casanova followed his example. The foreman inspected them, noted the absence of calluses, broken nails, grey scurf, then stared up at their faces. For a moment it seemed that he would turn them away, but the morning was cold and the men before him, despite the smoothness of their skin, were well figured. He grunted, the clerk inscribed their names, and Casanova conjured up a smile that was not entirely false, for in his breast – the hairs of which were already making nests for the vermin he had inherited from the onion-eaters – he experienced the thrill, beloved of naughty children and actors, of being taken for what he was not, at least, not yet.

By the water's edge they waited with the others for a boat to take them out to the bridge. The clouds broke. The rain dripped off their noses, collected in the gutters of their ears. It was not unlike being in the army again, which at nineteen, in the spring of 1744, he had joined in Venice and had served in, without the least distinction, until the winter of '45. The army – that absurd ragbag of an army – had at least taught him to withstand long periods of physical discomfort. One had learnt to put up with things, learnt that being wet and tired did not kill you, that any man had the capacity to thrive in circumstances which, in civilian life, he would consider intolerable. It was a lesson he had never forgotten.

The boat curved up to the steps. The next batch of workers, delicately shoving, clambered aboard. The ferryman pushed off, the little bowl of his pipe turned down to keep the rain out. The boat was very low, no more than half a finger between the gunnel and the orange and grey tresses of the river. A dead cat floated by, a rat hanging on to its tail. Too late, thought Casanova, to send Jarba back for the umbrella.

They disembarked at a jetty attached to one of the new piers. Casanova, rubbing at the red crease his new collar had worn into the back of his neck, gazed in wonder at the vitality of the works. Here at least, among the mounds of stone and timber, the ropes, derricks and pumps, the constant purposeful shouting, people were doing something useful, heroic even. Overhead, a block of stone the size of the Duke of Bedford's carriage traversed the air in a cradle of shrill hemp. Besides the labourers, numbers of runtish horses lounged patiently against the rain. The foreman came, riding over the water with his pug, the man all canine puff, the dog ripe with human malice. Orders were given and the workers moved off, slow and grey, a clotted smoke, flexing their hands, taking up their tools.

Casanova's gang was sent to the piling hammer: six hundred kilos of sleeping iron launched from its rubble bed by thirty ropes and sixty arms. The first hour was almost pleasant, Casanova exulting in his own power, even grinning at the foreman, who in turn observed him as though he faintly recalled him from another lifetime, some old feud between them. By the second hour, sweat stung his eyes and his heart swung in his chest like a ship's bell. He glanced, somewhat guiltily, towards Jarba. His insistence that they enter the new life together had strained Jarba's loyalty to the limit. It had been necessary to give presents, and even then, Jarba's expression had suggested he would rather try his fortune at the Exchange. House servants were so particular! But in the end, having promised Jarba that he would review the situation in, say, a month or two, and that he would not – as he had threatened to do in his first enthusiasm – get rid of the house in Pall Mall, he had prevailed. Now, his lips cracked, his chin flecked with dried slobber, Casanova winked at his valet, though what it must have looked like he had no idea. Not, he guessed, the kind of face to reassure a man.

After the third hour they rested and Casanova walked unsteadily to where the new arch on the city side was receiving its casing of dressed stone. The rain had given way to a sun of chewed brass, and London, smoky Atlantis, had risen into the morning, the dome of St Paul's draped in scarves of aqueous northern light. Over the hats and the dust, through the webs of rope, he observed, with a momentary pang, the commotion of the town, its semaphore of ladies' silks and golden sword hilts, of windows in austere buildings batting back the sunlight from rooms where who knew what agreeable, what peppery intrigues were hatching.

He turned his back on it and called to mind another memory heavier than any iron hammer, viz the Chevalier de Seingalt on his back like a beetle in the unlit parlour in Denmark Street, tears trailing from his face like black ribbons. Of the journey home he had only a confused recollection. It was like a painting slashed by a madman. On this shred, a man's amazed eye, large as an egg; on this, a pool of oleaginous light where a wretched girl suckled a child; on this, the old watchman, drunk and grizzled, holding up his lamp to gaze at a man distractedly passing . . .

All of us, thought Casanova grimly, all of us must make one such a journey as he had made that night.

Just as full sensation was finding its way back to his fingertips, the gong was struck, the foreman bawled, the dog jived like a felon on the end of its leash and the gang was set to work again. Ten years ago, thought Casanova, the effort would not have troubled him. Five years ago he could have shrugged it off convincingly. But now he found himself perplexed by limits he had not known before. There was a buzzing in his ears, his lungs felt as small as ladies' purses, his thighs were trembling, but each time the hammer swung into the air he felt himself purged of another orgy, another tasteless evening of champagne and cheating, another laborious seduction of someone's niece, another lie.

Hour four was best forgotten, was in fact forgotten in the difficulties of hour five. Hour six revealed the full elasticity of time, each worker immersed in a lonely epic of endurance, for to each of them it seemed that he alone was raising the hammer.

Another break; this one even shorter than the first. Ten minutes to slump against the stone of the new parapet and rearrange the strips of rag that held the skin in place against the lick of the rope. From their pockets the labourers produced flasks and bottles. Jarba and Casanova looked on, their blood still following the rhythm of the hammer, washing from toes to scalp and back again in ponderous waves.

'How is it,' asked Casanova, 'we have omitted to provide ourselves with some refreshments?' He looked around as if there might be a convenient place where they could procure quail's eggs and chocolate. Even an onion might not be unwelcome. An onion and a mouthful of water.

A figure approached them, face sealed with grey dust, large eyes like pools of amber in a wasteland. Not coming too close, he – she? – held out a bottle. Jarba pushed himself up to accept it and spoke to the stranger before passing the bottle to Casanova. Casanova drank, sputtered, wiped his lips with the back of his hand.

'What is this, Jarba, that the creature has brought us?'

Jarba said: 'It is English gin.'

'And the creature's name?'

Jarba enquired. The personage answered him in a whisper, then took back the bottle and rejoined a group of labourers who were hunched in the lee of a large derrick.

'Her name,' announced Jarba, 'is Miss Rosie O'Brien.'

'Ah,' said the Chevalier, reaching down to finger a lace cuff he was no longer wearing. 'We must find some way of thanking her.'

The gang was set to carrying baskets, large wicker baskets filled with clay and rubble. Determined to prove his credentials as a good worker, Casanova seized the heaviest of them and staggered the hundred yards to where another group was raking and pounding the rubble into a base for the causeway. His second basket was even larger than the first. He bent to it and dragged it into the air. Immediately, there was a vile singing in the muscles of his back and for a moment he was holding the basket only with his gambler's fingertips. The foreman watched him, the dog lolling its head, stretching its neck as if to ease some symptom of canine lunacy. Casanova lumbered forward. Rosie O'Brien came up beside him, her own basket laid easily in her arms as though it were loaded with petals or goose down. She turned to him, his face now as grey and stiff as hers, and spoke to him – in English? Gaelic? – explaining, so it seemed, how the baskets should be held, lightly, just so, in the unflexed sling of the arms.

'Ah, *grazie. Molto grazie.*'

He started to bow, felt his weight shift dangerously forwards and pulled back at the last moment. The girl walked past him, unloaded her basket on to the heap and was lost for a moment in a pillar of grey-green dust, like Daphne, fleeing from Apollo, transformed into a tree.

For the last hour they worked by the light of torches. Tiredness did not apply; each was carried by the work, riding its broad back, resting upon it, so that when the gong sounded and they gazed, surprised and stupefied, at the starless sky like wakers from a profound sleep, they could hardly stand. The morning's journey was reversed, the labourers queuing on the jetty, the oarsman pulling them across the stretch of river to the barnacled steps at Blackfriars.

'The first day,' said Casanova, as Jarba helped him from the boat, 'was bound to be the hardest.'

'Yes,' replied Jarba, tonelessly, turning away, turning west towards the lamplit squares, Pall Mall and home. Home?

'Dear Jarba,' called Casanova, catching his valet's arm, 'there are no feather beds for us tonight.'

'Mine,' said Jarba, 'is horsehair.'

'I always thought . . .' Casanova shrugged, Venetian style, denoting something warmer and more complicated than indifference. The others were moving off, calling their farewells across the cold night air.

'You have seen the girl?' asked Casanova. 'The one with the bad teeth who shared her drink with us?'

2

They found her among a group walking in a straggling crocodile into Holland Street. The newcomers, too weary even to scratch themselves, tagged along at the back as the crocodile moved up Puddle Dock Hill and wriggled through Dean Court into St Paul's churchyard. On the cathedral steps men in horsecoats were confabulating as they did on the steps of cathedrals everywhere, and in the darker fringes women stiff with cold waited to mutter something wanton to passing trade. They did not waste their art on the labourers. The labourers had their own doxies; uglier, poorer, more ruined than these.

On to Cheapside, past Bow church, the Royal Exchange, into Leadenhall Street. Casanova had been walking, staring blindly at his feet. When he looked up, something of the world's substance had been drained from the surroundings. These streets, these buildings, with their air of weary danger, he had not seen them before yet he knew them from his night walks through the quarters of the poor in Rome and Paris; knew their smell too – mank, slurry, the cheese-rind reek of poverty.

Somewhere in Whitechapel the crocodile turned sharply and dived down steps luminous with filth into a cellar cook shop. The workers slumped on to the benches, leaning their elbows on tables where hog-fat candles burnt in bottle necks, pale flames blistering the air. A woman of astonishing obesity, as inscrutable as a shogun, stood at one end of the room by a fire ladling victuals into bowls. A child, Sophie's age perhaps, rickety, her skin as yellow as the candle flames, handed out the bowls and picked the coins from the labourers' palms. Casanova peered at what she had brought him. Substances sized like dormice slid beneath his spoon. It did not appear like food at all, not the kind one is expected to put in one's mouth, but looking up he saw that everyone was already eating, concentrating, threading the slop from bowl to mouth, the men's stubble jewelled with fat. Now and then they stopped, breathed deeply and went on.

After the first mouthful he ate gratefully, despite the difficulty of holding a spoon between puffed and bloody fingers. He scraped out his bowl, scoured it with a piece of bread and even joined in the chorus of belches. Several voices then began to shout for drink. The cook, with a key on the end of a long chain wound around the bulk of her hips, unlocked a cupboard; the child teetered again between the benches, the bottles hugged against her tiny breasts.

To the side of Casanova, a middle-aged man with dimpled fists and the chubby, melancholy face of a disappointed grocer, hearing the hushed Italian pass between the Chevalier and his servant, addressed them in the same language, and confided to them – glancing left and right as he did so – that he was an Austrian, name of Kasper, a refugee in hiding from Maria Theresa's secret police. He knew everyone. There would be no difficulty obtaining a bed for the night or for as many nights as they wished. He, Kasper – tapping the side of his nose – would be their guide in this swampy underworld. They shared with him a bottle of porter, the Austrian spiking his portion with a dozen drops of laudanum, patting the phial containing the drug and saying cheerfully: 'This is what stops me throwing myself into the river!'

Casanova looked for Rosie, saw her sleeping at the next table, her face, anxious and exhausted, laid on the hard pillow of her powerful arms. How easy it would be to rescue her! The money he had in his purse – which weighed in his pocket like the secret contradiction of his intentions, his little *borsa* of hypocrisy; enough in there to buy the cook shop, perhaps the whole street – could set her sleeping in sheets of cool linen and send her out in the morning dressed by gold, by English guineas. And then? A month of happiness, of her stunned relief, of disbelief, before he tired of her and left her to survive as a type of Charpillon, but without the Charpillon's market-commanding beauty, nor the protection of those piranhas she lived with.

The glands beneath his arms and in his groin were swollen by the beginning of some low continuous fever. He did not need laudanum. He was high on the salt of extremity and moved, almost beyond words, by the rugged beauty of these faces that surrounded him, the faces of old campaigners who had seen and suffered more than could readily be made sense of. There was not one of them who did not have some limp or squint, some small or spectacular deformity. These were the cream of the island's wretched, the survivors, sold out of workhouses or foundling hospitals, the poor-hole their one sure inheritance. It was an honour to be among such a people. One would like to salute them, to paint them, write strophes in praise of their doggedness.

He rubbed his eyes, felt tearful and pleasantly remote. A woman clambered on to the table and jogged her way through country dances while the men sang in a circle at her feet and beat time with their mugs. What did Lord Pembroke with his three shaves a day, his fighting cocks, his everything-comes-easy, know of these simple pleasures, the camaraderie of those who had nothing but each other?

'Are you also in hiding, signore?' asked Kasper, his face pushed close to Casanova's. 'Your secrets are safe with me, signore.'

3

The boarding house was on Petticoat Lane and the only light came from a bonfire in the middle of the street where those who could not pay tuppence for a bed inside huddled round the flames, begging without hope from passers-by.

At the door of the house an old woman, guarded by a giant in sailor's pantaloons and a coat so recently stolen it still gave off the whiff of a Hanover Square supper party, collected the money, sliding it into an old woollen stocking that muffled the clink of the coins. Inside, Casanova gagged at the stench from some vaguely glistening cesspool in the well of the stairs. He pressed his fist to his mouth, and holding with his other hand to Jarba's coat-tail, he ascended, expecting at any moment the creaking wood to give way beneath him. From all around – there seemed to be no doors in this house – came the susurration of troubled dreamers, the brawling, lonely baritone of drunks, the mewing of hungry children.

On the third floor – the fourth? the fifth? – the labourers entered a room at the rear of the house. On a score of mattresses, most of which had burst and vomited out their straw, sleepers lay promiscuously tangled, possessions in rag bundles tucked between them. A kind of sodden light leached from a lantern hung on a nail above the boarded fireplace. Jarba and Casanova picked their way towards a bed less populated than the others and eased themselves into the stew of human air beneath the blanket. The other occupants, one of whom appeared to be the Austrian, stirred but did not wake.

On his back, gazing up at the shattered plaster of the ceiling, the Chevalier was reminded of a night twenty years previous, crossing the Marches outside Serravalle with that rogue Franciscan, Staffano, and how they had sheltered together in the house of a large peasant family and, while they slept, two crones, strong and smelly as she-goats, had attacked them for their purses or else to suck the young flesh from their bones. A tremendous fight had ensued, Staffano swinging his staff, the women shrieking and ducking . . .

A tide of exhausted laughter swept quietly through his chest. *Porco zio*, those were the days! From Serravalle he trailed his youthful shadow to Rome, to the Pope's slipper and to the little satin pumps of Lucrezia and her sister Angelica; to Cardinal Colonna, who had employed him to write love letters; and to the arbours of the Tivoli and the Frascati, where surely some version of himself was still walking with a girl and eating watermelon until their mouths were as red and sweet as a baby's.

Should he have stayed in Rome? Had that been his mistake? What times he had enjoyed there! That quality of the light and the way power smelt when one was close to it, like a very, very expensive whore. But to wish it back was to wish for time to unravel, to be a dog barking at the door of the past.

Goudar had been right, of course, (may sea monsters suck his brains through his nose); they were – had been – with their wit and their good legs and their willingness to walk into rooms others shied from, creatures of a similar strain. He had always suspected that Goudar had no parents, that he had been spawned autogenously from the stale air of some hotel room hired by the hour. And he too lacked proper origins; a mother of sorts, but his father could be the Doge or the Devil or merely some *mangiamarroni* who frequented the theatres where Zanetta had danced. Thus, bereft of those genealogies that tell a man what he is, what he is supposed to be, they had been forced to invent themselves. In Goudar's case the experiment had been, at best, a very partial success – the body of a man, the head of a mink rat – but for himself, ah! it had worked almost too well. He was exactly what the silk-wearing classes had needed: a truly accommodating fellow with a scrap of genius who, like a Venetian canal, was all the more charming on account of his corruption, the shimmer of his pollution. Very well. For years he had been distracted by his successes, by the world's applause, but now . . .

Something was burrowing into the skin of his thigh. He did not care; the sensation was remote, and vermin were enough like men to be tolerated upon occasion. Tomorrow, he thought, they could clean the room, find fresh straw for the mattresses. Some pictures for the walls? A new life. Jack Newhouse. Man of the people.

4

On their way to work the following morning it was as dark as when they had lain down, darker it seemed, for there were fewer lights about at this hour. A watchman had a brazier in front of his shelter; a priest hurried by with a boy who carried a lantern; a glow seeped out from a cellar where figures could be glimpsed labouring with knives at long bloody tables. But the labourers did not see each other's faces clearly until they were in the cook shop, breakfasting on what they had not finished the night before, the soup in the woman's pot which, like a pot in a fairytale, seemed inexhaustible.

There was no singing, no conversation, only the noise of their eating, which sounded like a hundred men walking across a boggy field, walking slowly, patiently. How was it, he wondered, they did not scuttle on their bandy legs into the houses of the rich, slay the fat banker and his wife, gorge themselves on brandy and pistachios? What was hanging to them? Or the plantations, or the hulks? What had they to fear? The problem, decided Casanova, probing the growth of his beard, was that they had no leaders, no unity, no idea of themselves. They thought themselves fortunate if they were not required actually to starve to death, like that woman who had been found naked and dead of famine in Stonecutter Street only days ago. Twenty such a month they said, pulled from London houses, and this in a town where the Lord Mayor's coach was so heavy with gold, so studded with ornament, that six fine horses could barely drag it through the mud.

Even before they started to haul the ropes, threads of fire burned along his back. He fortified himself by remembering feats of stamina that had amazed society. Who had forgotten Sulzbach and the great piquet game with D'Entraigues du Pin? The two of them at the gaming table for over forty hours, relieving themselves in pots brought to the table and eating nothing but some iced shrimp soup on the second day. The game had only ended when D'Entraigues, reaching forward to play one more losing card, had collapsed on the table and was carried from the room by flunkeys and not seen again for two days. As for himself, he had required nothing more than a light emetic administered by the casino surgeon, and three hours' rest before joining the company at dinner. How impressed little Mam'zel Saxe had been! Such a pity it had to take place in a mule's behind like Sulzbach.

His arms felt as weak as a child's. It was pride that gripped the rope, and when, after the second hour, his blisters broke and blood wept between his fingers, he grinned at it, gritted his teeth and redoubled his efforts, amazed to find that even now, hauling himself to a kind of gritty sainthood, too exhausted to swallow, he was making eyes at Rosie O'Brien. He liked Irish girls. He had sold one once to the King of France. Boucher had painted her portrait.

Filling their baskets side by side under a sky the colour of fried pig's liver, on the afternoon of the third day, Casanova slipped his large, rag-bandaged hand into Rosie's – the skin of her palm as hard as tortoiseshell – and sighed to her as effectively as he had ever done in rococo drawing rooms or among the topiary of a palace garden. It was not, it seemed, a simple matter to step suddenly out of a part he had played for so many years. The instincts adhered; indeed, they seemed to contain him. He began to wonder if, as a man, a life, he were any freer than a turnspit dog which when set at liberty can only run in circles.

On the fifth day, a man died.

He had been working in the new cofferdam, shoring up the walls against the blunt head of the river. There was a cry – which may have been the man himself or the warning of a friend, seeing the wooden sleeve of the dam suddenly bulge inwards -- then the dam was gone, two of the wooden stakes cartwheeling freakishly in the air. The labourers ran to the parapet, staring down to where the water, after a moment's boil, had already resumed its calm. A boat was launched, picking its way amid the debris. There was no sign of the man and no one imagined he could have escaped as none of the labourers could swim. For ten minutes the boat circled about, the oarsmen peeping through the scales of the river, prodding it. Then someone called from the bridge and the boat turned back. Mylne was standing up at his table, the plans braced with stones, the architect's young face faintly shocked as though he had received a rebuke. The foreman, with dog and stick, herded the gangs back to their work. Hands curled around the still-warm hafts of tools. Casanova heard the sound of someone, a boy or a woman, softly crying, but could not see who it was, as if the sorrow were not specific to one person but came sobbing out of the air between them all. On London Bridge the wagons continued their journeys; smoke ascended peacefully from the leaf-burning in Cuppers Gardens on the South Bank. By nightfall it was assumed that the tide would have carried the body as far as Greenwich, or even to the sea. The dead man was put away, his memory, like his body, hidden, carried off by unseen currents.

5

The idea for the strike was born on the sixth day of labour, during the third hour on the hammer.

'HEAVE!'

So were the first seeds of comradely distrust. (Were these sons of bitches pulling their share? Was he pulling for two? For half a dozen?)

Casanova brooded. He wished Jarba would stop looking at him like that. It was not valet-like at all.

6

On Sunday they rested, they lived. The labourers, paid in the tavern late on Saturday night – the foreman in cahoots with the landlord – staggered from their mattresses dumb with drink and made their way to the pawnbrokers' to redeem their scraps of finery. Then, the men in shirts they had inherited from dead fathers, long-dead grandfathers, the linen scrubbed and tenderly darned until it had the frail luminosity of a holy relic, and the women in bonnets woven from straw that had grown in Wicklow or Connemara meadows in the time of Queen Anne, trailed out in their tens and hundreds through the northern arteries of the town – Goswell Street, Bishopsgate, Brick Lane – to court among the brick stacks, to watch dogfights, to drink and to crack each other's heads good-naturedly with shillelaghs.

Casanova went with Jarba and Kasper to Dolly's Famous Steak House on Paternoster Row. There – faces shining with the icy rust-coloured water from the street pump they had washed at – they ordered great smoking steaks with onion gravy and buttered potatoes, and three bottles of the most bloody wine in the house, but Dolly, shelf-breasted, imposing as a storm cloud, would not have them in, not with their bridge dust, their dosshouse vermin. They left, as haughtily as men in such shabby jackets were able, and bought provisions from a pastry shop on Fleet Street, narrowly avoiding a meeting with the great lexicographer as he sailed from the door of the Mitre tavern in animated conversation with his little Scotsman. For an instant Johnson looked directly into Casanova's eyes and – still talking – seemed momentarily confused before bowling into the road, arm in arm with his protégé, between a troop of militia and the tumbrel of a butcher's boy.

At Moorfields, the air was scented with bonfires. Sitting under a tree near the Bethlem lunatic asylum, Casanova unfolded his plan. The Austrian nodded his head excitedly, his mouth full of cinnamon cake. He knew what needed to be done: secret names, pamphlets, code-words, invisible ink . . .

'But we must behave like reasonable men,' interrupted the Chevalier.

'Of course,' said Kasper, breaking the last custard tart into three unequal parts and eating two of them. 'We shall be polite. The English like to pretend they are such reasonable people.'

They considered their demands, setting them down with a

smudge of charcoal on the back of the pastry paper as the sun stretched out their shadows. By dusk, at the hour one must first breathe on one's fingertips for warmth, there were nine points.

1. No more than four hours in a day labouring upon the ropes.
2. Compensation for smashed limbs.
3. Nine shillings a week for all adult workers.
4. The decent burial of the dead.
5. Medicines for those who fell into sickness.
6. A provision of beer or (at Casanova's insistence) wine at the morning break.
7. No workers to be beaten by the officers of the Company.
8. The proper employment of children under seven.
9. No labourer to be turned away without good cause.

A tenth point eluded them.

'Must there be ten?' asked Casanova. 'Have we not dealt with the most urgent matters?'

'Ten,' replied the Austrian, 'is to be preferred. It will seem otherwise that we could not think of a tenth point. It will make us ridiculous. What is your opinion, Jarba? You, more than we, see with the eyes of the oppressed.'

'Signore,' said Jarba, who had been sitting a little apart from the others, looking at the asylum glowing in the sunset, 'there is not enough blood in your scheme. If the foreman's throat were to be cut. Or if the architect were to be hanged from his own bridge ... but since you ask, let me say that these demands will lead to nothing but our being flogged and thrown into the river.'

The other two were staring at him in amazement. 'I cannot imagine where you have got such ideas,' said the Chevalier. 'However, you have provided us with a tenth demand.'

He scraped a piece of dried custard from the paper and wrote:

10. No labourer is to suffer reprisals for bringing these most just considerations to the attention of the Company.

'No doubt,' said Jarba, 'there will have to be speeches.'

'Indeed,' replied Casanova, 'there must be speeches.'

'Quite a few,' said Kasper, squeezing his knees and grinning at his fellow conspirators. 'The people expect it.'

Jarba laughed: a sound like a little handbell which nonetheless seemed to carry over the whole of Moorfields. Even the rooks, those scruffy birds, circling over the elm-tips, appeared to laugh with him. Casanova turned his back on him, wondering as he did so what on earth it was they were doing in this place.

7

That night, Casanova gave Rosie a cake of Corinth raisins. They were stood together by the corner of White Chapel and Angel Alley, observed by a softly creeping audience of dogs and beggars. She held the cake in her hands, examining it in the light of the area's one streetlamp. Her breath betrayed a drowsy whiff of gin. She sniffed, peered at him with brimming eyes. Gently, he took the cake from her, broke off a piece and fed her, his fingers grazing her lips, her teeth. It was the most delicate, the most truly lewd thing he had done in years.

8

In the cook shop on Monday evening, the labourers solemn with exhaustion, the air thick with the reek of bones, Casanova roused himself, climbed upon the table and clapped his hands. For a moment his gaze snagged on the eyes of the cook-shop mistress and he faltered, just as once before, faced with such a look, he had dried up before the Inquisitors of the Republic. He turned away, cleared his throat and began to speak, pausing, and sometimes forgetting to pause, for Jarba to translate.

'My friends, I know what the rich are like. You have no idea how tedious their lives are to them. We should pity them! Every day like the last – cards, the theatre, dinner with some man who in private slanders you. Why is it so many shoot themselves? Because it is easier to pull a trigger than to get out of bed in the morning. Their wealth, their freedom, bring them no joy. Behind the walls of their mansions they envy you, fear you, hate you. They know their lives are useless. But you, who raise monuments to man's civilisation with your blistered hands . . .'

It may be, thought Casanova, that Jarba is introducing *mots* of his own invention, for there was more hilarity than he had expected, more in fact, than was strictly proper in a speech that treated of the nobility, the sublimity of the working people. Jarba looked up at him. He said: 'They wish to know if you will buy them liquor.'

Bottles and mugs – the mugs so dirty one did not dare to examine them too closely – were given out. The labourers drank. Rosie smiled at him. Now they listened, regarding him, this shark-nosed foreigner, with new respect.

Casanova took the pastry paper from his breast and flourished it above their heads. He read the demands, operatic now, convinced of his part, stamping the table as he read, his words filled with anger towards he knew not what, some injustice that no list could ever rectify. As each demand was translated the labourers waved their mugs and whistled. By the sixth they were cheering, by the eighth it was as rowdy as a bear pit, and when he had finished, a dozen of the drunker men lifted him on their shoulders and marched around the shop with him, singing like heroes.

'I come from such as these,' murmured Casanova, 'and now I have returned.'

There was something shocking in the thought, but he trembled with the pleasure of confession. He would have liked to have run, that very moment, to Lord Pembroke's house and told him. He would have liked to have shouted it at court and seen the powdered faces, brittle as Sèvres china, turn away from him.

Rosie stretched up. He felt the hot nuggets of her fingertips. 'We are one!' he cried. 'We are one!' And the labourers, as though they had been waiting for his command, ran with him full tilt through the door, cracking his head so hard on the lintel he fell back, dazed, blinded, borne through the wretched streets on a gondola of howling strangers.

9

When he woke, his head pillowed on Jarba's chest, his ear upon Jarba's heart, he sat up, felt the crusty extra crease in his brow and climbed cautiously to his feet, following the dry riverbed of light to the stairs. Several people – it was hard to be sure how many – were sleeping there, their bodies rippled awkwardly over the steps. Others lay in dark corners where the stairs turned, rustling as Casanova passed them and sending his hand to his pocket for his little Venetian oyster blade.

At the street door he nodded to the old woman. She had an infant on her knees, a great-grandchild perhaps, which rested its head in a perfection of ease against the empty wine-sack of her breast. The doorman was there also, smiling sentimentally and forgetting to change his expression as he looked up at Casanova, so that for the briefest moment they regarded each other like brothers.

Outside, the Chevalier relieved himself in the broad stagnant stream of filth that ran down the middle of the street, and was buttoning his breeches when he saw, flitting out of the house, the shade of Rosie O'Brien. He signalled her, a piazza-crossing, arcade-threading 'Tssst!' She came to him and he hauled her into his shadow, into the coil of his arms, and kissed her, one dirty mouth pressed upon another.

They walked together, journeying through thieves' markets, thieves' towns, the inhabitants huddling round their fires, inspecting their loot of ladies' handkerchiefs, gentlemen's watches and those little purses which men going out at night fill with a guinea or two for the footpads and highwaymen to steal, their true wealth stashed about them more secretly. Some among them called to Rosie and exchanged rapid sentences with her. All the while she held Casanova's hand, tightly, spreading over him a mantle of safety. Without her they would have gutted him for his shoes, for his teeth, even for his guts perhaps, which might have earned them sixpence from the tripe-sellers or the ancient guild of pie-makers.

Was he the first? How many others had she taken on this odyssey through the secret filaments of the town, wandering like Eurydice in hell between one uncertain island of light and another? He glimpsed the walls of the Tower, then they turned left, away from the town, and passed through Wapping. Twice they were forced to hide from the crimps of the East India Company who passed them in fast hushed gangs, hauling from the drinking dens anyone too weak, to drunk to flee them. Between the wooden hovels the masts and webbed rigging of the shipping stood out against the horizon of the far bank: galliots, smacks, oyster boats, brigs-of-war, Company barges, schooners, hay-boats and barques. From a cellar door came a burst of Urdu, and those men, arguing furiously in the middle of the street, were they not speaking Russian?

At last the city ended – a house, a ruined barn, a field. The river, unencumbered but for a half-dozen fishing boats, glided peacefully between its banks. The breeze tasted of estuaries and the dark was soothed by the peeping of river birds. On the bank by a willow tree – a tree she must have had in mind all night –

they lay down and embraced, cooing in their separate tongues and moving from intimacy to intimacy, collecting each other's breath, touching each other as though in search of secret doors. It was too cold for much undressing and they caressed each other through skins of sour fabric, pulling aside layer after unwashed layer until their fingers strayed on to the palp of the other's flesh. This, considered Casanova, beginning to riot in the girl's limbs, is how gods and sparrows did it, clenched under the public sky, racked by the moment. He had almost forgotten this.

Afterwards, the grass that had been beneath them uncurled and smelled momentarily of spring. He told her. She did not understand him, his words, but laughed anyway, kindly, and they returned together, honeymooning in the dog-haunted streets, their endeavours blessed by clouds of pre-dawn drizzle. In the dosshouse they resumed their slots; Rosie lay between a pair of dreaming girls, perhaps her sisters; Casanova rested his head again on Jarba's chest, synchronised his breathing with that of his servant and felt, as sleep stole through his senses, something like happiness, like pity, like

10

By the time they must walk to the bridge the drizzle had lengthened into rain, and rain so rich in soot it left black streaks on their faces. They walked in their usual huddle, coughing and cursing, the street mud lapping over their shoes. Casanova was sorry the weather was not better, for when the fishermen used to strike in Venice they always chose a fine day for it, making a festival out of a dispute, keeping everyone entertained and making themselves so popular the Serenissima always surrendered the extra ducats. He wondered if they should not delay, but the rain stopped abruptly as they ferried across to the bridge and he took it as a good omen. The foreman's dog greeted them, hurling itself the length of its leash, eyes bulging, enraged to see the draggled army back again, as though each evening when the workers departed it believed they were leaving for ever.

The gangs formed up in platoons and dispersed to their stations. Hands dragged from pockets reached up for the familiar ropes. The cussing and spitting intensified. There was a moment's terrible unhappiness, the foreman sucking in his breath as though inhaling the collective will. At the other end of the bridge the architect was apparently watching them, though through the caliginous air his face was as featureless as an egg.

'HEAVE!'

They dragged the ropes, fists swelling with blood, the ninety-seven aches in shoulders, back and legs rediscovered precisely where they had bloomed the day before. Who would have thought that hair could throb?

'HEAVE!'

The hammer rose, swung and fell. A monstrous heartbeat. The city's monstrous heartbeat.

'HEAVE!'

Porco miseria! Had they made the hammer heavier? Were these fraternal dogs actually pulling at all? He glared at them. Why did they avoid his eyes?

'HEAVE!'

The signal was to be the bells of St Bride's ringing eight o'clock. Then they would let go of the ropes and, with Jarba and Kasper flanking him, Casanova would walk to the architect's table and present their demands. Perhaps, he thought, his mouth dry as a griddle stone, the architect would invite them to sit at his table and they would have a glass of wine together.

'HEAVE!'

Today it felt as if they were lifting the whole city, dragging it up by its roots: cathedrals, jails, bordellos ... There was an ominous rasping in his chest, an inner surf, though actually the sound was more like the noise of money pushed across the green lawn of a gaming table; and the clicking of his shoulder joints, was that not like the click of the dealer's abacus? It had been good to be good at something and he had been good at that, in the days when his luck had held and it was effortless. Good at talking too, and keeping a cool head, and knowing when to leave. Good at many things.

'HEAVE!'

What if, for some reason, the bells were not rung today? In this miserable climate one could not see the sun to guess the hour. With his gaze he tried to catch Jarba's attention, but his valet, his co-conspirator, was already in a dream of exhaustion. How frail he looked. When he pulled the rope his teeth showed like those of a sick horse.

'HEAVE!'

Would they never ring?

'HEAVE!'

'HEAVE!'

At last, their music sullen in the dense air, the bells of St Bride's announced the hour. Casanova closed his eyes and counted. Five, six, seven ... seven or eight? Who cared. As the hammer drove into the pile he let go of his rope and walked, lightly, strangely, as a man in a dream. The foreman was watching him, the dog also, a loop of brilliant drool hanging from its lower jaw. Alerted by the unexpected hush, the architect glanced up from his plans, frowning, his dividers gripped in his hand like a weapon. Casanova could hear footsteps behind him though he dared not look round to see who was with him, to turn round as though he were afraid it might only be the echo of his own feet.

Mylne stood. He looked like a boy general unexpectedly approached by the haggard commander of the opposing camp. Casanova smiled. He had an incurable regard for any young man on the make. Pulling out the proposals from his shirt, he offered them with a bow. Mylne accepted them, nervously, as if the sweat-blurred, rain-blurred paper might scar his fingers. He looked round at his secretary, his draughtsmen, his chief engineer.

'Monsieur,' began Casanova, an odd chilly feeling at the back of his neck, 'you are the young genius at whose command the air is spanned by stone. I am but a humble worker. Yet these proposals – the work of several hands – are so palpably just I have the greatest confidence that they shall find favour. If I might expound upon the first point ... ?'

There was a look of baffled anger on the architect's face. One of the other gentlemen, concealing his mouth with his hand, whispered into Mylne's ear.

Casanova asked: 'You understand French, monsieur? Italian? Jarba!'

He looked back. Yes, honest Jarba was with him, face like polished grit, staring towards the dome of St Paul's. Kasper was also there, though his expression suggested that he had merely stepped away from his duties for a moment to apologise for the unfortunate behaviour of a colleague.

'Meester Mylne . . .' began Casanova again, but what was the point of it all? These men thought he was mad. Nothing would be changed. Nothing. Ever.

The architect passed the paper to the foreman. The foreman, as if making one of those chains of paper children holding hands, tore the ten proposals into halves, quarters, eighths, sixteenths, then mashed the pieces into a pulp and fed them to the dog, which ate them with an unexpectedly gentle manner, like a governess dining on a stewed pear.

There was one of those hiatuses; everyone waiting for someone else to speak or to perform. Mylne sat down, cleared his throat. The foreman started to loosen his grip upon the leash. Casanova's brain was quite empty of ruses. A little rhyme went through his head, an idiotic Venetian ditty the whores on the Calle delle Post used to sing:

> *Alla mattina una messetta*
> *Al dopo dinar una bassetta,*
> *Alla sera una donnetta . . .*

He was aware of a commotion behind him and wondered, with a sinking of his heart, if the others had at last decided to join him. A shout went up. The gentlemen at the table no longer appeared interested in him. They were walking hurriedly to the

parapet which was already thickly lined with workers. Casanova
followed; taller than most, he leaned over the hats and pigtails
and saw below a boat riding the current beside the submerged
cofferdam. He did not at first understand. The play was going on
without him. He had been forgotten. His performance had been
a complete failure. And then he saw that the river, in its wisdom,
had given up the body of the drowned man. Two oarsmen were
hauling it over the stern of the boat. The water had stripped the
dead man of his clothes, all but a black woollen stocking hanging
from one of his feet like an eel that had unsuccessfully tried to
swallow him.

They stretched him on his back in the centre of the boat,
sprawled, his flesh shiny as though glazed with fresh egg whites.
One of the oarsmen, shaking the water from his hands, carefully
untied the handkerchief at his neck and, seeming to hesitate a
moment whether to cover the dead man's face or genitals, finally
laid the cloth over the open eyes, the icy coral of the lips. The
labourers, each according to his faith, mumbled a prayer or
made a sign and followed the progress of the boat towards the
shore, but Casanova, working his way along the bridge behind
their backs, half running, stumbling over stone and timber, was
staring at another boat two hundred yards downstream, where
a gentleman in blue and a lady in a red cloak were being rowed
in leisurely fashion towards the sea. The pang he felt he could
not have explained, yet as they became lost among the hulks
and barges, the scurrying water traffic, it was as if they were
the last two inhabitants of his world and when they were gone
the little island of his life would be empty. For a moment he had
his weight on the parapet wall as if he intended to heave himself

over and swim after them, but Jarba was standing beside him and the Chevalier had no telescope to give him, no parting gift.

11

The evening of the abortive strike, Casanova sent Jarba back to Pall Mall to fetch two bottles of wine. Jarba returned, smelling of shaving soap and fresh linen. He had a hamper with white wine, cold chicken and macaroons. He also had the Chevalier's second-best winter overcoat with its fox-fur collar and engraved steel buttons. Casanova slipped the coat over his shoulders and they sat together on Savoy Steps, their drinking illuminated by the lights from Somerset House.

'A coat,' said Casanova, pausing to pour the last drop of wine on to his tongue and wipe the chicken grease from his lips with a napkin, 'is a very small concession.'

'Yes,' said Jarba, who was wearing his own, 'very small.'

'They have not beaten me, Jarba.'

'No,' said Jarba.

'I cannot go back to the old life.'

'No,' said Jarba, 'not yet.'

'There is no reason, however,' said the Chevalier, peering hopefully into the hamper, 'why we should not make ourselves more comfortable. The others are accustomed to it. Their skins are thicker. You and I on the other hand . . . Is there more wine, my friend? You brought just the two bottles?'

The next evening – for they had not, as Casanova had expected, had in truth hoped, been dismissed from the bridge, a fact as surprising as it was disconcerting and one that could only be attributed to the Company's reluctance to antagonise the workers so soon after the discovery of the drowned man's remains – they consoled themselves with a second hamper, better stocked than the first. Iced cheeses, apple cakes, a modest allowance of champagne. When they had eaten, Jarba shaved his employer by the light of an oil lamp outside the Turk's Head coffee house on the Strand. Then Casanova, in that mood of egalitarianism good champagne occasionally provoked in him, took the razor, wiped it, and shaved his valet. They stayed in the coffee house sipping chocolate and dozing by the fire until at midnight the proprietor gently roused them and informed them that he was closing. Back in their lodgings Jarba took a candle from his pocket, fixed it into the neck of a champagne bottle and lit it, casting its homely glow over their faces. From his other pocket he took Casanova's lamb's-wool nightcap.

'I brought you this, monsieur.' He gave it to the Chevalier, who scrunched it in his hands, sniffed at it.

'Bless you, Jarba. I am certain that no one could begrudge me such a trifle.'

Jarba carefully trimmed the candlewick. 'No one could begrudge you that, monsieur.'

Casanova looked at him, closely.

Curiously, the little comforts they allowed themselves did not make the new life any easier. Fresh rolls and coffee did not help them to face the rigours of the bridge as well as gin and hardtack had. Nor did a nightshirt and clean blankets improve their sleep. Despite their nightly exhaustion they lay awake listening to the house groan like an emigrant ship in rising weather. Their fellow workers observed them with open suspicion. Even Rosie looked confused, smiling awkwardly at this man transforming himself before her eyes, this man who wore rags beneath a fox-fur collar.

On the following Sunday, while the house was quiet, they portioned off a generous corner of the room with drapes; space enough for two hammocks and a table. The landlady was persuaded with a piece of gold, chewing it a full minute before she would admit its authenticity. The doorman found them chairs and a table, found them no doubt in someone's drawing room, and in the evening when they lit their lamps the little room glowed like a child's den. Rosie and Kasper were invited for dinner. A cold salmon gleamed like silver bullion on the table, and for a while the four of them stood around it like celebrants of some archaic faith, devotees of a streamlined pearly saviour. Then Jarba worked at it with knives, the fish gave up its meat and Kasper kissed Casanova's hand. Rosie looked on, holding her fork as though it were a type of large insect, unknown to her and possibly dangerous. The Chevalier encouraged her with smiles and nods. He was surprised that he had not properly noticed how dirty – no, how filthy – her hands were. Was this the girl he had swum in beside the Thames? This urchin?

When they had eaten, and the only sounds were the rumbling in Kasper's belly and the familiar hard music of coughs and moans from the other side of the drapes, Casanova suggested a hand of cards. But the Austrian, though he swore he had once known, could not remember the rules of any game, and Rosie shook her head, her expression veering from embarrassment to anger. Already, Casanova had decided against asking her to share his hammock, and as the wine was finished, he stood to dismiss them. Kasper embraced him, leaning damply against Casanova's chest before fumbling his way back into the outer darkness. Rosie edged her way around the table. Casanova bowed to her and in his best English bade her 'Goodanight'. Not until she had gone did he ask Jarba what it was she had said as she was leaving, and Jarba, slinging the hammocks, answered over his shoulder:

'Who are you.'

'Who are you?'

'Who are you.'

They stayed for one more week, though no one now was invited to share their feasts; no one would have come. The labourers felt mocked. Their hardships, it seemed, were part of the stranger's private game. The Company had him followed, suspecting treachery from rival syndicates, fearing that he might row out one moonless evening and season the works with gunpowder.

'I feel,' said Casanova to Jarba as they sat on their own at morning break, 'like a glass shilling from which the paint has begun to fray.'

On the fourth morning of that last week, the first to have a true winter wind of the kind that pressed icy fingers deep inside their ears – the labourers bandaging their heads with rags and Casanova wearing the yak-skin flaps of his Mongol hat tied beneath his chin – the foreman turned them away with a quick westerly jerk of his thumb. No words were exchanged, no explanations, no goodbyes. Kasper, among the gang waiting for the next ferry, stared down at his boots. Rosie was already on the bridge. Casanova waved, certain for the moment that she was looking at him, then turned and took his leave. What, after all, had he expected? Had he imagined that he might tiptoe away from himself? It had been nothing but a kind of carnival, a dressing-up, a child's game, but as Jarba went up to the Strand to find a hackney carriage, Casanova had the sudden urge to run back to the foreman and bribe him to let him pass. Not until they were crossing the bottom of the Haymarket was he finally convinced that it was over. He decided to blame Jarba, then decided not to. As they entered the house, Mrs Feaver threw up the little sticks of her arms for joy. Could it be, wondered Casanova, that the old woman was in love with him?

12

For a week after their return they dragged upon themselves, like heavy quilts, all the luxury the Chevalier's purse and pocket-book could bring them. In the downstairs rooms, slung in silver cooling-bowls, there were grapes the size of a man's fist, hothouse pineapples, blushing out-of-season apricots and boat-shaped lemons whose skins glowed so brilliantly in the dark one might have read by them. There were flowers too, a profusion of them, grown in curious circumstances by gentlemen with scientific gardens in Kew, the enormous blooms, light and fantastically coloured, hanging their heads in the parlour like globes of peeled air.

Outside the house sedan chairmen lounged against the railings harassing housemaids and holding spitting competitions, waiting to lug the foreigner or his valet about the town. In the evenings there was a carriage to carry them to gambling rooms and supper parties through streets perfumed with the scent of braziers and roasting chestnuts. Money flew from Casanova like a host of golden moths. He spent as though money were a bug gnawing at his softening muscles, as though it were a fox nibbling at his entrails. When Jarba did the monthly accounts, blotting and then sliding the ledger across the table to his employer, the Chevalier shut the book with a thud. Much more of this and he would have to return to the bridge, or find another elderly lady in need of a charming embezzler.

To calm this fever of extravagance they visited Signor Dominecetti's Turkish baths in Chelsea. Here, spice merchants and worldly bishops loomed through the steam like sturgeon in a khan's aquarium, bodies democratically nude, only their faces, ruddy, expensively jowled, signalling their rank. Casanova eased his back against a pillar. The heat hung round his neck like a lover. Sweat, rich as clarified butter, filtered through the creases and wrinkles of his face. He looked at his hands, which, from gripping the rope, still had a kind of permanent curl like an ape's. He flexed them and thought of Rosie, the hammer, the innutritious sweat of labour. What a nice story it would have been if he had managed to fall for her! How was it one could not place one's affections where one wished to? Why could one not say 'I shall love this girl' and so begin to love her? Could not love be made, as, for example, a painting was made through the intention of the artist? Or like a good soup, through the labour and skill of the cook? The heart would have its orders: become enamoured of Miss X, adore Madame Y. And if Miss X or Madame Y should prove false then one would burn the canvas, throw away the soup, start again. Ah, poor Rosie! Now they were like the two ends of Mylne's bridge, destined each day to grow a little further from each other . . .

He rested his eyes. When he opened them again a man was approaching him through the steam. What a face! Like an altar boy on his way to rape a nun.

'My dear Seingalt!'

'Greetings, Goudar. This place is sufficiently like hell for you to be at home in it.'

'I am glad to see you back among us, Chevalier. The world thought you had fled into France to escape the charms of a certain young woman.'

'I trust you knew better.'

'I? Well, I heard a very remarkable story. A man who looked so like you as to be your twin was seen working on . . .'

'Enough! I was staying with La Cornelys.'

'Cornelys? Poor woman, they say it will end badly for her. I understand she shall shortly be arrested for debt and that none of her aristocratic friends will come to her aid.'

'It is true there are only certain times when she may leave her house in safety.'

'It is to your credit, Seingalt, that you have not abandoned her. It must have been dull for you, though. You do not quite look yourself.'

'You are my physician again? You begin to alarm me.'

'You must know I take as much interest in your wellbeing as I do in my own.'

'If you have come to borrow money, Goudar, you may see that I have none upon me at the moment.'

'Money! I think not. Indeed, I hear that you lost every hand at the Cocoa Tree last night. That must have been expensive.'

'If one cannot afford to lose one should not sit down to play.'

'True. But does not every man have some amount he cannot afford to lose?'

'You know very well I am not one of those who ruins himself with the turn of a card.'

'I know it, my dear Chevalier. We both have our systems. We keep our heads whichever way the cards are going. I was not necessarily speaking of money, however. There are other things a man may lose which in the end destroy him.'

'For example?'

'His reputation.'

'That mirage!'

'His luck.'

'Only a fool depends on luck.'

'His courage?'

'A Venetian cannot lose his courage.'

'His wits.'

'Nor his wits.'

'Himself, then.'

'And how could a man lose himself? Goudar? . . . Goudar!'

'You have not heard, monsieur?'

Before the Chevalier left to ride home through the country, Goudar leaned in through the little window of the chaise and invited him to a rout that night at Mrs Wells's house.

'Who,' asked Casanova, hugging himself inside his coat after the heat of the baths, 'will be there?'

'You need not fear,' said Goudar, laughing. 'The Charpillon is not invited.'

'I had not thought of her.'

'And yet she thinks of you.'

'Pah!'

Casanova pushed up the window, hard. The chaise lurched towards London.

13

Mrs Wells, procuress to the Quality, was celebrated for her parties: her 'squeezers', her 'drums' and 'routs'. When the Chevaliers Goudar and Seingalt arrived shortly after nine, the street outside her house was crowded with carriages, most with footboys on perches at the back, brilliant in the loaned splendour of their costumes, singing insults to each other and slandering each other's masters.

Inside, the rooms were choked with the best people or, more truly, the second-best people, all looking over each other's shoulders for someone more interesting, more influential, to speak to. The men were red-faced, drunk, bored; the women in voluminous gowns collided softly with each other, their eyes like weapons. In the midst of it a quartet were sweating over their instruments, though for all the music one could hear they might have been pulling their bows over strings of slack cotton. What a roar of talk! Even the most delicate matter must be bawled into the ear of one's companion. There was no sign of anything to drink, still less of anything to eat. The heat made Casanova long for lungfuls of cold smoky London night air.

'Why,' he shouted into Goudar's ear, 'have we come here?'

'Eh?'

'Why have we come here? One can hardly breathe! I do not speak English. I shall catch a disease here.'

'Exactly!' shouted Goudar, almost knocked off his feet by a military gentleman elbowing past on his way to take a vomit. 'An excellent party.'

'You are a chattering slug, Goudar.'

'Quite so,' replied Goudar, nodding absently and making a sign to Mrs Wells, who was observing them through her opera glasses.

'You would pimp your own mother,' continued Casanova, a companionable smile on his face. 'Your breath smells of goat dung. Your beard-splitter is no bigger than a maggot . . .'

Thus, in desultory fashion, he entertained himself, speaking insults with impunity into the face of his fellow adventurer, his brother in arms. Only after several minutes, when his ingenuity was beginning to flag, did it occur to him that Goudar – whose replies were no more than a type of vocal blur – might be engaged upon the same game.

Suddenly, everyone was moving into the hall. Casanova and Goudar were swept backwards out of the drawing room and carried by the human tide until they washed up upon the bottom step of Mrs Wells's polished elmwood staircase. A few steps above them, Kitty Fischer, daughter of an immigrant German tailor and London's most regarded young courtesan, was eating a banknote served on a piece of bread and butter. Casanova recognised her, though they had not been formally introduced. The banknote was for a thousand pounds, a present from a rich admirer who took pleasure in young women eating his money. Here, considered Casanova, dazzled by the gems in the girl's dress, was a fitting emblem for the town, for the times. A girl eating cash, a girl transfigured, who would, had her nose been half an inch longer, have been sitting in her father's workshop sewing buttonholes by the light of a taper.

'One may still enjoy her,' said Goudar over Casanova's shoulder, 'in the usual way and for a fixed price. No ceremony is required. If, Seingalt, you are interested . . .'

What creatures they were, these courtesans! Women whose fame rested upon the notorious impropriety of their lives. Who were fêted for qualities that would be despised in a wife or daughter. He shook his head. He had known so many of them, the fashionable and the obscure, had dined with them, enjoyed their tricks, taken them in parks, in private supper rooms, in carriages; but some nights – and there seemed latterly to have been more of them – he could not pretend he had not seen the lie in the smile. He thought for an instant about Kitty's father. She was very young still, burning in the brilliance of her dress, the centre of so much dubious attention. Did she care? Had she the intelligence to despair? Well, it was too late for him to become sentimental about such things now.

When the bread had been eaten, the money corroding in the acids of the girl's stomach, the rout was finished. Everyone, like ghosts at daybreak, crowded through the front door, calling for their chairs and carriages.

'Where are they all headed?' asked Casanova, as he, Goudar and Jarba were jostled among the racket of iron-shod wheels. 'For that matter, where are we headed?'

'To Malingan's,' called Goudar, escaping ahead of them and burrowing through the crowd. 'A little supper party. We need only stay for a moment.'

14

Here at least there was wine to drink. Malingan filled the Chevalier's glass and watched him drain it, then filled it once more, prattling to him as if they had at one time walked around the world together. He introduced Casanova to two pretty women from Liège, also to their husbands. They talked about Liège though the subject was soon exhausted. They talked about England, and laughed at the manners of the English. They drank more wine. The women toyed with their jewels, their fans, their frills. They had not heard of de Seingalt, but of Casanova, of course, even in Liège.

The company was called to the table. It was not a grand table: some crystal, a little silver, most of it borrowed as Malingan had only his army pension and whatever he earned from cards to keep his house and family provided for. A tureen of fish soup arrived which Malingan's eldest daughter, Emilie, a girl as plain as a hymn-book, ladled into the bowls. Taking more wine, having tonight a real thirst for it as if it were July and he were sinking tumblers of *garbo* in the piazzetta, Casanova smiled at everybody, even at Goudar. If one could approach life, he thought, without the least expectation, one would often be agreeably surprised. He addressed himself to one of the young wives and contrived, before their bowls were empty, to brush her forearm with his fingertips. He intended, by the end of the meat course, to have tried something more fulsome beneath the table. Young wives were all for pleasure. One could deal with them directly for they had no maidenly virtue to protect. Their husbands were often relieved by such attentions, which left them free to drink or to gamble or to cultivate a mistress. Or even to sleep, for it was amazing the number of young men who, after six months of marriage, dozed half the night in a chair in front of the fire and then stole into their own beds for fear of waking their wives and finding themselves required to be gallant.

He was describing to her, in the most genteel language, some Japanese prints on an amorous theme which had been shown to him by a gentleman from Vatomandry, when the young lady, glancing over his shoulder and pulling a fishbone from the gap between her front teeth, interrupted him, saying: 'We shall have to find one more seat, monsieur.'

'Why so, madame?'

'Malingan has another guest,' she said. 'Do you know her?'

When the meal was done and the guests had pushed back their chairs – the men undoing the top button of their breeches, a servant setting up the card tables – Malingan whispered into Casanova's ear that he had had no idea, none, that the Charpillon was coming that night.

'Certainly I did not invite her. I hope you will believe me, monsieur.'

'A woman like that,' said Casanova, watching the Charpillon watching him over the rim of her wineglass, 'does not need an invitation. She is shameless.'

'I trust,' said Malingan, 'that you will not feel you have to leave us.'

'I shall not be driven away,' replied the Chevalier between gritted teeth. 'And I beg you not to whisper so in my ear. It will appear we have secrets.'

As Malingan went, Casanova noted the look that passed between him and Ange Goudar. He swallowed hard, stared furiously at the coloured whorls in the carpet, then, forcing himself to adopt the old maxim of an open face and a locked breast, he helped to move the furniture back against the walls so that the card-playing could begin in earnest. One of the ladies from Liège was lamenting that her party must depart for Ostend the following week, though they had seen nothing of the countryside of England.

'Madame,' began Casanova, seizing the opportunity to show his indifference to the new arrival, to gall her with a display of nonchalance, 'that is a state of affairs we must remedy at once. May I suggest that we make a trip, *en famille*, to the palace of Hampton Court? Thus you will see both the countryside and one of the finest buildings in England. Could anything be more pleasant? But it must be tomorrow or never.'

He had manoeuvred himself so that he stood between the Charpillon and the rest of the company, his back turned to the girl. If anyone had been in any doubt as to what he thought of her, this should make it plain enough.

'You may leave the matter entirely in my hands,' he said. 'I shall think of myself as an honorary Englishman. Now, we are eight in all, thus we shall need two carriages with four of us in each . . .'

'But we shall be nine,' came a voice from behind him, 'or were you thinking of going without me?'

He turned to her, feigned brief startlement to find her still in the room and, with his tone as icy as he dared, answered, 'Indeed not. I had merely miscounted. Nine is such an awkward number. However, the solution is a simple one. I shall ride. You may take my seat.'

'But there is no need for that,' said the Charpillon, walking forward and taking his arm. 'I shall sit on your lap. I trust no one will think it improper?'

The company smiled, simpered politely, as if the exchange had been one of those tiresome games which lovers cannot resist playing out in public. She was staring up at him now, impudently, and he was afraid of her, of the black water of her beauty. She stretched up and kissed the point of his chin; the company applauded. He said, 'I shall have the carriages here by eight o'clock.'

'Seingalt can always be relied upon,' drawled Goudar, and taking up a pack of cards from the table he shuffled them,

one-handed. It was a trick that Casanova had never quite per-
fected.

15

Another bad night: the Chevalier pursued through the *calli* of
sleep by men disguised in beaked white half-masks, their cloaks,
long black *tabarros*, creaking and snapping behind them like the
leathery wings of devils. He arrived at Malingan's ten minutes
before eight, blue bags beneath his eyes, the taste of earth on his
tongue.

The others were all sat around the breakfast table in excellent
spirits, particularly the Charpillon, who was addressed now
by the young wives as if, overnight, they had become the
fond repositories of each other's most intimate secrets. She
led Casanova to a chair beside her own and tried to tempt
him with swabs of buttered roll and spoonfuls of chocolate, but
though he had eaten nothing since supper the night before he
was convinced that he would choke if she succeeded in getting
the food into his mouth. The more tender her attentions, the
more sour he became, until, as they rose to board the carriages,
he was afraid that he would not be able to move, that his limbs
would have become paralysed by an ecstatic loathing of the girl
who now held out her hand to him. In this mood he was capable
of any crime, even the worst.

He took his seat, facing forward in the front carriage. Goudar
climbed in after him, then one of the ladies from Liège with

her husband. The Charpillon came last and settled herself on Casanova's lap, one pink-gloved hand holding the strap above the door, the other like a glamorous piglet on his shoulder.

At this hour the Sunday streets were almost empty. The coach rattled over mud still stiff from last night's frost. They passed beggars grooming their sores for the church door, and a troop of Quakers on their way to the meeting house, faces shadowed beneath their broad-brimmed hats. The movement of the machine juggled the Charpillon in Casanova's lap. At first it was no more than the irritant of an unasked-for caress, and he endeavoured to ignore it by recalling the names of every Doge of Venice since Pietro Candiano IV, but by the time they reached the Knightsbridge turnpike – the toll-keeper scowling at this noisy party of moneyed foreigners – the Chevalier had got no further than Tommaso Mocenigo and his body was in a seethe of arousal. How dispiriting it was to find oneself at the mercy of the crude mechanics of desire: how hard at such times to think well of oneself. The more he commanded his flesh to resist the more hopeless it was, as though clouds of opium were being blown through the hollow pipe of his spine. *Cospetto!* How bumpy the road was! Another pothole like the last and he would have to throw her on to the floor and take her like a spaniel.

He was rescued by Emilie's nose, which, in the carriage behind them, had suddenly started spouting blood. The coaches were brought to a halt and everyone climbed down, stretching and giving advice. They were not far from the river. A barge with red sails was passing, the bargemen sitting on their load of timber like bored children. Casanova watched them, their stately progress, perfectly silent at this distance, until his mind recovered its composure, then he shooed the women away from the stricken girl, took the handkerchief from her face and, remembering the old witch on the island of Murano who had cured his boyhood haemorrhages, he stopped the bleeding by the cunning application of his hands and the muttering of a half-remembered incantation. Soon the girl was able to stand, her dress spotted with the cherries of her blood.

'Shall we continue?' said the Charpillon. She was waiting by the steps of the leading coach, but Casanova, insisting that he keep a watch on his young patient, took hold of Emilie's hand and climbed swiftly into the second carriage. How kind he was! Everyone mentioned it. The seating was rearranged, Malingan agreed to ride beside the coachman, and the company set off again.

'How were you able to do that, monsieur?' asked one of the wives from Liège.

'Like this,' answered Casanova, fluttering his hands, then, seeing that Malingan's daughter was staring at him with calf eyes and had, quite predictably, fallen under his spell, he flashed his teeth at her, rested his head against the wood of the carriage, and slept. There was no one like Giacomo Casanova for being able to sleep in a carriage.

16

Despite its fountains, clock towers and stone heraldic beasts, Hampton Court was almost cottage-like by comparison with Versailles. There was no pall of majesty here, no sense of power fermenting in enormous painted rooms. Its ruddy bricks glowed in the noonday light, and on the gravel paths elderly gardeners wheeled their barrows as if it were not of much importance that they should ever arrive anywhere.

The party promenaded in the gardens, Casanova walking at the back of the group, the Charpillon at his side. He had tried at first to shake her off by going more quickly or more slowly or stopping to take a pebble from his shoe, but oddly enough they were talking quite companionably, like actors who, though still in costume, still made up for their roles, gossip together in the wings while awaiting their cues. Her grandmother was unwell but had been visited by the doctor. Her mother was in rather poor spirits worrying about the household expenses. The landlord was a brute. He delighted in terrifying them. Of course, once her aunt began to produce the Balm things would be more pleasant. Did Monsieur like her new gown? She had practically blinded herself with the sewing of it.

The day uncoiled. They admired things. At three they dined at a local inn and decided on one more turn in the gardens before the journey back to London. The path now was fretted with the long shadows of the topiary cones, and as they moved from light into shadow and shadow into light, Casanova found himself wishing that the path would never end. All the struggle of the past months, the confusion, the bad dreams, the slow burn of his unhappiness like a terminal dyspepsia, seemed to have happened to someone else, seemed suddenly unimportant. The important thing was – what was it? – the important thing was nothing at all! Strange. He wondered if the Charpillon would understand, and he was on the point of trying to explain it to her when she took his arm, slowed their pace until the others were almost out of sight and then, putting a finger to his lips to forestall any enquiries, led him back past the east façade of the palace, through a pillared gateway, and into the famous Hampton maze.

Here, in the twistings and turnings of the hornbeam hedges, the stillness of the afternoon was deepened. She took his fingers in her hand and guided him – left, right, left, left, right. The Chevalier could not decide how to assign the parts. Was he Theseus or the Minotaur? But the deeper they went into the maze the less he felt like anyone; simply a man led by a woman into the green heart of a garden.

In the centre of the maze they sat on a niche of warmer earth, a sunlit triangle. They had not spoken for several minutes and the silence had become a kind of pact between them, binding them. He knelt beside her and rested his lips against the flush of her cheek. She did not resist him, nor when he softly pressed her down on to her back and kissed her lips, lightly at first as if she were a sleeper he was afraid of waking, then more fully until there was no restraint, no self-conscious artistry, and he was kissing her as a man sometimes drinks, the bottle clasped in both hands, erasing himself with the fierceness of his thirst, the sweetness of the liquor.

She moved beneath him, she sighed, those moans of gorgeous distress, the little music of consensual ravishment that make a lover's brain reel. He plucked off his wig, tossed it behind him into the grass. Her skirts and petticoats were heaped up around her thighs, a creeping floodtide of silk and scented linen until at last – *O consolazione!* – the paradoxical eye that weeps most when best pleased, was hidden by nothing more substantial than the gauze of dusk.

He clawed at his breeches. He would have liked to have torn them off as if they had been made of tissue paper, but as he fumbled with the buttons something went wrong, a moment's inattention to the sensual weather within, and with a little gasp of horror he fell victim to that accident only really excusable in a novice. It was the kind of lapse that never inconvenienced him on those occasions when he had nothing more to lose than the price of a good supper or a little pride. Now, however, it took on the proportions of an authentic disaster.

Hoping the Charpillon would not have noticed, he went on more desperately, nibbling her, studding her with kisses, but it was not long before she shared the knowledge of his misfortune and sat up. She did not laugh as he had feared she would. She patted the coils of her hair, casually rearranged her skirts and delicately ignored him. He begged her to excuse him. Usually, of course, normally, ninety-nine times out of a hundred . . . Would she not accept it as a tribute to her beauty? If she would allow him a moment's grace all would be well again. And indeed, by a supreme act of the will, he was already recovering himself, which fact he proved to her by finally, abruptly, and at the cost of several threads and two gilt buttons, disrobing.

'I think,' said the Charpillon, after the briefest glance, 'that we had better find the others.'

He stared at her, slack-jawed. Had she been quicker she might have escaped him then, but she hesitated and as she pushed herself up from the grass he caught her arm and dragged her down again.

She said: 'I do not like the way you are looking at me, monsieur. Surely we have done enough for one day?'

'Are you insane?' he hissed. 'You really imagine I shall let you leave like this?'

Keeping hold of her with one hand he reached with the other into his coat pocket, took out his clasp knife, his little Venetian settler-of-all-terms, drew out the blade with his teeth and held it to her neck. He pricked the skin, teased from her throat a pigeon's eye of blood. Then, prompted by some dark inspiration from the cellar of the self, he pressed the blade against his own throat.

'Monsieur,' she said, feeling her neck and forcing into her voice a kind of terrified courage, 'you appear unsure which of us you should murder. If you do not make up your mind, and soon, the cold air will kill us both.'

She struggled to rise but he held her down. In a rapid voice, one he hardly recognised as his own, he spilled on to her face every insult a man can make to a woman. It was visibly darker by the time he had finished.

'What I am, monsieur,' said the Charpillon, 'I have to be.'

'I pity you,' he said, more drained than he could remember having been in his entire life.

'I pity you,' she replied. It did not sound like anger.

From somewhere in the park Malingan was hallooing them. The Charpillon, shaking herself free at last, stood up and brushed the dead grass from her dress. She gave the Chevalier one more long unreadable look then went on quick feet into the alley between the hedges. Where her head had been the first stars had opened against the diamond blue of the evening, their hard, disinterested light glittering above the silhouette of the palace chimney pots. Casanova, on his knees still, tumescent as a bull, the knife cataleptically at his throat, could not, for several long minutes, tear his eyes from them.

'You could not disguise your eagerness, signore. The secret of your charm was the cause of your undoing.'

'I am grateful, signora, that you will concede I had some charm.'

'Indeed, your history confirms it. Yet it seems it was not quite sufficient for the Charpillon.'

'That I never fathomed. I must suppose it so.' It was all so long ago, but had the Charpillon known how it would be in the maze? Had she always been one step ahead?

'Of course, signore, you were much her senior in years.'

'Pah. There is nothing remarkable in that, signora. It is well known that a young woman prefers an older man. Someone with more experience. More . . .'

'Money?'

'Girls' eyes light up at the sight of gold. It is the greatest aphrodisiac. They would rather have gold than a handsome face.'

'I would rather say, signore, that a man who has nothing else to offer must at least have money if he is not to spend all his evenings alone. But what of the young woman who ate the banknote?'

'The money was worth more to her in her stomach than in her purse.'

'And the Charpillon?'

'Was like any corn factor who in times of want drives up the price of bread, knowing that people will pay for what is both scarce and necessary.'

'Have you considered, signore, how you, in her shoes, might have behaved? It appears to me that you were as alike as two drops of water. But tell me this: you still believed she had no tender feelings for you?'

'I believe she hated me.'

'Though she had declared her love.'

'More than once.'

'You did not believe her? You preferred to put your faith in gold.'

He flinched. Had he, at some turning in his life, lost faith in the human heart?

'Signora,' he began, 'we are all born into the counting house. We . . .' but his words were lost in a sudden storm of coughing, of sputters and whooping inbreaths. He spat into his handkerchief, then, like an old woman, a venerable grandmother, he pushed the handkerchief up his sleeve.

'I have often wondered,' he said, glancing at the candle – how much was gone, how much remained – 'if when people talk of "love" it means to each of them something quite different.'

'No, signore, it means to each of them precisely the same thing, but you have abandoned your story and I wish to know what new scheme you had when at last you escaped from the maze.'

He shook his head. 'Did I escape, signora? I often doubted it . . .'

17

'There is a point,' said Johnson, hammering a tack through a piece of decorative holly above the window, 'where our understanding fails us. It is, if you like, the mind's kissing gate, beyond which language and intellectual vigour avail us nothing. We can never hope fully to explain ourselves, nor to perceive another in his entirety. That, monsieur, is the prerogative of our Creator.'

Casanova, beginning to feel the narcotic effects of so much tea-drinking, nodded his head gloomily. 'We are doomed to act out of ignorance.'

'No, monsieur. That would be to exaggerate the case entirely. On a hot day you drink off a glass of beer because you are thirsty. There is no mystery in it. However, certain of our actions, those that seem to defy our own best interests . . .'

'Such as my regard for . . .'

'Just so. Such courses are harder to fathom. In this case the normal operation of sublunary desire does not adequately explain the doggedness with which you pursue a creature whom you claim brings you nothing but pain. She is one young woman among others, many of whom, I have no doubt, would be available to you – to your magnetism or your purse. You are addicted, monsieur, as much to your unhappiness as to your pleasures.'

'In the Serenissima we say, "A man who cannot swim is drawn irresistibly to the water". But may we not save ourselves by reason?'

'Yes, monsieur,' answered his host, 'reason might do, had we the language for it, but much that passes for reason is not reason at all. We delude ourselves. This scheme you have now, monsieur, for becoming a man of letters, a scholar, a drudge, is just such an instance.'

'The profession has made you eminent.'

'It has made me old before my time. I have laboured like a beetle and had precious little in the way of reward.'

'But has the king not granted you a pension?'

'The equivalent of what you, monsieur, spend each year on new shoes.'

Casanova glanced at his feet, shrugged his shrug. 'Say what you will, it is a profession both honourable and genteel. I am convinced of it.'

'Whereas bridge-building,' said the lexicographer slyly, stepping back to admire his work, 'was merely honourable?'

Before leaving Pall Mall to spend Christmas with Johnson, the Chevalier had promised himself that the bridge must, for the time being, remain his secret. Yet he had scarcely passed through the door at Inner Temple Lane before he was confessing it, and by the time they had finished the first pot of tea the great logophile knew everything. Worst of all, he had not appeared in the least surprised, as if all along he had suspected Casanova of harbouring a mania for heavy engineering and sleeping in filth. One day, decided Casanova, I shall learn how to hold my tongue.

From the street below came the piping of children's voices. A

Christmas carol! Johnson filled his pockets with apples and went down to them. Casanova remained, warmed his hands at the little fire, then turned his back to it and lifted the flap of his coat, looking around admiringly at the snug room with its comfortable weight of books and papers and half-darned socks, its unwashed cups with their tidal lines of tannin. He picked up one of the lexicographer's tattered quills and sniffed at the nib. Let Johnson say what he would, after the last encounter with the Charpillon the urgency of casting off his old life was more apparent to him than ever. Surely, in the crucible of the mind, in the mysterious fire of a man's intelligence, such transformations were possible, though the bridge had taught him a valuable lesson: such changes must not be violent. What was inflated too suddenly was apt to burst, and these hands had been made to wield an instrument more delicate, more powerful than any pick or shovel. It was amazing he had not thought of it before! His reverence for the man of letters – the woman too – for more than once he had been to Madame du Deffand's and Mademoiselle de L'Espinasse's salon on the rue Saint-Dominique; his pleasure in browsing through the shops of the booksellers or the libraries of great houses; the almost swooning sensation of settling on to a window seat with a copy of some loved or long-sought-for book . . .

First, there would be a *History of Venice* in four or six volumes, the longest love letter ever addressed to that miraculous city. This he would follow with a tragedy written in a metre of spectacular difficulty – trochaic pentameters? End-stopped dactylic hexameters? Then a short philosophical novel in the manner of *Candide*, but of course, much better than *Candide*, chastising the follies of the age, eulogising the simple life. A man could grow old in such work, could even fail in it, without ever thinking himself despicable.

'It is wonderful,' said Johnson, coming in at the door, 'what happiness one may impart with the gift of an apple. Now, monsieur, I must put this Grub Street business out of your head.'

'Grub Street?'

'It is a place, no great distance from here, inhabited by hacks and printers and desperate poets. It is also a name we give to an aspect of the human condition. It is, monsieur, a mash of spoiled dreams, the Patagonia of the soul.'

'You are determined' said the Chevalier, 'to discourage me. You may try, monsieur, but you shall not succeed. A man must be allowed to change.'

'A man, my dear Chevalier, is what he is. He must make the best of it. Simply by changing his coat he cannot become something else . . .'

'On the contrary, do we not become in time precisely what we appear to be? If a man takes up a musket and goes to the wars, what is he – whatever he has been before – but a soldier? A woman, be she the most virtuous in Christendom, who takes it into her head one day to sell herself for a shilling, what may we call her but a whore?'

'Certainly we are at liberty to pervert ourselves, but that is not to change. You must know, monsieur, however we seek to push ourselves down our true nature will always float to the surface.'

'Like a corpse in a canal? Does not this belief of yours break your heart? Such impotence! Will you not allow us just a little freedom?'

'The freedom to pretend? I would not place much value on such a freedom.'

'This is a counsel of despair.'

'It is no counsel at all. It is but a statement of the facts. The sooner you are content to own yourself the sooner you shall have your measure of peace.'

'I can only say, monsieur,' said the Chevalier, somewhat testily, 'that you are not a Venetian.'

'True, and by merely speaking your language and riding in a *burchiello* I would not become one. But enough of this. It is Christmas Eve and there is a gentleman in the Parish of St Giles I should like you to meet.'

18

Once outside, Casanova wished he were wearing an extra pair of woollen stockings, for though he had been assured – and assured with relish – that the weather would become far colder, far nastier, he found it quite cold and nasty as it was. In the narrow alleys around the Temple he walked in the lee of Johnson's back while his guide hurled words into the face of the wind and the words whipped past Casanova's head like scraps of paper he could not possibly catch.

They took the boat to Westminster, then walked north, passing directly from streets of splendid houses, squat and prosperous like retired generals on a bench, to streets of squalor through whose narrow disastrous ways the great man-shadow – for so he had become again in this gloom – walked with his customary sureness. Was it possible, wondered Casanova, that the lexicographer had once known these haunts too well? What, if one were to dig down through the years, might one discover? A score of Johnsons, perhaps, each piled above the other like sacked or deserted cities.

'Not long ago, monsieur,' bawled the man-shadow, 'every second house in these parts was a gin shop. You will still find no shortage of highwaymen, bullies, common assassins and affidavit men here. You may tell them by their swagger and their fancy waistcoats.'

'And the gentleman we are visiting is one of these?'

'No, monsieur, he merely has them for his neighbours. The gentleman we are visiting has no waistcoat . . .'

They turned in at one of the meanest houses and mounted the stairs to the attic. Johnson knocked. A woman came to the door, a stub of candle in one hand, the other holding an infant, its little face screwed up like a ball of paper.

Johnson talked with the woman. Casanova heard his name and bowed; she gazed at him as if he had been the Grand Vizier of Damascus. Johnson placed a coin on the ledge above a string of washing that reeked steadily in the feeble heat from the fire. The woman started to sob. The infant woke and joined her. Other children moved indistinctly in shadowy beds at the end of the room. Johnson's hands, clumsy moths of comforting, hovered about them.

'Mr Pattison,' said the man-shadow once they were on the stairs again, 'is at his club.'

'It is not to be wondered at,' said Casanova.

They turned back east, down Holbourne Hill, Smithfield, Cheapside, striding side by side through the heart of the city – the City of Dreadful Night. In the tangle of streets beyond London Bridge, Johnson paused, looked around, sniffed at the laden air, then pushed open a heavy gate into the yard of a 'glass house'.

'Mr Pattison!'

It was the back yard of a small factory, the yard heaped with ashes beyond which the factory chimneys – discernible as slots of more solid blackness against the starless background of the night – still gave off luminous plumes of smoke, though in all other respects the place appeared deserted. Johnson called again and after a moment a head emerged from the ashes, like a seal from a grey sea.

'This,' enquired Casanova in a whisper, 'is the club?'

'One of several,' answered the man-shadow, and introduced the Chevalier to Mr Pattison, who had appeared phantasmally before them, brushing the ashes from his sleeves.

'*Enchanté*,' said Pattison, as if every day he met spurious foreign gentry in this place.

The three of them rambled in the streets, their cheeks pricked by nibs of icy rain, the wind brawling in the alleys. It was an unforgiving place, a wilderness, untouched by any festive light. At the corner of some unnamed street they entered a drinking house and took a table in the upstairs room. There were cock feathers and a paste of half-dried blood on the floor. Johnson, seeing there was nothing less alcoholic than strong beer to be had, ordered three glasses of hot flip, and a dish of peas for Mr Pattison, who, when the dish was set before him, ate with a trembling hand, swallowing without chewing until, after a choking fit, several of the grey balls reappeared and rolled over the table into Casanova's lap. Such was the expression on Pattison's face the Chevalier felt bound to return them. The poet thanked him and ate them a second time, more successfully.

'This gentleman,' said Johnson, indicating Casanova, 'wishes to be of our profession. What have you to say to that, Mr Pattison? Has the profession treated you kindly?'

Pattison smiled. It was a young face, coarsened by the effects of hunger and sickness but still with features absurdly sensitive, as if the clap of butterfly wings would have startled him. It was not a face that would ever see forty. He said – his words contained in breathlets, asthmatic gasps: 'My case is nearly hopeless, as you well know, Mr Johnson. I am as I appear to be and there are days when, for shame, I cannot bear to look my wife in the eyes. You may wonder how it is she suffers me and shares my poverty but, good soul, she knows that I must follow my muse, that I must live and die for poetry.'

'Pattison,' said Johnson, 'when he first came up to town with two or three poems of promise, raised on the strength of them a subscription for his collected works . . .'

'Which,' interrupted the poet, draining his glass and looking round for the potboy, 'I had not written, then or now. I write slowly. I cannot count on making more than one or two good lines in a month.'

'That,' said the Chevalier, 'is very little poetry to feed a family upon.'

'When he talks of writing slowly,' said Johnson, 'he is speaking only of his good lines.'

'Mr Johnson is right. Satires upon some lady suspected of being with child by her footman. Ballads on the life of some poor devil to be stretched at Tyburn. These I can compose at a rate that would astonish you. My best design was to follow the health of ladies with wealthy and loving husbands. If one fell ill I would wait to see which way it went. If she recovered, I wrote a hymn of thanksgiving for which I sometimes received a guinea. If she succumbed I wrote an elegy. I got five pounds once for a lady who died in childbed, though that was for the child also. These days there is a deal of competition. It is considered bad luck to have a poet outside your door, as though we were carrion birds . . .'

'For my part,' said Johnson, midway through the third round of drinks, 'the thought of having to sit down and put pen to paper makes me feel as if I had eaten a bad oyster. I will spend half of the morning staring at the pigeons on my neighbour's roof or in conversation with Miss Williams, and when at last I do sit and scratch something on the paper it is like dipping my fingers into boiling water. I stop, I sharpen the quill, I start to read some book I left open upon my desk the night before. I tell myself that I need only write a sentence or two, even a single word, but when I start I find the ink is too thick or too watery so I must stop again and make some more or send Francis out to Darley's. At length, however, I have my word and to keep it company I write another. Two words which, when I squint at them, look like two dromedaries making their way across a solitude of white sand. This is all very fine except that one of them looks so lame I am forced to put a line through it.'

'Oh my,' said Pattison, rubbing his hands with pleasure, 'now you have but one and one word on its own is a miserable thing.'

'It is indeed, sir, so I plunge my nib into the ink as if into the black heart of whatever demon it is who has put me to this torture. I should like to take a mouthful of ink and spray it over the paper. My hand is shaking so violently that the third word appears like anything, like a crushed spider. I stare at it, I rub at my neck – and thus dirty the collar of a shirt which was cleaned only the month before. I am longing for someone to knock at the house door or for the children in the court to make such a row I must run out and chase them away. Were the bailiffs to come and take me for some old debt I should be more relieved than alarmed. But no one comes.'

'Would I be right in thinking,' interrupted the poet, 'that the next thing you do is fall victim to Morpheus?'

'You know it, sir. A dead sleep, my head pillowed on the parchment, and when the clock strikes and I open my eyes I may see my mornings work, viz one word almost legible, one crossed out and one that might easily have been written in Uzbeg or Cherokee. It then amuses me to write several more words in this same imaginary language, after which I cannot go on without a pot of tea and something sweet from the larder. Thus, the whole sorry business starts again until the publisher's boy is sent up with orders from Mr Millar that he is not to leave without the promised manuscript . . .'

'And then?' asked Casanova, disconcerted by such a trivial, such an unheroic portrait.

'Then,' continued Johnson, 'I share a cake with the boy, take a fresh sheet of paper and work easily for an hour until the thing is done. That, monsieur, is writing.'

In the early hours of Christmas Day they returned to the glasshouse. The poet, who had only peas to defend him from the full effects of so much hot, sweet beer, hung like a floozy from Johnson's and Casanova's arms, burbling and singing in Greek, his broken shoes flapping like toy sharks. In the factory yard they laid him down. Johnson showed the Chevalier how to dig for the warmer ashes, and with handfuls of these, grey feathers, grey petals, they covered the shivering body of the poet until there was only his face, faintly apparent, lying there like a discarded dinner plate.

'Goodbye, Pattison.'

'Merry Christmas to you gentlemen. Tread carefully as you go. These ashes are inhabited by several young people of genius.'

'We shall mind our way. Goodnight to you once more.'

'God bless you, Mr Johnson. I dare not speak again or my mouth shall fill with the ashes.'

19

'His case,' said Casanova, as they came down Fleet Street under the teeming rain, 'is a severe one. Does he not prefer to go home on such a night?'

'No, monsieur,' answered Johnson, breasting the weather, 'he is used to his condition and will be snug enough in the ashes. In my experience, poets are tougher than prizefighters. It takes a great deal to kill a good poet, or even a middling one.'

'What is most surprising,' said Casanova, 'is that he does not doubt himself. It does not seem rational that a man could be so sure of himself when he is so free from worldly success.'

'True,' said Johnson. 'There are those who think he should be with poor Kit Smart in the madhouse.'

'That may be,' replied the Chevalier, looking in with a pang at an unshuttered window where several children, too excited for sleep, were gathered around the knees of their indulgent parents, 'but still I would call him a fortunate man.'

At Temple Lane, Johnson once more set about the business of tea-making, dropping kindling into the fire and then, on the burning wood, nuggets of sea coal, lifting them from the sack with chubby, dropsical fingers. Francis Barber was curled asleep on the window seat and the lexicographer's cat, a creature about the size of a pedlar's knapsack, was on the best armchair watching Casanova with blank intensity, an edge of pink tongue poking from its mouth.

They had changed out of their rain-soaked clothes. Casanova wore an old suit of his host's, some rough woollen stuff, which hung off him in such a way that he felt more draped than dressed. Above the fireplace, an old clock ticked unrhythmically. It was the sound of time lapping against them.

'I trust,' said Johnson, 'you have given over your mistaken ambition.'

'The Charpillon?'

'I was referring to your more literary delusions.'

'Not at all,' replied Casanova, catching a glimpse of his reflection in the teapot, his face fluid in the heated surface of the silver. In truth, as the evening had gone on it had become increasingly hard to imagine himself as anything. The fire, the cat, the rain; all these seemed to possess a reality, a specific gravity, far greater than his own. The cat, he thought, seemed aware of his discomfort and to be savouring it.

'Now,' said Johnson, his voice echoing from the inside of a large cupboard behind the door, 'I intended you to have this in the morning but it is morning enough now.'

He came back to the table with a small parcel, roughly wrapped with printer's paper and tied with a length of faded ribbon.

'It is a small production of mine,' said Johnson, 'concerning the son of the Emperor of Abyssinia who, in company with his sister Nekayah and his old philosopher, has several adventures in pursuit of the meaning of life.'

'Which they discover?'

'They do not, monsieur. I think it may be a very good book for you. I composed it during the evenings of a single week in order to defray the costs of my mother's funeral.'

'You buried your mother with a book!' said Casanova, immediately wishing he had expressed himself differently, but the other merely nodded.

'Ay, with a book.'

Casanova felt himself bound to make a gift in return. How awkward it was! Why had Jarba not reminded him? Still, it may be he had something. A silver button from his coat, perhaps, or . . . He excused himself and went upstairs to where his coat was drying over the back of a chair in Johnson's sleeping chamber. The last time he had worn this coat . . . well, he would rather not think about the last time. He put his hand into the left pocket, fumbled round in its depths and drew out the little stoppered bottle. He smiled at it, sourly, then returned with it to the parlour.

'It is,' he said, as Johnson peered hopelessly at the label, 'a cordial, a nostrum, a famous tonic. It is called "The Balm of Life".'

Johnson shook him by the hand. 'My dear Chevalier,' he said, 'you have done a kind thing. You have seen that my health is not of the best and you have brought me something that may, God willing, alleviate my discomforts.'

'Did I not promise it the first time we met?'

'You did, monsieur, indeed you did.'

They drank the Balm – Johnson insisting that Casanova have a share of it, which, reluctantly, he did – then they mounted the stairs to bed, the lexicographer going ahead with a candle in a jar. In Johnson's room they shook hands then removed their outer clothes and lay down in the bed together. Johnson said his prayers, apologising that they should be in English, but that it would be improper, unpatriotic even, for an Anglican to pray in French. Casanova did not pray. He lay, listening past the other man's mumbling, to the rain on the window and the rain in the street below, a deep sound, a long exhalation. When Johnson had uttered a last amen, he blew out the candle. There was still some light from the embers of the fire and the two men, snug beneath the covers, began to talk, first, briefly, of politics, then, for a long time, about women. Johnson spoke of his wife whom he admitted had never been much of a beauty, and who in later life, having endured with him the indignities of a poor writer's lot – 'You have seen it tonight, monsieur' – took to her couch, comforting herself with liquor and romances, for which he did not blame her in the least.

'I was an awkward lover, monsieur, never the kind of man a woman might step out of her house to watch come down the road. I am ashamed now to think of what kind of husband I was. It was as though I carried little blown eggs in my pocket and was, in my clumsiness, forever crushing them. The truth is I have never known what to say to a woman other than to say what I would say to a man. You, monsieur, you seem to have made a study of the subject. Tell me, then, what in your view is the surest way to win a woman's interest?'

Casanova took a deep breath. His success with women seemed to him now somewhat mysterious and to have been the fruit of a certain kind of innocence. He had never – certainly not in his youth – considered what was best to do, he had merely done it, unthinkingly, as though reaching into a bowl for peaches. There were of course innumerable tricks – the use of cantharides, bouillons, opiates, cocoa leaves. Laughter often brought success, and certainly nothing was gained without a little boldness. He scanned his history: on the parade ground of the past his conquests formed up in colourful platoons but their numbers mocked him, evidence not so much of his virility, his attractiveness, his infallible technique, as of some manner of partial blindness. Would it not be better if he could recollect two or three women, known and honestly loved? His success was also his failure. The logophile, with his memory of a plain wife and an awkward passion, had a better story to tell.

'Monsieur,' he said, having pondered these things for a while and attempted to distil from his experience one clear glass of wisdom, 'it is as the old saying has it: "What is right for Fatima will be wrong for her sister".'

'Then,' said Johnson, 'the art lies in knowing which of the two one is speaking with?'

'You have it,' said Casanova, chuckling at the inanity of it; and on they went, talking almost to themselves, a soft dreamy kind of talk, the words almost indistinguishable from the rounded vowels of the rain, until the influence of the Augspurghers' syrupy nostrum cut them off. Something dense landed on the end of the bed, circled, and finally settled on Casanova's feet.

'It is only Hodge,' said the man-shadow. 'Have you ever seen a cat laugh? I saw a dog once . . .'

But Casanova, easing himself a little closer to the fatherly warmth of the man beside him, his mind cut loose by the drug, by fatigue, by the music of the rain, could already hear himself, as though across a great distance, beginning to snore.

He woke early – too early – into one of those unseasonable hours that greet troubled minds everywhere; the pale hours when the longing for consolation and the knowledge of its absence are most perfectly matched. He had been dreaming of Solomon Kephalides, the surgeon who had operated on him in Augsburg to cure the disease La Renaud had given him. In the dream, which returned to him now in rags of memory, the surgeon had flayed him, exposing a body sticky and fibrous like the pulp of an unripe date, like a pupa in its birth gel; but also like something decayed, something rotten. How unsettling Nature's symmetries were! The way, for example, the sounds of pain and pleasure were so often indistinguishable . . .

A creaking floorboard; the stealthy shuffling of stockinged feet crossing the room. The Chevalier peeped out of his skull properly for the first time that day. By the light of the dawn he saw the lexicographer stood at the end of the bed putting on a coat – Casanova's lovely coat! – easing his arms into the sleeves, shrugging the silk over the stumpy wings of his shoulders and drawing himself up into a kind of parody of the Chevalier's bearing. Then, having examined himself for a minute in the hand mirror from the dressing table, his poor sight struggling with the poor light, he slipped off the coat, hung it again carefully over the chair and crept back to bed, his face lit up by a smile of illicit happiness. Casanova quickly shut his eyes, feigned sleep. It was not something he wished to think about. He would let the day begin again, much later.

PART THREE

1

'Ready, ladies?'

On the feast of Epiphany a large carriage, trunks and parcels wrapped in canvas and lashed to the roof, stood outside Casanova's house in Pall Mall. The street door of the house was open, and after a moment the Chevalier himself appeared in his travelling clothes, arm in arm with Grandmother Augspurgher. He lifted her up into the coach and a minute later came out of the house with the others. Several neighbours, in gloves and mufflers, looked on from a distance as the women boarded. The last out was Jarba, hatboxes slung over his arms. On the doorstep, Mrs Feaver stood shivering to wave them off.

The coach creaked through the blowsy morning light. Flocks of wintering birds flew overhead, and as the last fine house was lost to view the land spread out on either side, purposeless and deserted.

Of course, when Casanova had first suggested to the Charpillon that they go together into the country, she had laughed at him. That he had expected. The Country! In January? Then, when he had persisted, painting for her little verbal landscapes, glimpses of the English arcadia in which they could, away from the malign influences of the city, cease this foolish tormenting of each other and at last decently come to terms, she had spoken

185

to him as though his horse had kicked him between the eyes. Did Monsieur not realise that everybody who was anybody fled from their estates almost as soon as the first leaves fell? And when he had still persisted – for there is a point one must reach in these discussions before anything useful may be done – when he had stubbornly gone on telling her that he knew very well all that she was saying, had himself already considered all such objections but that in time, a few hours even, she would start to see the wisdom of his thinking – then she had mocked him, saying, what did he imagine they would do together – shoot ducks? Play whist until the spring? Finally she had ignored him and turned away, picking with a needle at an old piece of embroidery, but Casanova, determined that in all their dealings together he would at least have one small victory, had taken from his pocket the bills of exchange, fanning them in front of her face. There had been no need to explain to her what such weighty papers might achieve. She knew well enough that one may knock a house down with paper, that one may bring nightmares to fruit.

That should have been the end of it. The Augspurghers could not risk his taking the bills before a magistrate, but somehow he had failed, or rather they had poisoned his success by insisting that if the Charpillon went the whole family accompany her. They even had a lawyer, some prematurely aged functionary from Stara Zagora, a man humid with greed, who had drawn up a document on several pages of plump vellum and bound the Chevalier and the Chevalier's pocket-book to the Augspurghers' will. Clause one – and more than a dozen had come after – stipulated a fifty-guinea monthly allowance to be paid on the first of each month to Madame Augspurgher, in advance. Casanova had protested, the

Augspurghers had insisted. He had threatened, they had called his bluff. He had signed. It was, he imagined, like being flogged with lengths of ribbon; after the ten-thousandth stroke, how it stung!

The further west they went, the poorer the roads. They clung to the straps, the luggage thundered overhead. At one point – and God alone knew where they were, for it seemed to Casanova that they were already westering off the map – the nearside wheels of the machine disappeared into a rut as deep as a grave and the passengers were piled together in a heave of hoops and heavy coats. Half an hour later they were forced to climb down and walk – all but Grandmother Augspurgher, who waved back at them with mittened hands – when the horses were unable to drag them up a hill steeper and more mired than the rest. The last of the women's good humour, which from the start had been in the shortest supply, vanished entirely when one of the horses went lame and they were stranded, rocked by the wind for two hours waiting for a replacement. Only Casanova, veteran of countless journeys worse than this, maintained a gimballed disposition and sought to rescue these inauspicious beginnings with tales of coaches disappearing in the snow, of horses slipping over the side of mountain passes, of highwaymen and snapped axles, of attack by wolves, even – one afternoon of maddening heat while posting to Seville – by fighting bulls. The women stared out of the windows. They did not care about the Chevalier's stories. They had stories of their own.

Late in the afternoon they reached their destination, jouncing down a final hill, squeezing through a lane so narrow the hedge-rows sucked wetly at the sides of the carriage, passing through a miserable, smoking village, passing a church, crossing a humpback bridge, scattering a flock of sheep and pulling up outside a long, L-shaped two-storey building, its front smothered in ivy, its windows tightly shuttered. In a garden leading down to the road, a cow grazed on a rosebush, and by the gate, watching the carriage approach, a man and a horse were sheltering under the skirts of a beech tree.

'*Votre vache*,' said the man, the landlord's agent with whom Martinelli, on Casanova's behalf, had arranged the renting of the property at ten guineas a month, '*et votre jardin . . .*'

He opened the front door with a key the size of a wine bottle, then went to the windows and, after struggling a moment, pulled open the shutters. The room was not improved by light. On the floor, a fossilised sea of undulating flagstones, stood a long gouged table, a dozen rustic chairs, and a clavichord that sagged on its spindly legs and grinned at them, gap-toothed, like some man's mistress put out to grass when he could no longer bear the sight of her.

At one end of the room was a fireplace, the largest the Chevalier could remember having seen outside of a castle, and on the shelf above, two books, the only two in the house, in the county perhaps.

They trooped about behind the agent, up and down narrow staircases which in Casanova's imagination were haunted by the footfall of crapulous, disappointed men. They peeped into rooms where, at their entrance, the air leapt back astounded. Four-poster beds, made it seemed for a race of midgets, lay exhausted on the bare boards while wardrobes and mirrors and tatty commodes looked on like distant relatives at an expiration. On the walls of the corridors were pieces of shot fauna and paintings of country scenes, of prize bulls, duck shoots, hounds larking woodenly beside their expressionless young masters. As the agent opened the shutters in each room they had another view of the anonymous countryside, a view of woods and now and then of the back of the house where the two sides of the L formed a kind of courtyard and a walnut tree grew and a sundial stood dumb under the clouds and a bench leaned back drunkenly beneath the bare branches of the tree. Everywhere there was the smell of mice, of too much weather.

When they were gathered again in the main hall, the agent gave Casanova the key and rode away over the fields. How expressive a man's back can be! And how strongly for an instant the Chevalier felt the temptation to follow him, to flounder in his boots through the sopping grass until exhaustion, or night or some tumult of the weather, stopped him in his tracks. He braced himself. The Augspurghers and their little servant girl were huddled in the middle of the room: Grandmother Augspurgher on one of the chairs, tatting, the aunts and the mother beside her, still wrapped in their capes, lips pursed as though sucking on pieces of liquorice, or something more bitter than liquorice. The Charpillon leaned against the table next to her mother, arms folded across her bosom, her gaze turned inwards, brooding. Now and then she made a little noise, something with her tongue and teeth, and each time she made it Casanova was frozen for an instant in mid-thought, as if it were the noise of a tuning fork struck against some tender part of his brain.

'Jarba, did we not pack some brandy?'

He smiled at them all and made agreeable noises, but his charm seemed useless now.

In the end he fetched the brandy himself.

2

All night the hulls of storm clouds grated against each other. Tiles were snatched audibly from the roof and several times Casanova was woken by little purses of icy rainwater bursting on his face or falling with dull thuds on to the bed. Next morning, he lay staring at the unfamiliar walls. Not London, not Dubrovnic . . . Where? He sat up. His head hurt. He had slept in his clothes, his cloak for a blanket. The room was bitterly cold. He swung out his legs and wrapped the cloak tightly around his shoulders. On the floor beside the bed his glass was waiting for him with an inch of brandy still in it. He drank it, felt for a moment violently unwell and then much improved. He stopped shivering and went to the window, massaging his neck. Rain, of course, but the sky was backed by a moist and swelling silver light.

He went into the corridor and listened. There was no sound of anyone else moving about. Two pinched-looking rodents observed him from the wainscotting where they were breakfasting on a scrap of leather. The Chevalier greeted them in a whisper then made his way down the stairs, feeling as if he had been brought to this house in his sleep, as if he had seen none of it before. In the hall their baggage was piled just as they had left it the previous evening, and on the table the empty brandy bottle lay on its side beside one of the Charpillon's earrings. He weighed the earring in his hand, disentangled a chestnut hair from it then went to the door, sliding back the bolts and stepping out under the shelter of the porch. A crow, in a flurry of black, alighted on the tip of a lonely, skeletal buckthorn tree on the other side of the lane. Somehow it balanced there, swaying, then hopped clumsily into the air, fell, swooped and rose over the trickling valley. He wondered where the cow had gone, if it had survived the storm.

He closed the door and went to examine the fire which, with wood from one of the chairs (they had attacked the chair like savages, smashing it on the flagstones), had provided some comfort for them the night before, but the ashes now gave only an imaginary warmth as if they were nothing but the picture of a fire. He sniffed, shivered again and with the reflex of an inveterate browser, took down the books on the shelf, blowing the dust from them and spelling out their titles. The first, with most of its pages uncut, was *The Setting of Corn* by Sir Hugh Platt, while the other, much handled, was Harris's *List of Covent Garden Ladies*, but the edition was so old that most of those it listed, with their tantalising names, their lubricious specialities, would now be grandmothers or dead of the pox.

He sat and leaned his head against the chimney piece. The stone there was worn into a smooth shallow bowl, as if for three hundred years people had leaned their heads back in just this way, in this place. He squeezed the books and smiled. Who was the last man to have held them, to have looked dutifully through the one and then flicked furtively through the other? A taste for the women listed in Harris's was always a symptom of chronic melancholy.

Happy men did not go to such women, as the women themselves well knew. Happy men stayed at home which was why the bagnios did such brisk business. He stood and placed the books back on the shelf. He would have liked to have embraced the man who bought them, to have caressed him like a brother.

3

The Augspurghers, who from the first had taken for themselves one side of the L and established there an independent state in which a man could only have been an intruder, appeared at midday, all of them coming down together, Grandmother Augspurgher at the front with her needles, her nods towards the empty, more shadowed corners of the room.

The Augspurghers' maid, Jarba and Casanova himself had been hard at work for hours. They had swept and scrubbed, bringing in buckets of icy, slate-coloured water from the well at the back of the house and sea-coloured rainwater from the wooden butts outside the front door. The cobwebs had been brushed from the windows. A tall country dresser had been dragged in from another room and set with glasses and china. They had foraged for wood and found in one of the outbuildings, where tools with frayed leather strapping and rusted blades hung from the walls like prisoners in an oubliette, a cord of timber dry enough to burn. There were lamps on the table and – a last domestic touch – a young cat, perfectly white, curled up on the floor as near to the fire as it could bear.

For a while, though they could not entirely disguise their pleasure at such a scene, the women complained of the discomforts they had suffered during the night. The damp beds, the inexplicable noises, the explicable ones. They were quite sure someone had thrown stones at the window, and as for the smell emanating from a corner of their room it defied all description. They were sure there must be something buried there, something large.

'A camel?' said Casanova, who for some reason had been thinking of camel hunts on the salt flats outside Cadiz.

'And where,' said the Charpillon, 'will we find a hairdresser in such a wilderness?'

'A large rat,' declared Aunt One, 'or a dog.'

'My dear Mam'zel Augspurgher,' said Casanova, taking the Charpillon's earring from the pocket of his waistcoat and giving it to her, 'we have no need to be fashionable here. We may wear our hair like troglodytes or seamen, or shave it off entirely like lunatics.'

'Surely there are no camels here,' said Aunt Two, looking towards one of the windows.

The Charpillon took her earring. She muttered: 'You are the lunatic, monsieur, with or without your hair.'

'Will you not all sit?' invited the Chevalier. 'I shall be your waiter. I shall bring you your breakfast.'

'Wicked beast!' cried the servant girl. The cat had its claws in the back of her leg.

'I cannot bear my egg too hard,' called Madam Augspurgher to Jarba. 'A hard egg would almost kill me.'

Jarba put eggs into a pan to boil. He had his back to the women and seemed to be speaking something to the water, putting a spell on it perhaps. The coffee had been made. The pot was like a little dog sitting up to beg. Casanova carried it to the table, smiling and feeling in his chest an unexpected pulse of hopefulness. Might they not, at the last, be some kind of family? Might things not, for once, all work out for the best?

The housework continued all day. The maid had smuts on her face from cleaning out the fireplaces. Jarba's hair, a fine coppery frizz, was powdered with dust from beating the furniture. The Chevalier, in shirtsleeves, wielded a broom, set the pictures straight and evicted the hens from the kitchen.

The room next to his sleeping chamber – apart from a man's hat left mouldering upon the floor – was completely bare. The air here seemed less troubled than in other rooms and he decided to take it as his study. As paterfamilias and tyro author he should have such a room; at the very least he would need somewhere to hide from the women. It had a view overlooking the garden, the beech tree and the lane. The rain had stopped, and when he looked down he saw the Charpillon with the cat in her arms walking on the path.

From an apartment on the opposite side of the corridor he recruited a couch, a solid table, a writing stool. Then, with Jarba's help, he carried Goudar's chair upstairs. It had already been the subject of several awkward questions. Why of all things did he wish to bring a chair into the country? Did Monsieur think that they had no chairs in the country? It was fortunate that none of the older Augspurghers had ever been employed at Madame Gourdan's establishment on the rue des Deux Portes or there might have been some difficult explanations. As it was, he merely informed them, standing in the hall at Pall Mall, staring at them and drawing himself up to his full height, that the chair was important to him in ways that they were not qualified to understand. *C'est tout.* He placed it now in a corner of the room near to the window and tried to remember what Goudar had told him about its operation. The springs were armed by a switch on the back: this way off, this on. Or this on and this off. Or . . . He did not expect to have to use it. Surely she would come to him, if only out of boredom. But if she should not . . . He looked back from the door and nodded. Jarba disposed of the stranger's hat.

Outside, Casanova searched for the Charpillon. He had hoped they might play together with the cat, but she was not in the garden now. He picked up a stick, a good stout Johnsonian sort of stick, and decided to walk about his new domain, inspect it, perhaps even have some thoughts on improving the land. He trusted that anyone observing him from a distance, watching him with a telescope, say, or double-barrelled opera glasses from the woods above the house, would take him for a countryman, a gentleman farmer, a gentleman farmer poet, as Virgil had been. He came to the walnut tree, touched the clammy bark, came to a thing in a field which appeared to him at first like the wreck of a small boat but which, after a few minutes, he realised was a plough. Then, beside a little pond of brilliant, impenetrable green, half a mile from the rear of the house, he discovered a pigsty with a black pig inside and he reached over the fencing to scratch it between the ears with his stick. The creature raised its snout, its shunted face, and grouted the air, its eyes polite and fearful as though uncertain whether it were being caressed or gently beaten.

'Were you also,' asked Casanova, feeling a Brahmanical connection to the beast, 'a man once?'

The sea-light of morning had gone now. The sky was smoky, indifferent. Walking back to the house he glimpsed, across the open hillside, another man out walking, a neighbour perhaps, his greatcoat blowing around his legs. The Chevalier raised his stick in salute but there was no answering gesture. He was glad to be in the house again. He realised that he did not much care for the smell of soil. Personally, he preferred a good, dirty canal.

4

Days fell like droplets from the end of a bough, gathering slowly to the tip, trembling there a moment, then falling more suddenly than one had expected. On Sunday morning – and they could not at first think what day it was – they were drawn to the windows by the tolling of a bell. The sun was properly, defiantly out for the first time in weeks, and the countryside glittered as though the fields had been spread with thousands of panes of glass. The entire household hung from the windows, calling to each other until their faces tingled with the cold, and for half an hour, as they prepared themselves for church, there was a buzz of inconsequential chatter which, noted the Chevalier, tying a lilac cravat in the mirror, was very like the sound of human content.

The mood was tarnished somewhat by the oozing slabs of mud that lay along the lanes, and by the time they arrived at the church the service was already in progress, though there were only a half-dozen men and women in the pews, and in the aisles a half-dozen dogs that licked at the moss on the walls or sniffed the corners of crumbling tombs for the bones of former grandees.

The parson, airborne in his rickety pulpit, paused as they came in, and seeing the quality of their coats, bowed deeply. Casanova nodded and sat with Jarba and the women on a pew marginally less derelict than the rest, flicking through the tatty prayer book, fidgeting with his cuffs and counting the change in his pockets. The parson rambled on, occasionally, with an oily smile, addressing himself to the fashionable strangers. There was an attempt at singing. There was a dogfight. Two children ran in at the back of the church, shouted something and ran out, laughing. At least one member of the congregation was too drunk to sit up, and during the discourse slithered with painful slowness to the floor. They mumbled the responses, stood up or sat down as the service required, busy with their private thoughts or else with heads as empty as soap bubbles. Whatever sense or beauty the ritual once embraced had long since evaporated, leaving only a piece of dull theatre, an hour of lassitude, of mild physical distress.

Was this not a model, considered Casanova, of his own existence, his own life broken up into rituals as empty as these? He was afraid that he had lost something, whatever it was that had enabled him to lie on his back beneath the moon and be shuddered with the joy of living. Could he now, as he once had done in an attic room packed with light on the Place Royale in Paris, dance on his own across the wooden floor with no music other than the singing in his blood? He remembered this much: that at one time it had seemed to him the greatest good fortune imaginable to be a man, to wake up, to lie down, to feel the weight of himself as he descended a flight of stairs. He prayed for a minute – and he had not pimped for cardinals without learning how to pray – silently petitioning a reprieve from whatever force it was that snaffled the human heart and dried up the faculty of wonder. To his left Jarba was sat, looking like a man who had come to terms with everything. Fleetingly, the Chevalier was tempted to strike him.

In the graveyard the oldest stones had almost sunk without trace into the earth and the air was reduced to a permanent twilight by a gang of ancient yew trees. The newcomers presented themselves to their fellow worshippers: a Sir Somebody and his wife, a doctor, a farmer, a retired notary, a pair of damaged elderly female twins and the parson himself, whose name Casanova remembered for a moment and then forgot. There were promises to call. The notary or perhaps the doctor shook Casanova vigorously by the hand as if he had succeeded in selling him a sick ox. All the men stared at the Charpillon, despite her puffy eyes, the sour-cream complexion of her face. She did not bother to be civil. On the way home she sneezed so violently she almost fainted.

On Monday, as if by mutual agreement, no one got out of bed. It was surprisingly easy. Casanova woke and dozed, sometimes opening one eye, sometimes the other. He dreamt of rain and, when he woke, saw it on the windowpanes, the whole world liquefying.

On Tuesday he was roused early, before it was properly light. A figure, whom his nose informed him was female, leaned over the bed.

Had she come to him at last?

He reached out blindly, brushed a hand, clutched it, then immediately let go.

It was Madame Augspurgher. Her daughter was with fever: shaking, vomiting. Pain in every limb and joint. Monsieur was responsible, bringing them to this horrid place! Did he not know how delicate she was? What a fragile constitution?

For once he had not been dreaming of the rain but of a night at the Ridotto in Venice playing *biribisso* with Ange Goudar and losing heavily. He dragged himself from the bed, groped for his surtout and followed her to the far end of the house where the sick-watch lamp was burning. The Charpillon was lying straight out in the centre of the bed with that formality peculiar to the dying or to the newly dead. On either side of her sat the aunts, their noses red with cold and with unhappiness, each holding one of the girl's hands. In a truckle bed in the corner of the room the grandmother was staring at the ceiling as if someone had left her a message there and she was trying very hard to read it. Casanova bent over the Charpillon.

Sickness was occupying all beauty's old rooms. Her hair was the brown of dead grass, her eyes, peeping through half-shut lids, were the blue of cheese mould. He stretched down his hand to touch her, then drew back, afraid. What was this malady she had? He was suddenly very sure that he did not want to die in this place, burning up with one of those fevers no doctor could slow by as much as an hour, or one of those lingering sicknesses that did the worm's job while you were yet alive. The aunts were looking up at him. It was not a friendly gaze. The Charpillon groaned, or something groaned inside her. He spoke her name, cooing it two or three times, as one might call up to a lover's window in the dead of night.

What was it Goudar had said about doubt? That they should fear it more than the stiletto? Before Munich, before London, what had his speciality been, his true métier? Certainly it had nothing to do with the seduction of women which was a common trick, like a conjuror pulling coloured handkerchiefs from his sleeve. No. His successes had all derived from an ability to convince others that he and he alone had the solution to whatever difficulties confronted them. The King was impotent? Casanova had the answer. The minister needed extra revenues? Casanova knew where to find them. The abbé was in love with his brother's wife? Casanova knew what to do. Later, with the aid of a great deal of coffee, of cunning, of gambler's luck, one discovered a way, or, failing that, one convinced them that it was so. People were perfectly willing to be imposed upon when it suited them, when they were sufficiently desperate. If all went well you would be wealthy for a month, a year even. If you failed . . . then a horse with sacking on its hooves would, by morning, put you beyond the reach of your enemies. It was more than mere duplicity. It was more useful, more interesting. To say a thing – to say it with conviction – was halfway to doing it. He had cured little Emilie. Why not the Charpillon?

He reached down, softly detached the girl from her aunts, gathered her into his arms and carried her to the door of the room.

'I shall cure her,' he said, 'you need not be afraid. It will take exactly three days.'

It took five.

5

He did not send for any physician or apothecary; he knew what damage such men could do. He warmed his bed with embers in a pan, then tucked her in and tended her. Jarba brought up the necessary things: the nourishing drinks, the basins of boiled water. From his personal medicine bag the Chevalier took out a dozen bottles and lined them up on the mantelpiece. Most of them looked doubtful: old amatives, or proprietary poisons like the Augspurghers' Balm of Life. He was tempted to ask them to make up a batch of the Balm, put it to the test, but they would only tell him they needed a ground narwhal horn or a shrunken head or the finger clippings of a saint. He picked out a bottle of 'Dr Norris's Fever Drops', pulled out the cork and sniffed it, then threw it and all the other bottles out of the window, into the garden.

For days he hardly slept other than in snatches as he crossed the room or wrung out a cloth. He cleaned her, changed her linen, eased her thirst a drop at a time. Washing her, wiping the bitter sweat from her breast and back, from the soft buckler of her belly, he was not indifferent to her charms. A beautiful girl, even when she coughs like a miner and smells of rotten fruit, is still beautiful. The flush of fever imitated the coital glow; her sighs mimicked those he had drawn from her briefly in the maze. There was nothing now to prevent him from taking liberties. She was at his mercy. Could he not lay himself upon her like a compress, a salve, a delirious dream? For hours his mouth was dry from the heat of his thoughts but his hands went on, benign and businesslike. To stop her grinding her teeth to a dust he slipped between her lips one of the supple fingers of his gloves.

For half a day, as the fever reached its crisis and a blue glaze of pain spread around her eyes, he sang for her, songs from that complicated and ill-lit time, his childhood. In the corridor the women kept their vigil. He heard them there, scratching about like mice, whispering like ghosts.

On the sixth day, having succumbed at last to a few hours of sleep, he opened his eyes to see the old Charpillon inhabiting her gaze once more. She was lying very still, suspended in the luxury of her recovery, though her face was overlaid with an almost imperceptible veil, a fly's-wing of suffering, and at the corner of each eye a new crease that nothing could erase now but Death. He sat forward. She did not smile at him but uncurled the fist of her left hand which slowly he reached for and took with his own. He could not speak. He was too sad to speak, and too happy. In another minute, half a minute, the moment would have passed and the longing, the hopelessness, the endless scheming would start again. What could be saved? What lasted? Both he and this girl in the bed would go down into the dust with their smallness and stupidity intact, chattering and plotting on the edge of the grave, laden with grudges. For now, however, it did not signify. In the little O of the moment he was as rich as he had ever been.

She said: 'You do not look well, monsieur.'

He nodded. It had been coming on for hours, for weeks perhaps. The shivering, the cat's-tail of nausea in his belly. The oddest expression on the face of the moon.

'I feel,' he said, 'quite wonderful.'

The Charpillon climbed slowly out of bed. Casanova climbed in.

'So, signore, the Charpillon became your nurse and you became her patient?'

'That is so, signora.'

'She was a good nurse?'

'She cured me of the fever.'

'In three days?'

He shrugged. 'Three days, four days ... Who knows, who remembers. What is the hour, signora? Already it seems dark to me. Should we not light another candle?'

'This,' said his visitor, in a voice like evening, like sand through a glass, 'still has an hour to burn.'

The Chevalier sniffed. Finette whimpered in her sleep then settled again. What name had they given to that little cat at the house? He remembered it on the bed while he was convalescing, rolling on the curl of its back and nibbling at his fingertips. Neigeux, Flocon de neige, Boule de neige? The rain had been turning to snow then. Impossible weather but beautiful. At night he heard the foxes scream. London was a thousand miles away, and Venice, the Serenissima, another planet.

'When you had both regained your strength, signore, no doubt your friendship was more intimate. More pleasing to you both. More romantic?'

He would have liked to have shouted at her: 'You know! You know!' but breath was precious now, he must harbour it. He touched his face, reminded himself, then said, quietly and in the voice of one resigning himself to a night or a lifetime of bad cards: 'For a while it seemed so, signora, but in truth, it was business as usual.'

6

'I would rather be miserable,' said the Charpillon – they were all at the table together, the shutters shut, the fire spitting and snapping in the hearth – 'than bored.'

Casanova raised his eyebrows. In truth he was as bored as she was and it had become difficult to pretend otherwise. He was, however, determined to be the last to admit it. 'A party?' he said. 'Is that what you wish for? Cards? Company? Dressing up?'

'Monsieur,' said Madame Augspurgher, who in the country had become increasingly ragged as if, bereft of the compacting pressure of the town, she had slowly begun to explode, 'we have been at our wits' end with nothing but hills to look at.'

Casanova turned in his chair. Jarba was sitting on the chimney seat, reading. For the first time, Casanova noticed that his valet possessed a little pair of folding spectacles.

'How much of the wine did we bring from London, Jarba?'

'Six dozen bottles, monsieur,' answered Jarba without looking up. 'Champagne, claret, madeira, tokay. Some were broken on the road.'

'Six dozen . . . It might do for a small entertainment.'

'And there must be food,' said the favourite aunt, threading her needle; all evening the women had been working on the tapestry. 'Even in the country we cannot expect them to starve.'

'Jarba?'

Jarba shrugged. 'There is the pig, monsieur.'

'Ah . . .'

'Or the cow?' said the second aunt.

'We might allow them to draw straws,' suggested Casanova. Other than a man or two he had never killed anything larger than a cockroach.

At ten o'clock – for there was nothing to stay up for, nothing more entertaining than an owl hooting to its mate – the women retired, all of them going together, as they always did, like a disciplined force from the field of battle. Jarba closed his book, slipped it – rather secretively, to the Chevalier's mind – into his pocket, and bade his employer goodnight. The little servant girl was already in bed. Casanova sat up alone, moody, restless, fantasising about cobblestones and smoke, the perfumed crush of the opera house, the weave of little streets that led you who knew where. Banks! Newspapers! He was even nostalgic for the prisons. What use was the countryside to a man of his talents? It was a place to hide in, or to cross with a loaded gun between one city and the next. And he had not written a word other than two letters to Johnson which were full of lies, of absurd posturing.

He yawned. The cat turned its belly to the heat. He was about to leave – he had already blown out the lamps, keeping one small candle to light himself upstairs – when his eye was caught by the sparkling of the threads in the tapestry on the end of the table. It was the women's usual practice when they had finished sewing to roll their work up and take it with them to their quarters. Tonight, however, they had left it undone, surrounded by their needles and coloured spools, their pin-cushions and scissors and thimbles. He slid the candle along the table, then leaned forward over the light as if leaning over a little pool to study his reflection. In the centre of the work, the main figures were almost completed. A girl with tresses of red hair was riding on the back of a white bull beside the blue-and-silver weave of an ocean. In the background, other figures, less distinct, looked on. The subject of the tapestry was immediately apparent to him. The beauty on the bull's back was Europa, daughter of Agenor and Argiope, Phoenix's sister. The bull, of course, was Jove, who had thus figured himself the better to steal the girl's modesty, for when he appeared to her at the seashore in Tyre with his heavy dewlaps and milky hide, he had seemed so gentle and lovely that Europa was not afraid of him and felt quite safe upon his shoulders.

Why, wondered Casanova, admiring the Augspurghers' needle-work, had they chosen such a theme? What was it but the story of an outrage, of a god concealing his nature in the innocence of a beast like a blade sheathed in leather? But as he looked, leaning more closely, it struck him that there was something curious in the picture, something unexpected which did not tally with the old story at all. He held the candle over the cloth, careful not to spill any of the wax, and as he moved the light, patches of the tapestry came alive. The bull, which should surely have had a demure but implacable expression suitable to a god, seemed instead to stare out forlornly at the cunning stitching of the surf, while the girl, for all her youth and lightness, clutched the jewelled horns in her fists and drove it forwards. Even the onlookers – observed more closely – appeared to linger on the beach, tense with the knowledge of what was coming, ready perhaps to hold their hips, to roar with laughter . . .

'Very well,' he muttered, going up the stairs, his shadow, candle-flung, ghoulish and looming at his side, 'but the thing is not finished. Not yet.'

7

Jarba wrote out the invitations, and in his old sea boots went through the snow to deliver them. Casanova was at work in one of the outbuildings. He was building a faro table, hammering a beading of nails a hand's-breadth from the edge of the table, then, cooking up a glue of flour and water, he fixed to the centre of the table a suit of spades in two rows, ace to six on the first row, seven turning the corner, then eight to the king on the second, the king finishing opposite the ace. He made a little box for the banker to draw the other cards from. He enjoyed these simple jobs. He liked the way one forgot oneself while hammering in a nail, the way one whistled between one's teeth and how, looking up, one was pleased and surprised to find the world in place again, as though, in some way, that was what one had been making all along.

Later – and he left it as late as possible – he shot the pig with a duelling pistol from a distance of fifteen paces. The pig hopped backwards with a ball in its brain and fell into the snow, twitching for a moment. They tied a rope about its back legs, suspended it from a bough of the walnut tree and cut its throat. It bled into a bucket. The Augspurgher women stood around with knives. They had butchered more than one pig in Franche-Comté. Despite the cold they had their sleeves rolled up to their shoulders.

To Casanova, their faces seemed very white and perfect. The servant girl was hunched by the bucket, stirring the blood to stop it clotting. He could not watch them. He retired to his study and cleaned the action of his pistol. When he looked out later from a window on the corridor, there was a churned scarlet cloud beneath the walnut tree.

On the following Saturday – the twenty-third day of January, Year of Our Lord 1764 – the local gentry, their wives and hangers on, trudged in muddied finery to the gate of Casanova's country house. Torches burned in the garden and rows of champagne bottles were plugged into the snow, dark green bells smoking with cold. Casanova greeted his guests at the door, helping them to brush the snow from their shoulders, their hats. Some of them, the doctor in particular, seemed to have primed themselves with liquor before setting out. They looked at the Chevalier, with his half-dozen sentences of English, his indecently direct gaze, with open suspicion, and for a moment there was a kind of stand-off, a grisly English awkwardness, with the guests in a gang by the door as if they might all rush off into the night again like hens before a fox.

The Charpillon and her mother took charge. Jarba started to fill the glasses and the servant girl, chattering to herself and wielding a blade as large and sharp as a new moon, cut tranches of pork from the spitted carcase of the pig. Soon the room was roaring. The farmer sang, the parson risked a jig with the Charpillon's favourite aunt; the pig was pared down to a rabbit. At eleven o'clock, Casanova winked at Jarba and they moved together to the faro table, Jarba – as croupier – going to the opposite side of the table to Casanova who was, naturally, the banker. The Charpillon clapped her hands and invited the guests to play. She was at her most delectable tonight; pearls – presents from the Chevalier – in a milky loop around the blush of her throat, and in her hair a score of brilliants spangling like stars. Shuffling the cards, Casanova remembered Kitty Fischer, that young tree struck by lightning on Mrs Wells's stairs, and how the men had ogled her with good-humoured awe. Think of the Charpillon in such a dress! She would drag the antlers from their heads, send them pounding and hollering through the woods, moonstruck, blissed. He realised that he was proud of her, that he admired her tremendously.

At first they played for shillings, then, their faces flushed with excitement, the shillings became guineas and banknotes appeared. For an hour, Casanova's mind in comfortable harmony with Jarba's, he saw to it that no one lost too heavily, too fast. The room was hot now. The women fanned themselves, dabbed at their faces with perfumed handkerchiefs. The men loosened their stocks; some had stuffed their wigs into their pockets, the tails hanging out like disgraced cats.

The baronet they had met in the churchyard, a lively old gentleman with little trumpets of silver hair in his ears, won a hundred and forty guineas playing 'sept et la va'. The Charpillon was at his side, one hand – how well Casanova knew the weight of that hand! – on the shoulder of the old man's coat. She murmured to him; his eyes glistened, he nodded and placed his guineas, his banknotes as large as county maps on the card she had chosen for him, the queen of spades. Lost to the new game, the new girl, the baronet was playing '*quinze et la va*' and thus stood to win fifteen times his original stake. Three hundred guineas! Should he profit from the next coup his income for the year would be increased by perhaps a third, enough – for a week or two – to buy a girl of his own. Casanova drew the banker's card from the top of his deck. For a moment it occurred to him that the Charpillon, who amid the wine and the hubbub had evidently been keeping cool mental lists of all the cards played, might seek to punish the bank and humiliate him, but the banker's card was the queen of diamonds.

'Bank wins,' said Jarba.

The baronet flinched then stared at the table. The room was suddenly quiet. The parson cleared his throat as though to begin a sermon, and the Charpillon moved a few inches from the old man's side. Casanova smiled.

'Jarba,' he said, 'please return the stake to our neighbour. We are playing for our entertainment. Nothing more.'

Jarba slid the money back along the table. The baronet protested, the rims of his ears crimson with embarrassment, but finally he was persuaded to accept. They had all been warned. No one now would be able to complain he had been robbed before it had been shown to him that this was a game with teeth. They started again, roused, each searching in himself for what he might have of the spirit of extravagance. Casanova looked fleetingly into the Charpillon's eyes. There was something in this glance, something behind the flash of mutual congratulation, that was wistful, regretful, perplexed. Then they dropped their gaze to the cards. They concentrated.

The Chevalier's watch said four o'clock before the last of the gamblers had left, clutching his winnings or his confusion. Jarba and Casanova sat up alone, drinking a last bottle of champagne which had been kept hidden for the inevitable celebration. Jarba received his croupier's cut. Casanova took the rest – gold, paper money and notes of hand – dropping them into his pockets without counting. He knew from the extra weight as he stood up how much he had made. A good haul from such an out-of-the-way crowd.

He bid Jarba goodnight, kissed him, and as he ascended the stairs sang softly.

> *Sonno usar con gli amanti arte e driturra*
> *prodighe e quelli dan tutto il cuor loro*
> *e si tirano a se l'argento e l'oro . . .*

He gazed for a moment towards the women's wing and wondered what the odds were of stealing the Charpillon away from under the noses of aunts and mother and grandmother, then, with a shrug, he went to his study, set down the candle on his desk, picked up his pen and stared at his own half-formed reflection in the window, his mind, anaesthetised by drink, by gambling, curled inside his head like a dog in a dreamless sleep. He had been in such an attitude some minutes when he began to suffer the strangest sensation that he was not alone in the room. Could one of the gamblers have stolen upstairs to wait for him? One of the baronet's men – for the money had not been returned a second time – crouched in a far corner of the room with some instrument of revenge in his fist? Very slowly his hand edged towards the candlestick. In similar circumstance – Odessa? – he had done well by flinging a lighted candle into his attacker's face, sending the man staggering and giving himself a few precious seconds to find a blade. The villain escaped but had left a trail of crimson splashes leading to his master's door. By noon the whole town had known of it . . .

No noise? Surely nothing human could be so silent.

He stood, took up his light and turned so fast the flame was a line of fire dragged through the air.

'Come out!' he hissed. 'Come out, you chestnut-eater. Come, let me sew your lips together!'

Such insults certainly give a man courage! He stepped forward. Someone was sitting in the chair, in Goudar's infernal throne, his mechanical flytrap. Casanova slipped the knife from his pocket, sliding it from beneath the gold and silver coins, but before he had it open it had fallen from his hand and clattered on to the floor.

'*Porca miseria!*'

He crossed himself.

'*O porco dio!*'

In her nightdress, her hands and legs trapped by the springs, her hair standing out from her skull like wisps of smoke, Grand-mother Augspurgher was staring at him with the eyes of the dead.

For what seemed the longest time Casanova had the same startled glassy grimace as the woman in the chair. He saw himself, very clearly, trussed in a tumbrel riding beside his own coffin, the Augspurghers waiting at the foot of the gallows to hiss at him as he climbed the hangman's ladder. Were they already searching for her? No? But how long before one of them woke and saw the empty bed?

He knelt, told himself he had been in tighter corners than this. First he must release her from the grip of this monstrous invention. Sweet heaven, why had he not broken it over Goudar's head the moment he had set eyes upon it? And what in the name of the Serene Republic had the old woman been doing here? What madness, what dream had inspired her?

He reached round and ran his hands over the back of the chair until his fingers encountered a small button midway between the rear legs. He pressed; nothing happened. He pulled it, pressed again, struck it with the side of his fist. Suddenly, the hooks shot back into their housing and the seat dropped forward, delivering Grandmother Augspurgher into his arms. He stifled his yelp of horror and laid her down on the floor. The room was like a furnace though there was no fire. He thought to close her eyes but could not bring himself to touch her face, the delicate wreath of wrinkled skin. What if – dead though she undoubtedly was – she were suddenly, with those sharp gums of hers, to bite him?

Easing off his shoes, he went downstairs. Jarba was clearing up the evening's entertainment, flinging empty bottles out of the front door into the snow. He must be drunk, thought Casanova, or was this how he always cleared up?

'Pssst! Jarba!'

Jarba turned, looked, nodded, then lobbed another dead man out the door. Casanova tensed, but it fell like a coin dropped into a well so deep that its splash was only heard in dreams.

8

She was found next morning in the garden, almost buried under a fall of fresh snow. By the crystalline web of her hair a wine bottle leaned like a headstone. It was the Charpillon who found her. Casanova and Jarba had been carefully searching elsewhere. Soon, all the women were in the garden, even the serving girl, who stared at her mistresses, impressed at last by the glamour of their grief. The weeping was terrible. It was unrestrained, frightening. The Chevalier, watching through the window in the hall, felt his skin tingling as if he were about to suffer a herpes attack. Even the cat had sidled off and hidden itself in some secret place.

Jarba said: 'You should go to them, monsieur.'

'In a moment,' said Casanova. 'Soon.'

In the Serenissima one died as cheerfully as one could, easing life off like a silk stocking while the rest of the world, with its busyness, its endless appointments, made as little fuss as possible. One saw the red boats, of course, on their way to the cemetery at San Michele, but one tried not to let them spoil an entire day.

'Jarba . . .'

'Yes, monsieur?'

'You think Death is a man or a woman?'

'My death, monsieur, or yours?'

They wrapped Grandmother Augspurgher in a sheet, brought

her in and laid her on the faro table. She was as stiff as plaster.

'How could she have got there?' asked the Charpillon, her eyes already bruised with crying.

'Perhaps, my dear, Jarba threw her out with the bottles,' said Casanova. He had not slept. He was becoming hysterical.

Oddly, all the women had black dresses. Even the little serving girl was soon attired as if she had packed for a funeral. Jarba and Casanova made black armbands for themselves by cutting out the back of one of the Chevalier's waistcoats. A candle burned by the dead women's feet. A little pool of greasy water was spreading over the faro table and dripping on to the floor. No one ate. No one spoke. When, at the end of the day, with whimpers and loud snuffling backward glances, the women helped each other up to bed, Jarba looked his employer in the eye and said:

'Monsieur, she cannot stay here.'

Casanova shrugged, nodded. 'But where can she go?'

They went outside and walked around the house then emptied one of the rain butts, wrapped the old lady tightly in her sheet and lifted her inside, packing the space around her with snow as though she were a consignment of sherbet or Sicilian figs. They sealed the lid with a rind of candle wax then carried her to the outhouse where they had found the firewood. On the side of the butt Casanova scratched with his ring

VIVAT PERPETUA.

'It is what we say of Venice,' he whispered, stroking the wood.

It was three days before the roads were clear enough for a carriage. Brilliant yellow, it came up from the local posting inn, the names of a dozen English market towns painted on to the sides and a figure with winged feet, a Hermes, pointing forward to the next destination. The barrel would not fit through the coach door so they lifted it into the basket at the back, wedging it into place with the other luggage. After looking at it a while and becoming tearful again, the women took their seats. Jarba too, for the Charpillon had insisted that he go with them. 'He is the only one with sense,' she said.

Casanova, who, ever since the old lady's demise, had been looked upon with naked suspicion, did not protest. Now he stood under the beech tree waving his goodbyes and watching the machine with its precious cargo slither drunkenly between the wintry hedgerows. They disappeared; then he saw them again, a mile distant, creeping up the hill on the other side of the village, cresting the brow, pausing there a moment as the coachman fixed the tackle for the brakes, then sinking beyond the Chevalier's sight, leaving him staring at the little slot of daylight where they had been.

He swallowed, went back into the house, went heavily up the stairs and lay down on the Charpillon's bed. Her scent was still there. It was not an expensive perfume but now, overwhelmed by his solitude, he inhaled it as though it were the ether of life. He tried to sleep, reciting to himself exchange rates – francs to guilders, guilders to kroner, kroner to drachma, drachma to shillings – but sleep would not come, and when he moved his head he felt something press his temple from under the pillow. He pulled it out. It was the novel he had seen in London while sitting in her room at Denmark Street. He began to read it, some French nonsense, yet the story, with its bad style, its ridiculous ideas, enchanted him. He flicked over the pages, grateful to have found such a perfect distraction, and had reached the end of chapter five – the young hero had just discovered another of the heroine's suitors hiding in a dovecote – when a rose tumbled from the pages on to his face. The flower had been pressed and dried and had left a faint shadow of itself in the book. There were no thorns upon its stem, only tiny dark wounds where he had broken them off for her the first – the second – time they had met. He touched the petals to his lips, then sprang off the bed and raced down the stairs, out of the house, through the garden, splashing in the slush of the lane . . .

'MARIE!' he cried, his voice echoing over the valley. 'MARIE! MARIE!'

'My dear Johnson,' he wrote, sitting up in his room that night, boozy and insomniac, 'perhaps I should write a story first. A little fable about a man in the country trying to make sense of his life, a man who has done everything but who has nothing and who runs from one disaster to the next like a blind man in a fire . . .'

He held up his candle to the window. Did he imagine there would be some answering glow, that somewhere in that blue dripping world another light was being held up, another pair of eyes staring out? He leaned a little closer to the glass.

PART FOUR

1

In a flowing ankle-length coat of quilted Chinese silk, its tangling dragons glistening with London drizzle, the Chevalier de Seingalt shouldered his way through the crowd in the market. Something in the quality of the place, its cloistered walkways, courtyards, flights of old stone steps, the cries of the porters, of the boys who ran about with long-handled nets and, of course, the birds themselves, their whoops, caws, piercing whistles, their shrieks, reminded him of Fez where once he had warmed the sheets with a girl and her twin brother in a room full of flies above their father's workshop, the noises of the souk drifting past the intricately carved shutters, arabesques of light patterning the whitewashed walls . . .

'We must,' he said, turning to Jarba and waking from this sad but agreeable daydream, 'find an intelligent bird. One capable of learning some little expressions of endearment that I shall teach it.'

Many of the marketeers were old sailors, one-eyed or with a hook for a hand, some with their faces tattooed, some with bones through their noses or chiselled teeth. They walked barefoot over the floor, carrying on poles cages with Myna birds and. cockatoos, canaries or quetzals. A pair of pelicans were displayed waddling on a leash, and in a corner of the courtyard a flamingo shivered and balanced on one leg beside its tobacco-chewing, one-legged owner.

After an hour they purchased a young parrot, a fine-looking bird with a plumage of grey and red-tipped feathers, though it was more for its homesick sighs that Casanova bought it, as if it were remembering Madagascar, or an old life swooping over the waters of the Limpopo. They took it to Pall Mall and placed the cage on the dining table. Mrs Feaver cooed to it through the painted bars, feeding it scraps of truffle and pieces of dried polenta, while the bird, dropping its liquid turds on to the floor of the cage and turning its oddly mobile head from side to side, regarded them, nervously.

Lord Pembroke called while the Chevalier was browsing in his little library, wondering which strophes, which delicate rhyming couplets, he might lodge in the creature's memory. His lordship admired the bird. He agreed that the Charpillon was sure to be amused.

'So you did not manage to secure her in the country, Seingalt?'

'The country, my lord, is best left to painters.'

'I must warn you, Seingalt, that many people are laughing at you. There are several gentlemen who have wagered large sums on the outcome. One – whom I shall not name – has a thousand guineas on the Charpillon keeping you out of her bed.'

'Then the gentleman has already lost his money for I have been in her bed and can bring witnesses to prove it.'

'No, my dear Chevalier. The terms are very precise. You must have been not only in the girl's bed, but in the girl . . .'

'That, my lord, will be a very nice matter to corroborate. What if I were to lie?'

'Will you lie?'

'Of course not. But tell me, what if I were successful and she were to lie? One cannot expect a woman to broadcast her complacency.'

Lord Pembroke, lounging by the fire, examining himself in the mirror there, and touching, amorously it seemed, the skin of his cheek, chuckled dryly. 'You really imagine, Seingalt, that the whole world will not know of it even as you are climbing back into your breeches?'

'It seems I must enjoy her in public, then.'

'Privacy,' said Lord Pembroke, 'is a luxury of the poor.'

'How so, my lord?'

'Because the world does not care what they do, so long as they do not riot – more than once or twice in a year.'

Casanova tapped the bars of the cage. 'May I enquire upon which side his lordship has laid his money? I know you are a man who loves to hazard his wealth.'

'It is true, I could not resist it. However, you must see that it would be unfair to us both if I were to satisfy your curiosity.'

'Then I must assume that you have bet against me. But surely it is most unjust that I, who have pursued the Charpillon at considerable expense, will gain nothing, even when I succeed with her, as I am still confident of doing. Would your lordship entertain a second wager? A private one? Jarba will draw it up on paper, or if you prefer we could settle it with a handshake, which I know is the English way.'

'Let us do both,' said Lord Pembroke. 'Then there can be no confusion.'

Jarba sat at the table and wrote from the Chevalier's dictation.

When he had finished he passed the paper to Casanova, who read it through quickly and handed it to Lord Pembroke.

'Are you satisfied with it, my lord? If within twenty-four hours I have not enjoyed all the Charpillon's favours then I shall pay you the sum of five hundred guineas. If I succeed . . .'

'You shall keep your money and have five hundred of mine.'

'Would your lordship care to put his name to the document?'

'By all means . . .'

'Now we may shake hands.'

'Twenty-four hours,' said Lord Pembroke, consulting his watch. 'I shall call on you. What faith you have, dear Seingalt, in your parrot!'

2

It was seven o'clock; threads of silvery rain embroidered the darkness. Casanova, his chin snug in the fur nest of his collar, went to Denmark Street by hackney, the birdcage on his lap, the parrot swaying daintily on its perch.

'*Je t'adore, je t'adore, je t'adore . . .*' murmured the Chevalier, for there was no time to teach the bird any more complicated phrase. '*Je t'adore . . . Je t'adore . . .*'

Despite Jarba's advice – and Jarba was addicted to good sense – he had not informed the Augspurghers of his coming; indeed, they could not even know that he was back from the country. Naturally they would still be in mourning – the old woman was barely a week in her grave – but what was more tedious than lounging about in black, speaking in whispers and trying to outdo each other with sighs? What tyrants the dead are, and what a welcome surprise for the Charpillon to see the Chevalier at the door with such an unexpected gift.

'*Je t'adore . . . Je t'adore . . .*'

The hackney turned into Soho Square. He glanced at the unlit windows of Cornelys's house. Had her creditors already seized her? The rain on the coach's window made the whole world seem as if it were under water. He felt a sudden pang for something he could not quite name. For *pidocchi* soup perhaps, or for Zanetta, or for 1750. God knows, a little sunshine would not go amiss.

'*Je t'adore . . . Je t'adore . . . Je t'adore . . .*'

They turned out of the square, turned right and then left into the narrow sleeve of Denmark Street. He rapped on the roof with his cane; the hackney rolled to a stop. How quiet London was tonight! He paid the old coachman who, with a little cry of 'Hup!', moved off, leaving Casanova in utter darkness, unable at first to distinguish the Charpillon's house. If only someone would . . .

A door opened. The Augspurghers' little maid, her face sulphurous in the light of her lantern, peered out into the street. Casanova stepped towards her and was about to call when another figure appeared, who, leaning quickly to kiss the servant, the girl embracing him with her free arm, the Chevalier recognised as the Charpillon's hairdresser. The scene enchanted him – so unaffected, so wholesome! He was tempted to declare himself and offer them the price of a room in one of those inns on the edge of town that catered for the urgencies of young sweethearts, or to pay for them to have an evening at the

Temple of Flora in Lambeth where it was said any enormity might be committed in the name of love; but the young man stepped suddenly into the hall and the door was closed, sealing the street in darkness again.

Was it possible that someone – Lord Pembroke? – had sent word? Had the Charpillon got wind of his return? Was she even now preparing herself to receive him? It would be a pity to call while she was at her toilet and have to sit for half an hour with her mother and aunts while they talked of Grandmother Augspurgher and flicked accusing glances at him. Timing in these affairs was everything; all the books agreed. He would wait a while in the doorway of the house opposite and go in when the hairdresser came out.

He sang to the bird in a whisper: '*Je t'adore . . . Je t'adore . . . Je t' adore . . .*'

Droplets smashed on the stonework of the porch where he was sheltering. In the mud of the street the rain sounded like a thousand ivory balls spinning in a thousand roulettes. No one passed. No one wanted to be out on a night like this. He was afraid the parrot would take a cold.

'*Je t'adore . . . Je t' adore . . .*'

The watchman hurried past in a canvas cape, head down, and called the hour, the light of his lantern dancing over the puddles. It could not be much longer now. What incredible designs was the Charpillon having her hair worked into? What pileous sculptures was the young man creating on that lovely head?

'*Je t'adore . . . Je t' adore . . .*'

Water – icy, muddy rainwater – was seeping through the seams of his shoes. If he stayed any longer he would not be fit to present himself. And what if he got chilblains, or his piles, which had plagued him ever since his imprisonment in the Polombi, swelled up and chased all thoughts of pleasant dealings from his mind? No, he must go in or go back; but if he returned home now he would forfeit his guineas. Lord Pembroke, the young dog, would be hugely amused, which is to say the whole of the West End would be amused.

He picked up the parrot cage, stepped carefully across the mud-river of Denmark Street and knocked at the door. No answer. He knocked again then, feeling the door give beneath his knuckles, he pushed it open and stood dripping with the parrot cage in the unlit hall. How careless of the maid to leave the door unbolted. Then he realised she had done it so that her beau, when he left her, could steal out of the house more secretly. Cunning girl! He set the cage down, opened it and lifted the parrot out.

'*Je t'adore*,' he murmured, '*je t' adore* . . .'

The bird stood calmly on his sleeve. He stroked the blood-warm feathers and started, very slowly, to feel his way along the passage. The faintest, softest glimmerings of light showed beneath the parlour door. His heart was beating as though he had been running. He put his ear to the wood. Ah! He could hear her now. Was she . . . yes . . . she was sobbing. Poor Marie. How she must have loved her grandmama! Should he leave now? No doubt that would be the decent thing, but there was the little matter of Venetian pride, of the laughter of strangers. And there was something else, something perverse yet irresistible, a force that gathered in the small of his back, impelling him forwards.

He smoothed the head of the bird, took a deep breath and opened the door.

At first, so intent were they on their combat, staring hard into each other's faces, urging each other on, they did not see Casanova, hovering, half in, half out of the room, as if it still might be possible to step back into the passage, into the rain, into some other place where he would not be required to play so ridiculous a part. Then he was upon them, charging them, the bird on one hand, his cane grasped in the other, raised. The Charpillon let out a shriek and tumbled the hairdresser out of her lap so that he lay an instant on the carpet, stunned, shiny with pleasure, comically engorged. With a desperate contortion he managed to take the first stroke of the cane on his back. It made a wet sound. The parrot, squawking furiously, launched itself into the air, beat clumsily around the room and disappeared through the open door. The hairdresser, bleeding from one ear, clutching at his breeches and bawling a mixture of insults and pleas, hobbled frantically behind the shelter of the sofa where Casanova followed him, striking with his cane and kicking like a man who knew precisely where to kick, like a man who had studied the art of kicking and knew where the nerve bundles were, the ganglions, the medullae delicate as orchids. It was the Charpillon who saved her lover's life, throwing herself at Casanova and for a moment trading blows with him as though they were a pair of boxers. Clearly it was not the first time she had used her fists and though Casanova's punches were harder, she dealt him three to every one of his. He backed off; the hairdresser, taking advantage of the respite, threw open the parlour window and dived headfirst into the garden. In the same moment the Charpillon's mother and aunts entered the room like Swiss guards and battened on to the Chevalier's cloak, dragging him back to the wall and wrestling with him there until the noise of the front door, its hollow, ominous slam, returned them, a middle-aged man draped with middle-aged women, to something like themselves. They panted, avoided each other's eyes, then started to speak, to accuse, all at the same time, as if in an operetta.

'Oh!' wailed the favourite aunt. 'She will catch her death out there. Foolish man!' She brandished her fan beneath Casanova's nose.

'Sneaking into the house like a thief! Look, she has not even taken her shoes!' cried the mother.

'You are a bully, monsieur,' said the second aunt, 'scaring poor Marie out of her wits . . .'

'She will be murdered for certain,' said the mother, wringing her hands and sniffing.

'You will be responsible, monsieur,' said the second aunt, meaningfully, 'if anything happens to her.'

'And how,' answered Casanova, feeling like a stag at bay, 'how do you suggest I conduct myself when I catch her submitting to the embraces of her hairdresser? Should I be calm? Philosophical?'

'Tush, monsieur,' said the mother in a more conciliatory tone, 'the young man means nothing to her. It was merely high spirits.'

'The young are impulsive, monsieur,' added the favourite aunt. 'Were you not impulsive, monsieur, when you were young?'

'Impulsive, madame?' shouted the Chevalier, his face in spasm as if he had just bitten off the end of his own tongue. 'Impulsive? You have spoken like a bawd, madame. Your niece is a . . .'

'What,' interrupted the second aunt, 'do you intend to do about her? Sure she has fallen into some cellar. Why do you not go out for her?'

He meant to say, to lean down close and yell into her face: why the devil should I? But she was right. A young woman out on her own on such a dark, vile night ... It was far from safe. It was downright dangerous. What if something were to happen? Undoubtedly the responsibility would be his.

There was silence for a moment. Various articles of clothing, intimate articles, dangled from an arm of the sofa. He looked away and noticed the serving girl staring in around the jamb of the door, mouth open. He sent her for a light. For an hour under the tumbling rain he searched, then returned to the house. Had she come back? She had not. The women looked at him as if the girl's blood were smoking from his hands. Among the jagged circles of his thinking he could not decide who was in the wrong here. Had he, Giacomo Casanova, the Chevalier de Seingalt, not been put upon in the most spectacular way? Cuckolded by a hairdresser! And if she had dealings with the hairdresser, why not with the grocer's boy, the street-crossing sweeper, the rag-and-bone man?

Then he saw himself, a tall and notorious foreigner, bursting into this house of women, waving a parrot in their faces and assaulting their hairdresser whose ribs would be tattooed with bruises for a month to come. And how could she have betrayed him, to whom she had made no promises? What understanding had there been between them? Could she not claim that he had persecuted her almost from the first moment they had met? A coldness flowed in the marrow of his bones. He excused himself and went full pelt to Pall Mall, roused Jarba, roused the cook, sent Jarba for the watch, then led the party out into the night, shining his lantern into the glistening viscera of streets and alleys, steps and courts. There was no trace of the Charpillon, no sign of anyone. They pressed on, wiping the rain from their eyes, hurrying through inky pools, hopping over the frothy plaits of kennel streams, crying like the ghosts of drowned men the drenched syllables of the girl's name.

Twice more he went back to the house in Denmark Street and twice more set out again. He had reached that pitch of depletion where his body was an object that squelched at the side of him or beneath him, or sometimes above. It was only when Jarba, during the night's last wretched quarter, took his hand and escorted him to Pall Mall and up to his room and undressed him and sat him by the fire that he realised how far gone in weariness, in spirit, he truly was.

He sobbed. Jarba comforted him, Jarba with his measured presence, his eyes that had seen men leap over the sides of ships and never break into the light again. They would search in the morning. They would find her. No doubt she had gone to the house of a friend. Little Miss Lorenzi perhaps.

'Thank you, Jarba,' murmured Casanova, allowing himself to be led like an invalid towards the heaped coverlets of his bed. '*Caro* Jarba . . . Do you think this rain will ever stop?'

There was no answer. Jarba had gone. The Chevalier tried to say his prayers, but when he closed his eyes he saw, in endless replay, not the Charpillon and her hairdresser making the beast with two backs on the sofa, but himself, as he must have seemed from their perspective, running in with his mouth like a strip torn from the white of his face, a kind of monster . . . '

His watch ticked like a beetle on the cabinet beside the bed. He was suddenly very sure that he would not sleep, not without a bullet in his head.

His pistols were about somewhere, his long-barrelled terrors, his pig-slayers. In one of the travelling bags? Or had Jarba put them back in the bottom drawer of the chest? Could he persuade Jarba to load them for him? The thought of stumbling around the room looking for powder and shot was too miserable. It might be simpler to hire people, killers by appointment, who would come into the room in dancing-pumps and smother him with their gloves. Surely in a great city like London such people existed.

The candle flame hopped upon the wick, sizzled, phutted and died. After a minute or an hour, he heard the window open across the street and then the voice he had heard so often, calling like a muezzin, its mysterious message. He stared out from his own windows. He saw nothing. The rain fell all night.

The first news was not good. A runner came from Denmark Street with a note saying that the Charpillon was still not found. Casanova paced the floor of his house until, muttering to himself and chewing at the cuticles of his nails, he strode along Pall Mall and up the Haymarket beneath the canopy of his cumbersome umbrella, the rainwater lapping over the tops of his shoes. Everything had assumed the same colour, a kind of silvery grey, so that it was difficult to be sure where the roofs met the sky or where the steps of the houses were separated from the street. Even the people, seen at a slight distance, had the same silvery look to them, like church spires in the Netherlands.

The Charpillon was home. The servant girl told him this at the door, frowning as though she had instructions to frown and had been practising in front of a mirror.

Might he call on her mistress to see how she did?

He might not. No visitors other than the doctor. And the surgeon. And the apothecary. And the apothecary's boy. And . . .

'Will you at least tell me, child, what is the nature of her trouble? Is there any danger?'

'You have destroyed her,' called the Charpillon's mother, appearing behind the maid's shoulder. 'I have never seen her so poorly. The shock has stopped her courses, monsieur.'

'Her courses?' he repeated, dully, unsure of the sense of this ominous expression. 'Is there nothing I may do? If you will not let me see her at least allow me to pay for her care.'

He pulled from his pocket a well-filled purse. A grey-and-red-tipped feather came with it and spiralled on to the doorstep. They both stared down at it a moment.

'There is enough here, madam,' said Casanova, holding out the money, 'to ensure that she receives the best attention.'

Madam Augspurgher looked at the purse and made an odd little movement with her head, as though in her brain she were rolling a marble into a pocket. 'Money!' she said, contemptuously. Then she took the purse and quickly disposed of it among the folds of her gown.

The doctor arrived. He pushed past Casanova into the hall, the house door was closed, the bolts shot home, top and bottom. Casanova waited again across the street, looking up at the

Charpillon's window and seeing in his mind's eye the physician's grave expression, the doom-denoting shake of his head while the women, clutching their rosary beads, reciting decades, snuffled into little handkerchiefs.

When the doctor reappeared at the door, Casanova ran over and, much to the doctor's alarm, climbed halfway into the carriage with him. The only English he could bring to mind were some gambling terms and two or three sentences of flattery. The doctor, imagining that he was being robbed, threw a handful of coins into the Chevalier's face, then struck him in the chest with the boss of his cane. Casanova staggered backwards, lost his footing in the mud, and before he could renew his attempt, the doctor had shut the door and the carriage was rocking towards Holbourn, its wheels throwing up arcs of water like some manner of ingenious mobile fountain.

Casanova walked home, counting his footsteps. It was seven thousand two hundred and twelve steps from the Charpillon's door to his own.

3

Throughout the day messages passed between the two houses. Sometimes the notes – he did not know which of the Augspurghers was writing them, they were all unsigned – offered a crumb of hope: Marie had spoken some words; she had taken a little broth; she had smiled. Then the following message snatched it back: she had a fever; she was ranting; the doctor would not answer for her.

The last note, delivered by the unspeakable Rostaing at dusk – a weird green twilight in which the furious smell of the sea was clearly discernible – was the worst.

'Monsieur, she has forgiven you.'

Forgiven!

He lit candles for her in the chapel of the Bavarian ambassador then hurried to Duke Street and lit a dozen more in the chapel of the Sardinian ambassador. On his return he slept for two hours, lay awake and came downstairs at first light to be told that the cellar had flooded and that everyone was afraid that if the rain continued another two days the river would burst its banks. Casanova hardly heard them. He nodded; shrugged. What did it matter to him that the city should flood? Let it.

At nine o'clock, unable to bear any longer the absence of news, he took a chair to Denmark Street. The chairmen, miserable in cloaks of rain, ploughed the water with their shinbones. At the Augspurgher house the windows were shuttered. The rain streamed off Casanova's upturned face. His cries were echoed by dogs. No one answered his knocking.

In the water at his feet a child's shoe bobbed like a little boat. He picked it up, turned it in his hands. The shoe was an omen and not a good one. Absently he thrust it into his pocket. At the same moment the door swung open and a man in black holding a coat over his head hopped into the street. Casanova darted forward and seized the man's shoulders.

'You are a doctor, monsieur?' But even as he asked he saw the bands and gown of a priest. He let go of the man and stood for a long time, aware that the serving girl was watching him as though she wished to tell him something, but when he looked towards her she quickly shut the door.

So, he had killed her. Of course. It was plain from the start that one of them would destroy the other. Their lives had been pointed at each other like daggers. He took out his pocket-book and, folding the notes – he did not trouble to count them – he pushed them through a crack at the top of the door. There was no purpose now in trying to speak to them. Very likely they would set the law on him, in which case he would not trouble to defend himself. He started to laugh. His clothes were plastered on to his body, the curls of his wig were ruined, his stockings black with the stream-born filth of the streets. At Pall Mall he stripped in his room and left his clothes in a sopping pile on the floorboards. He stood in front of the mirror and stared at himself with the eyes of an undertaker. How inevitable this now appeared to him. No amount of scented powder, of gold, could help a man to escape such a moment. One might postpone it a while, deafen oneself with babble and cards and minor frauds, but now it had come to him – the rain-coloured silence of truth – and he was finished.

One imagined such a moment would be terrible, but he felt as though he had at last arrived at a destination he had long been travelling to. He was not afraid of it and the sadness was bearable. At some level, perhaps, this was what he had desired all along, to be brought to such a point. If so, then his one regret was that the Charpillon should have discovered her own end in helping him to find his. There was about that something unspeakably clumsy, something that could not be forgiven at all. He pressed his lips against the mirror, kissed himself goodbye and turned away.

From the wardrobe he fetched dry clothes, dressed carefully in a suit of French grey and sat at his table to write the necessary letters. It was almost pleasurable, for as each letter was written and sealed with wax it was another matter he need never think of again. The paper mounted up; he lit a candle, sipped at a glass of brandy. What an amazing number of people he knew! To those he knew best his letters were the shortest. They would understand. They would hold the letters in their hands in Venice and Rome, in Paris and Königsberg, the broken seals in black flakes on the table-top, and they would understand. It was that kind of century, that kind of life.

He was still writing the following morning. He had sharpened the quill so often it was now no longer than his little finger. Should he take off his rings? He twisted them, eased them off for the last time and lined them up on the desk. He flexed his fingers, cracked his knuckles. Then, after blotting and sealing the last letter, he opened the shutters; it was still raining, though more lightly now. He gazed slowly around his room and made a number of small adjustments. He imagined them coming in, friends and strangers, turning over his books, going through the drawers, perhaps stealing things – souvenirs of the great Casanova!

When he was quite ready he went downstairs, took the umbrella from its corner by the door and went out of the house. He did not want to see Jarba. Jarba would look into his eyes and know everything. Poor fellow! He had not had much luck with his employers.

Outside, his mind unburdened, freer than it had been in months, years perhaps, Casanova felt remarkably good, and for ten minutes as he strode east out of Pall Mall he was as alive to the world, to its endlessly variable surfaces, as only a condemned man could be. In the gunsmith's opposite the Mew's coffee house in Charing Cross he purchased several boxes of lead shot, as many as he was able to cram into his pockets. Outside again he walked more slowly, and by the time he reached Whitehall Steps to take a boat to the Tower – the site he had chosen for his translation – his neck and shoulders were aching from the weight of the shot, his feet sinking deep into the mud, so that he moved with as much difficulty as if he were already beneath the surface of the river.

At the steps the water was so high the boats appeared on a perfect level with the street. Casanova signalled to the oarsman, then, fearful that a slip would end the whole affair in a precipitate and unsatisfactory manner, he gripped a wooden post, balanced under the fins of his umbrella, and swung one leg, cautiously, into the stern of the boat.

'Seingalt!'

He looked round, straddling the water, furious that this, his last journey, so sad and beautiful in the rain, should have been interrupted.

'Seingalt!'

A carriage with four glistening black horses stood in the road beside the wall of the privy gardens. For a moment Casanova wondered if he could ignore the voice – such a rude and imperious voice – and pretend that he had not heard. In half a minute he would be in the middle of the river, then nothing in the world could call him back.

'Seingalt!'

Heavy as three men, he sighed, swung back his leg and dragged himself towards the carriage. Lord Pembroke leaned out.

'You have not shaved today,' said Casanova. 'I have never seen you with a beard.'

Lord Pembroke touched his chin and frowned with distaste. 'I have been in Moll King's all night. At two o'clock I lost my estate, my title, all my clothes and even my watch. Had I left then I should not even have possessed a pistol with which to shoot myself. I might have called on you, Seingalt, and borrowed yours.'

'I take it,' said Casanova, feeling as if he were having a conversation in a dream, 'that you won the next hand.'

'I did, and now some other devil is ruined. Where are you headed?'

'Nowhere, my lord, in particular. Merely taking the morning air.'

'An unhealthy thing to do in all this rain. It drums on men's skulls and makes them Bedlamites. Come into the carriage. I am going to my barber's and then I have a little celebration in mind which I should like you to attend. It will cost you nothing.'

Casanova started to make his excuses; Lord Pembroke waved them aside. Finally, deciding that the delay of an hour or so made very little difference when one was about to step into eternity, he collapsed his umbrella, hauled himself into the carriage and sat opposite the young lord.

'Tell me, Seingalt, have I won our little wager?'

'You have, my lord. The money is waiting for you at Pall Mall. You may have it whenever you wish.'

Pembroke chuckled. 'And have you finally given her up? If so, I trust you will not object if I try my luck.'

'I have no objection, my lord. It does not matter now.'

In the barber shop Casanova plotted how he might excuse himself, for the thought of the celebration – which would undoubtedly be some manner of orgy – filled him with an insurmountable disgust. Several times he was about to speak but each time he only opened his mouth and remained silent. Lord Pembroke's face was steaming under the hot towels. The barber, surrounded by his tackle, his braiding pins and crisping irons, his leather rollers and long spiral machines for frosting the hair, stropped his razor and stroked the blade on his palm. The Chevalier flinched. All his resolve was draining away from him. What was he doing in this barber-shop limbo? He felt as if he should never be able to move from his chair, that he would sit here for ever, nauseated by the smells of powder and singed hair, but somehow – such was the lunar pull of right behaviour – when the moment came and his lordship's face had its customary sheen, its girl-smoothness, he was able to drag himself back to the carriage. Frankly, he was amazed that Lord Pembroke could not see that he was in the company of a dead man. Or had his lordship perceived it immediately, even from a distance? Would his lordship have any interest in saving Casanova's life?

They stopped at a tavern in Dirty Lane. Lord Pembroke ordered a private room and cold meats and mentioned the names of four women who seemed well known to the landlady. Soon, servants came carrying trays of food and wine. Casanova sipped a little of the champagne. It was surprisingly good. He nibbled at a piece of cold pigeon. Odd to think that an hour ago he had believed he would never eat again.

'Musicians, my lord?'

Four men, led by one of the servants, shuffled into the room.

Each carried an instrument in one hand and rested the other hand on the shoulder of the man in front. Of course, realised Casanova wearily, one cannot have an orgy without blind musicians.

The women took longer to arrive, detained perhaps by some other saturnalia in some other tavern with another young lord and his foreign friend. When they came in they were laughing and shaking raindrops from their fingers. Lord Pembroke introduced them and the musicians started to play, their discoloured eyes half open, the expressions on their faces cringing and mournful as if they expected at any moment a hand to fly out of the darkness and strike them.

The women drank. Lord Pembroke drank. Casanova smiled at them like an indulgent parson officiating at a wedding he did not quite approve of. One of the whores, Celeste, a young woman from Normandy, settled herself on his lap. Her clothes were not of the cleanest; they had the smell of theatre costumes. He patted her hand, but when she moved to kiss his cheek he pushed her away, very gently.

'Are you unwell, monsieur?'

He told her it was nothing, a languor, a faintness that would soon pass; he did not wish to spoil the merriment. Lord Pembroke and the other women were dancing, stripping, throwing their clothes over their heads. His lordship called on Casanova to join them. The Chevalier waved, did his best to leer. 'I shall join you a little later. I am not entirely myself just now.'

Celeste slipped a hand between his thighs, felt his indifference and shrugged.

'Do you wish me to wake him up, monsieur?' she enquired, as though asking him the name of the capital of Peru.

He shook his head, removed her hand. He was amazed at himself. Even with a raging fever or crushed by the most purple melancholy, he had always been able to rouse himself, had always been able to eat what was in front of him. In order to rid himself of her weight – he had weight enough of his own – he said: 'I should like to see you dance.'

The others, naked now, were dancing an absurd jig. Celeste stripped off and joined them. Casanova glanced round at the door, wondering if it would be possible to slip out and rid himself of the lead shot – but where could he leave it? Would it not look very odd? Would not everyone immediately guess his secret?

He poured himself another glass of champagne and leaned back on the bench. At least there was a fire in the room. He yawned. What a spectacle they were making, these young people. Were they really enjoying themselves? It was hard to believe it. And did the musicians imagine they were missing something wonderful? Gods and goddesses cavorting in splendour like something out of Fragonard? He would have liked to have told them that it was nothing: four strumpets and a spoilt young aristocrat romping in a tavern room like overgrown children, yet without the dignity of children.

The dancing gave way to coupling. Casanova observed Lord Pembroke's technique with mild professional interest, as he would the work of another card player. He was not overly impressed but smiled encouragingly and raised his glass. Celeste, smelling more strongly after dancing, settled on his lap again and seemed surprised to find his condition unchanged.

How interminable it was! And what a relief when his lordship finally put on his clothes. Only with the greatest effort of will was Casanova able to rise from the bench. He dug a coin from his pocket and gave it to Celeste.

'Perhaps,' she said, 'Monsieur might ask for me another time, when he has more appetite.'

'By all means,' replied Casanova, wondering if he were in any danger of going through the floor.

They descended to his lordship's coach. The musicians were led off like convicts. By the time the carriage swung into Pall Mall the streets were thick with an unhealthy, pre-dusk darkness.

'I shall call for you at eight, Seingalt. We shall sup at Ranclagh. I do not like the look of you at all.'

'My lord, I do not think I shall be fit company. Perhaps another . . .' He did not have the energy to protest. 'Very well, my lord. At eight.' *Sequere Deum*. He staggered into the house, pushed the door shut with his heel and struggled out of his coat, which crashed to the floor, or rather splashed, for there was an inch of water in the hall. Jarba and the cook and Mrs Feaver, legs bare to the knees, were stood at the far end with buckets and brooms. Casanova slowly crumpled to the water's surface, kneeling amid pools of reflected candlelight that pulsed and sparkled like galaxies of unstable planets. He closed his eyes. All this water. It smelt like . . . smelt like . . . Home!

4

At eight, the lead shot stacked beneath his bed ready to be retrieved whenever he should be free of his social obligations and at liberty to drown himself, Casanova and Jarba were collected by Lord Pembroke's chariot. They went as far as the horse ferry at the end of Vine Street. Beyond, the roads were impassable, haunch deep in mud; deep enough in places to swallow a mail-coach.

Lighting their way with the coachman's lantern, they followed the path to the waterfront. The rain had not abated; the men turned out the sides of their hats to protect their wigs.

'I have never seen the river so high,' said Lord Pembroke.

'Is it dangerous?' asked Casanova, hopefully.

'In so much water,' said Lord Pembroke, struggling to erect the Chevalier's umbrella, 'what could be safer than a boat?'

They scudded over the black leather of the Thames. The waterman, complaining to himself, gripped his oar and looked about him hard as the current hurried them between Vauxhall and Tothill, the Battersea windmills and the Chelsea waterworks. They came in at speed, the boat grating its side against the jetty where a score of other watermen sat in jostling craft waiting for the tide to start its ebb. None but the strongest could row against the river in this mood. One of them was singing, and for a few entrancing moments the Chevalier, as he clambered up on to the slithery wood of the jetty, imagined it was his own language, something from Jamelli's *Merope* – but how could that be? The wind and rain were playing games with him. All these gurglings and splashings, these sonorous drippings, these hissing rain-skirts that swept like ghosts, like the white palms of the wind. Little wonder that a man imagined that he heard things.

The entrance fee at Ranelagh was half a crown. Lord Pembroke paid and then they passed into the warmth and geegaw splendour of the rotunda. Thirty chandeliers hung on long chains from the roof, and under their golden light a crowd some two hundred strong paraded around the great central pillar, the women's gowns sweeping the faded green matting of the floor. It was a more distinctive, a more elevated company than one found at Vauxhall. Men of the Million Bank, the South-Sea Company, the Levant Company, of Coutts and the Royal Exchange, in coats of cut black velvet, cruised confidently among the airier vessels of the nobility like coal barges at a regatta. Many of the faces – lords, noble wives, courtesans and fashionable artists – were well known even to Casanova. Was that not Lady Stanhope there with Caroline Fitzroy? And surely that was the Duchess of Grafton whispering in Lord Bristol's ear . . .

Around the circumference of the rotunda, tables were laid out for supper parties. Lord Pembroke, nodding to acquaintances, cousins, fellow members of Whites and the Hellfire Club, guided Casanova to an empty table and immediately ordered mugs of hot bumbo to drive out the damp from their bones.

'Tell me, Seingalt, do you not feel yourself reviving? Is this not an elegant scene?'

Casanova, leaning on his elbows, his eyelids as thick as walnut shells, inclined his head and thanked his lordship for his kindness. He thought: Is this how Lazarus felt waiting for Christ and the other meddlers to leave the village? Then the thought of Lord Pembroke as Christ almost made him giggle.

'There are some beauties here tonight, Seingalt. I cannot believe you have lost all interest in such things. Does not that girl talking to Horace Walpole make you want to eat a whole barrel of oysters?'

'Indeed she does, my lord,' answered Casanova, not looking.

'More bumbo,' said his lordship, 'and then I shall introduce you to whatever of these nymphs has taken your fancy.'

On the far side of the central pillar the orchestra began to play a minuet and a score of men and women gathered beneath the musicians' benches to dance, a slow and complicated walking which had something so irresistibly pleasing about it that Casanova, swallowing a mouthful of his drink, could not help but follow their movements and envy them.

How sticky life was! How very difficult to shed! If he did not nurture his coldness he would start to be afraid of what tomorrow or the next day he had resolved to do. He looked down at the supper plates, the savoury steam curling beneath his nose. Cautiously, he slid his fork into a corner of venison pie. The goodness of it almost brought tears to his eyes. He had hardly eaten a proper meal since returning from the country. He nibbled a little more.

We are, he considered, as the pastry melted on his tongue, imperfectly organised, our appetites blundering at life's teat even when the mind has said 'Enough!' One day perhaps we shall possess the ability to die at will, but who would then survive his own childhood?

'Seingalt,' said Lord Pembroke, frowning and cocking his head in a way that reminded Casanova of his unfortunate parrot, 'do you hear that noise? It seems to come from . . .'

'Noise, my lord?'

Jarba pointed at the chandeliers, where the glass, finely trembling, emitted a high and wavering note, just discernible above the music of the orchestra. Some of the waiters had noticed it too, pausing with their trays and looking up into the upturned bowl of the ceiling.

'You know,' said his lordship, tightly, 'we had an earthquake in 'fifty that brought all the chimneys down.'

'In 'fifty-five,' said Casanova, 'an earthquake moved the beam in my cell at Venice. I had been in solitary confinement for ninety-seven days. I thought God had come to rescue me . . .'

His gaze had returned to the dancers. Oblivious to the disquiet spreading in slow ripples across the rotunda, they went on with their stiff little movements, their orbits and eclipses. For the last half-minute Casanova had been studying the back of a young woman, her body of flowered silk, her cream-coloured skirts, her blue shoulder knots and on her feet – though one could not be quite sure at such a distance – shoes embroidered with blue satin.

Lord Pembroke was talking again, more urgently now, but Casanova did not hear him. It was the end of the dance. The woman, still with her back to him, raised her arms, her dimpled elbows, her hands cased in pink Swedish gloves. Casanova stood up. He was trembling. None of this made any sense. Had he started to hallucinate? Was it the drink? He stepped away from the table; somehow he had become entangled in the cloth and as he staggered from the alcove, glasses, plates and cutlery spilled on to the floor behind him. He did not pause, did not look to see what damage he had done. He was calling her name, shouting it, but she could not hear him yet; indeed, he could hardly hear himself for there was a deep rumbling in his head, a rumbling it seemed in everyone's head.

'Marie Charpillon!'

Her back tensed. He was only a dozen strides from her now, and from outside there came a dull, profound booming as though, in the centre of the world, the Devil were slamming doors. The musicians stood up at their benches like weasels, and under the swaying chandeliers, a dozen ladies swooned into the arms of their escorts.

'MARIE CHARPILLON!'

At last she turned. How frightened she looked, how pale, as if she really were a dead girl come out to dance. He reached out to her, one long and still ringless hand extended towards her throat, and had almost touched her when the doors of the rotunda burst inwards and snapped from their hinges, doors and liveried doormen flung high into the air by the force of the water. For a few seconds those at the far end were at leisure to watch it, this black disastrous force, this ravenous tide folding into its maw generals and waiters, dowagers and supper tables.

Casanova laughed; a single short bark. So, the river had come to him! Ranelagh did not have the solemnity of the Tower but no doubt it was more fitting that his life should be doused in a pleasure garden. The black edge was almost upon him. He steadied himself, half turned, than felt himself lifted, swung up like a child, his nose suddenly on a level with the lamps. Instinctively he filled his lungs; a last hug of air. Something

– a bottle? A boot? – struck his shoulder. He was dragged under, his coat was torn away from him, his shoes sucked off his feet. The river was stripping him like the drowned man at Blackfriars, spinning him in whirlpools, tripping him up with invisible currents, yet it was quieter here; just the sound of his heartbeat and the press of the water against his eardrums. He opened his eyes. The water was not as black as he had imagined it would be. Above him were pools of milky luminescence where the chandeliers were still throwing down their light.

His left hand had hold of the Charpillon's right; or was it she who had hold of him? Those tight gloves of hers had been peeled away like fruit-skins. Her arms were mysteriously white, her skirts pulsed like jellyfish, and around her head her hair floated in a bloody cloud.

He clawed the water towards her. Was it not a magnificent justice that she should die with him here, that he should be her suicidal executioner? How glad he was he had never learnt to swim! She was staring at him through dazed, tender, terrified eyes. She tried to pull away from him; she knew what he intended, what he was doing. As they struggled, a table drifted past and a man, still in his chair, a glass in his hand, sailed deeper into the body of the flood. Bubbles like a chain of pearls seeped from the corner of the Charpillon's lips. The air in his own chest was beginning to burn. Very soon he would open his mouth and take his first deep breath of the river. It should not be difficult for a boy from the Serenissima.

He held her in his arms now. She seemed to have given up; certainly she was no longer fighting him. Her hair caressed his face, her arms lay limply over his shoulders. He lifted her head. Her eyes, still open, were turned upwards, inwards, seeing marvellous things. A great sob burst from Casanova's mouth, an undulating, mercury-coloured bubble of unhappiness. He took his arms from around her waist, lifted her and – all his old famous power! – launched her, watching her ascend in a cloud of cream-coloured skirts until she was absorbed by the bowls of light and was lost to him for ever.

He exhaled, lay back, descended . . .

'Breathe, signore!'

He breathed. It was like the sound of something snapping in the air; like mid-winter midnight. Finette woke, shook herself, gazed up at him, her mysterious god. When his sputtering subsided he stretched out a hand to her, scratched behind her ears, reassured her. 'Not yet,' he whispered. She settled again; the easy movement of an animal between the waking world and the sleeping.

'Is that death?' he asked his visitor, who it seemed had moved her seat a little closer to his. 'One day forgetting to breathe, forgetting to tell the heart to beat, the blood to run?'

'That is half a death, signore, for if death is a forgetting it is also a remembering.'

He bowed to her in his chair, paused, then went on with the story. What else was left?

'It was the great flood of 1764, signora. Greater than any before or since. The wind and tides, the moon herself, had conspired. You will think I exaggerate, but I swear to you on the memory of my father, all the low-lying areas of the city were deluged. Only rooftops and the spires of churches showed above the water. Who knows how many lost their lives? Hundreds ... thousands perhaps. The poor for the most part: the rich it seemed were better at floating. At Pall Mall the river ran a hand's breadth

beneath the window of my room. For days I saw from my bed
– where Jarba, who had pulled me from the rotunda with the
merest spark of life in me, had left me to recover my wits –
the dead drift by like terrible lilies, the men face up, the
women face down, just as Pliny tells us. And it was not only
the human population which suffered. There were horses and
dogs and cattle, their swollen carcases covered with black crews
of carrion birds. Terrible, and such a stink! But the English are
a resourceful people and like my own they are used to water.
The dead they collected in nets and took to those hills that
stood above the water and which were now island cemeteries,
like San Michele. The rain stopped. The sun appeared. The king
and queen in the royal barge rowed into the city to encourage
the people. And though many were starving, they stood on the
roofs and waved. Yes, signora, it was a disaster that began to
be a holiday. The watermen rowed their fares where once there
had only been carriages and cobblestones. Children leapt into
the water from chimney pots. I even saw, signora, a frigate of
His Majesty's navy with all its pennants flying, moored by the
opera house . . .'

'And you were able, signore, to enjoy this unexpected apparition of your native city, knowing that you had murdered your
tormentress?'

'I had not murdered her. Perhaps I had even saved her. Quite
soon afterwards I saw her – a little pale, to be sure – being rowed
across the park with her aunts and mother and the Chevalier
Goudar.'

'The young lady had more lives than a cat.'

'I believe, signora, that she could outwit death at every turn.'

'Every turn but the last, signore. But tell me, you were relieved to see her? Were you at last free of your infatuation?'

'Signora, I could hardly tell you what my sentiments were on seeing her. It is true that beneath the water of the rotunda I had renounced her. I no more thought to be her lover, nor was I any longer jealous of her hairdresser. All my exploits had failed – my pursuit of the Charpillon, my attempts to – what was it? – to make myself anew, to revolt against the part which life had assigned to me, to revolt against God. I even lost the better part of my fortune to the floodwaters, as so many did. No. When I came to myself again I began to cook. A special dish which wise men prefer to serve cold. I am sure you have heard of it, signora . . .'

5

Two weeks after the flood, the city still in the grip of the river, Casanova went by boat at dusk with the constables. The magistrate, having seen the bills of exchange, had already issued the necessary warrant. All that remained now was for Casanova to point out which of the women were to be taken into custody.

They rowed through Soho Square. The shutters on the top floor of Carlisle House stood open and a girl in a blue mob-cap leaned out to wave at him.

'Monsieur!'

'Sophie!'

The waterman brought the boat under the window. Casanova, who in his youth had learnt the trick of standing in a shell of swaying wood, reached up and took his daughter's hands.

'There is to be a party,' said the girl, bending down to him. 'The grandest party Mama has ever given. We shall pay off all our debts! Will you come, monsieur? It is on Sunday evening.'

'The tickets are four guineas,' said Madame Cornelys, thrusting out her head beside her daughter's. 'To be paid in advance. In gold.'

Casanova counted out the coins from his purse and held them up to his daughter. Madame Cornelys disappeared, returned, and passed down a ticket. The Chevalier said: 'You look weary, my dear Teresa.'

She raised one of her mouse-skin eyebrows. 'And you, Giacomo, look as if you have not slept since you came to this city.'

'Where are you going?' asked the girl. 'Will you not come in and dance with me again? Who are these gentlemen with you, monsieur?'

At Denmark Street the constables clambered in through the window of the Charpillon's bedroom.

'That's one of them!' called Casanova, pointing to the Charpillon's mother, who was sitting, perfectly amazed, on the end of her daughter's bed. She screamed. The aunts ran in, ran out. The constables pursued them into the corridor. From the window of the adjacent room the Charpillon's head emerged. At first, Casanova was afraid she would cry mercy. If so, this was her moment; he did not think he would have the strength to resist her, but with her white face mottled with rage she cursed him . . .

'May you die forgotten! May you die a beggar with your nose rotten as an old cabbage stump!'

The constables, frowning at Casanova though at the same time evidently enjoying their work and taking a certain pride in the mayhem they left in their wake, returned with the older women, who clung to each other, shouting out for the whole street, shouting as loud as cherry-hawkers, the injustice of it all. The boat pulled away. Madame Augspurgher waved her handkerchief to her daughter, who remained at the window reaching out towards her as the space between them widened.

What a monster I am, thought Casanova, dark and gleeful under the folds of his cloak, but what joy there is in revenge! Little wonder that whole cities, whole nations, become addicted to it.

They could not take the women to any of the usual lock-ups. Those were all buried beneath tons of water, sudden tombs for their prisoners: the doxies, the wild drunks, the street-sleepers, pick-pockets, those of the 'canaille' whose names and histories were lost entirely with their last breath. In place of the lock-ups, several church towers and belfries had been requisitioned and it was to one of these, to St Mary-le-Strand by the Royal Palace of Somerset, that the constables now directed the boat. They tied up at a large decorative urn on the roof and the women were passed over the balustrade like bundles of sticks, sharing their captivity with a dozen big-lunged boys who had been caught swimming down into shops and looting. As the boat cast off the Chevalier felt the women's stare pressed like a knuckle between his shoulder blades, but he was invulnerable to their anger, shored up by the iron of his own. It was tit for tat. When struck, strike back harder. We learn the rules of life in the school-yard.

6

On the Sunday Casanova and Jarba went to the amusements in Soho Square. All the streets and alleys leading to the square were busy with boats, large and small, for Cornelys had invited everyone and everyone was coming. Hastily but ingeniously constructed jetties extended out from the house, almost as far as

Charles Street. There were lights and singing and several hilarious collisions. It was a crisp winter's night, the moon rocking in the cradle of the waters.

Inside the house, in the banqueting hall, there was such a crush at the tables only the strongest guests could move their elbows to wield their knives. Those on the outside of the room found themselves shuffling in an interminable queue that had no obvious point of arrival, that moved only because it moved, victim of its own mysterious volition. Casanova, wedged beside his valet, drank off a glass of warm champagne and scanned the hall.

He began to work on a woman with seahorse earrings who moved, drowsily smiling, immediately to his right. After they had exchanged some dozen sentences – demanded even by the etiquette of Low Debauchery – the Chevalier was still uncertain of what language she was speaking. Hungarian? Yiddish? But she comprehended him well enough, and as they passed the door they escaped the procession and went together on to the roof where he unlaced her between the chimney pots.

His second conquest was a cultured English woman, the leader of a salon, a bluestocking, whom, after a short discussion of the Comte de Buffon's *Histoire Naturelle*, he managed to pleasure without the necessity of leaving the room.

The third was a school companion of Sophie's, a girl full of energy and curiosity whom Casanova instructed in one of Cornelys's pantries, surrounded by truckles of high-smelling cheese and tubs of salty butter. Her schoolgirl French was a delight – '*dites-moi, s'il vous plaît, qu'est-ce que c'est que ça, monsieur?*' – her lips tender as prawns.

The fourth was the youngest son of a wealthy Huguenot family, silk merchants in Spitalfields. Casanova, at his most tender and skilful, drugged the boy with pleasure and led him back into the room as the eldest son.

The fifth turned out to be the first. She shrugged, spoke to him again in her incomprehensible language, and slid under the billiard table in the library with him.

Once more in the fug of the banqueting hall, two o'clock striking, the bell-note carrying sweetly over the floating town, Casanova discovered the Chevalier Goudar at his side.

'What a joy to see you here, maestro,' said Goudar, neat as a mosquito. 'I have been observing you. I am sure you will agree it has been an evening worthy of your old self. I congratulate you.'

He took Casanova's hand, heavy again with rings now, and kissed it.

'Goudar!' said Casanova, snatching back his hand and wiping it against his coat. How he wished he could have flung this Mephistopheles out of the window! But Goudar was indestructible. Goudar would only be at an end when Casanova himself was. He said:

'Is she here?'

'The Charpillon? Indeed she is not. You have always made the mistake, monsieur, of thinking she is a heartless creature but in truth her heart is as kind as your own.'

'She is at home, then?'

'With eyes red from weeping. I do not blame you for what you have done but you should beware of her vengeance.'

'I shall not be moved, Goudar, if that is your mission. Those harpies shall stay in their belfry until I receive payment in full.'

Goudar grinned. Was that pity in his eyes? 'I do not think that shall be long, monsieur.'

'How so?'

'My esteemed colleague, while I am the first to praise your talents, which are – there is no use denying it – extraordinary, you must allow me to believe that on occasion I see things more clearly.'

'Perhaps, Goudar, because you are as feeling as a lizard. As a lizard's tail.'

'Each man, monsieur, must act from that part of himself which is least weak. My temperament is cool compared to yours. I am well equipped by nature for the role of observer, confidant; even, dare I say it, of counsellor.'

'In other words,' said Casanova, 'nature has equipped you for a spy. Do you have advice for me, counsellor?'

'Since you ask for it,' replied Goudar, 'and since, despite everything, I am determined to be your friend, my advice is that you make your next conquest a reconquest.'

'I have already done so,' said Casanova. 'The fifth was the first.'

Goudar said: 'I was thinking of La Cornelys.'

'Teresa?'

'Then,' continued Goudar, looking closely into Casanova's eyes, 'you would not have to leave the house tonight.'

'A warning? If your intention is to alarm me then you have failed. Jarba is with me, also the waterman. You must know that I never venture out without the means to defend myself.'

'Even so, you would do well to go home in the daylight. Is a night with Cornelys such a drab prospect?'

'I am not in the habit, Goudar, of changing my plans for fear of ruffians. If these creatures you warn me of are determined they will find me tomorrow or the next day. They will not be deterred by the light. If they are not such men then I have nothing to fear. They shall be scared off with a shout, like street dogs.'

'Monsieur, it is the answer I expected of you. I have done my duty.'

'Indeed, you need not reproach yourself.'

'We shall meet again, monsieur.'

'Tonight, perhaps?'

7

It was past three in the morning and most of the remaining guests were asleep in their seats or sprawled on the table surrounded by crystal and the savoury carnage of the feast. The woman with the seahorse earrings was curled up on the carpet, smiling at her dreams. Casanova stroked the side of her face then whistled for his boatman and set out for home. There was still a moon but it was low now, so that in some streets there seemed to be swarms of silver bees over the water while others were as dark as those tunnels that run secretly beneath the streets of all cities, dark physical echoes of the world above. Since the flood the sounds of the city had changed. A cat wailing in Cock Lane could be heard in Golden Square. A man hammering in Ludgate could be heard everywhere. Voices drifted on the water like waste paper; words and sighs and whispers whose owners were nowhere to be seen.

It was, thought Casanova, the language of the newly dead, their last disembodied utterings, their lament.

They bumped into the body of a drowned horse which span slowly away from them, glossy and swollen with corruption. Then, fifty yards from safety, as the boatman steered his craft into the end of Pall Mall, a voice called:

'Good night to you, Seingalt!'

'Who are you? Who is there?'

Boats, at least three, pulled from the shadows.

'So,' said Casanova, reaching into his pocket, 'Goudar was a true oracle. Jarba! Ask what it is they want of me.'

Jarba hailed them. A shape in the bows of the nearest boat called back. Jarba said: 'They are officers, monsieur. They have come to arrest you.'

'But today is Sunday,' said Casanova. 'A man cannot be arrested on Sunday.'

'No, monsieur,' said Jarba, 'today is Monday.'

In the darkness there was the unmistakable sound of a pistol being cocked.

'Where must we go?' asked Casanova.

'Before the court,' said Jarba.

'Now? At this hour?' He did not like the idea of a night court. What colour of justice was dispensed in the flickering of lamps and tapers? It was the kind of thing they did in Rome or St Petersburg; he had not expected it here. The English, perhaps, were being infected with continental ideas, but he was not yet alarmed. He had been arrested in too many countries before now for the experience to have any novelty, yet as they followed the lead boat – there was one abreast of them and one behind

– he began to wonder if he had been very rash in disregarding Goudar's warning. The law was a net in which the more one struggled the more one was enmeshed. It served many gods, of which Truth was merely one, and not the most important. He took hold of Jarba's hand, squeezing it as if to reassure him, though it was he himself who sought comfort from the touch.

They were heading east, into Cockspur Street, into the Strand, past the end of St Martin's Lane, the Coach and Horses tavern, the ironmongery of Freke and Bliss on the corner of Castle Court. Past Lumley Street and Oliver's Alley, then left up Southampton Street and into the great piazza of Covent Garden where already there was some activity in the new floating market in the centre of the square. An old man and a boy glided past in a skiff loaded with turnips, but they looked only briefly at Casanova, as if the space between their world and his were too vast for the mind to leap across at such a sluggish hour of the day. As for the galleries around the edges of the square, they could not be seen at all. Heaven alone knew what questionable types rolled together now in the black of the sunken jelly houses, the silted glitter of the bagnios.

The constables tied up beside the Bedford coffee house. A light blinked above them; a man with a lantern stretched out of a second-floor window and let down a rope-ladder.

'They have brought us,' said the Chevalier, gazing around quickly to be certain of his bearings, 'to the playhouse.'

Jarba spoke to the nearest of the guards; a quick to and fro of voices.

'This,' said Jarba, 'is where the magistrate sits now, his own house being drowned like the others.'

'Well, then,' said Casanova, a large hand on his shoulder pressing him forward, 'no doubt all is as it should be.'

He started to climb.

Inside, they were led by the lantern-bearer, who strode on without waiting for them, leaving them to grope their way through a series of small, cluttered rooms, the old workshops of the playhouse. From the beams, gowns and coats decorated with a mock sumptuary of glass sequins and painted threads hung and swayed, faintly sinister, like the victims of some revolutionary tribunal. Then a short flight of stairs, a narrow passage and a low door on which the lantern-bearer knocked, three times.

The effect of the sudden space they now entered, with its torches and candle-branches, its familiarity and simultaneous strangeness, was so disorientating that Casanova could not at first take another step. They were at the top of the theatre, the one-shilling gallery, opposite the stage. Below, the proscenium and the boxes were completely submerged. Props and scenery from some unlikely drama floated on the water. On the benches of the gallery and in some of the boxes near the front of the theatre, clusters of men and women, who had looked round when the door opened, had already returned to the demands of their own business. Some of them, from their wigs and dark coats, were clearly functionaries of the court: now and then one jumped up and called out a name. Others, clutching sheafs of paper or with their heads bowed together in harassed consultation, were perhaps plaintiffs or relatives waiting to have their case heard. Who the rest were, sitting with their pies and oranges, their bottles, pipes and newspapers, Casanova could only guess. Insomniacs, perhaps, or members of the theatre company. There was an air in the place of measured chaos, of boredom, of fear.

The magistrate – not the plump, venal fellow who had issued the warrant for the Augspurghers – was sat at the very top of the gallery, his eyes bandaged with a length of black silk tied in a bow behind his head.

'Why does he wear such a thing?' whispered Casanova, wondering what new English eccentricity he was about to encounter, and wondering whether it would cost him dearly.

Jarba said: 'It is Sir John Fielding. He is a blind man.'

'A great advantage,' answered Casanova uncertainly, 'in one who must judge.'

He sat on the bench to wait his turn. It was the same seat perhaps where, among the press of the rabble, the anonymous apple-thrower had launched the fruit that struck Grandmother Augspurgher when – four months ago! – they had all sat below in the pit watching *Artaxerxes*.

At last, shortly before five, he was called.

'James Casanova! James Casanova!'

With Jarba at his side, he was led across to a space three rows beneath the magistrate's seat so that his head was on a level with his judge's knees. The knees themselves were covered with a thick blanket against the cold.

'Casanova?'

'I am here, signore.'

'You are also known as the Chevalier de Seingalt?'

'That is so.'

'A citizen of Venice and sometimes of France. Do you wish

to inform the court of any other nations you favour with your citizenship?'

'I am sure, signore, you are fully informed of my history – and may I congratulate you on your faultless Italian. Have you visited the Serene Republic, signore?'

'You understand, Seingalt, why you are here?'

Casanova spread his arms. 'Your officers were not inclined to tell either myself or my valet of the charges against me.'

'Then I shall tell you with what you are charged. A young woman has made complaint of you and says she goes in fear of you doing her some mischief. Unless you may defend yourself to my satisfaction it is my duty to sentence you to perpetual confinement in the prisons of His Majesty the King. You may speak now or else accept in silence the decision of the court.'

For a moment Casanova had the sensation that these proceedings did not affect him at all and that some other man was being tried here, some other wretch on the verge of losing his freedom. He found himself thinking of Sophie, and briefly saw the child before him, her little blue cap like a blue flag of innocence. What did she have in store for her with such a mother, such a father? *Povera figlia*. More than beauty or brains he wished her luck, or if not luck, then courage. He would find some way of helping her, that is if he ever got free of this madness. What a night it had been! What he would not give now for a bath, a dish of chocolate, bed, a warm bed with cool corners to stretch his toes into . . .

When he looked again – had he been asleep on his feet? – Jarba was standing by the magistrate's chair. Sir John nodded, then spoke to his clerk.

'Marie Charpillon! Marie Charpillon!' cried the clerk.

Like night-corn blown by a breeze the crowd on the benches rippled, and from their midst came the Charpillon, her mother and her aunts, the older women seeming thinner and somehow partially erased by their confinement, their faces pinched with fatigue but with their eyes still as hard as the buttons on Casanova's coat. He would have liked to have spoken to them. He felt suddenly ashamed.

'We shall continue,' announced the magistrate, 'in the French language, so that all parties may understand each other. A man's liberty is at stake. Also a woman's, for a woman who may not walk the streets unmolested is not free. Marie Charpillon, is the man before me the one you complain of?'

'He is, monsieur.'

'He has threatened you?'

'On numerous occasions.'

'He has laid hands on your person?'

'He has beaten me, monsieur. Beaten me grievously. He even held a knife to my throat so that I despaired of my life.'

'Is there more?'

'Monsieur, I hold this man responsible for the death of my grandmother. He forced us to go with him into the country where the air is very unwholesome.'

'You have no more complaints?'

'None, monsieur, other than that this man has terrorised myself and my family for half a year.'

'Very well. Monsieur Casanova, what have you to say in your defence?'

'Only this. That if it is against the laws of England to be the

dupe of a cunning and shameless young courtesan, to fall foul of
the intriguing of her unnatural family, to be driven to the brink of
insanity and despair by this young woman's monstrous infidelities,
then I am indeed guilty, though the very worst of your prisons can
offer me no torment like that I have suffered at the hands of the
Augspurgher family. I might mention, monsieur, that they owe
me six thousand francs.'

'I,' said Lord Pembroke, who had appeared at the scene as
silently as an eel, 'have undertaken to repay the debt, though
as the defendant owes me five hundred guineas, it is he who is
in debt.'

'*Bravissimo*,' said Casanova, clapping his fingertips, curling his
lip. It was such a perfect sneer his lordship stumbled backwards
as though he had been shoved.

'I do not like this case,' said Sir John, reaching up to adjust
the band around his eyes, 'for I begin to sense there is much
to answer upon both sides. Were I not constrained by law, by
decent precedent, I would have the two of them shackled and
sent out into the square in a holed boat. I fancy they should
soon learn to co-operate. Tell me, Monsieur Casanova, if you
were to be released, would you seek to harm this woman or her
family?'

'Monsieur, I would not. It is true that I wanted revenge for
I have never been treated so abysmally by any woman. Now, I
want only peace.'

'Peace? The peace to do what?'

'To be what I am, monsieur.'

'And what is that?'

'An abuser of women!' shouted the Charpillon.

'A destroyer of families!' chorused the aunts.

'A mother's nightmare!' called the Charpillon's mother, flourishing her hands at Casanova as though she were a magician and the trick were intended to make him vanish. 'Can Your Honour imagine what it is to have a young daughter pursued by such a man? Such a cynical man. I believe in his heart he hates all women. He would like to see us all ruined.'

'Monsieur,' said Jarba to Sir John, 'may I speak?'

Among the party around the magistrate's chair there was a sudden hush. Sir John turned his head towards the source of the voice.

'You are the accused's valet?'

'I am.'

'He treats you well?'

'As a man treats a valet.'

'You may speak.'

'Monsieur – with respect to my employer, the Chevalier de Seingalt, whom some call Casanova – I have seen his dealings with this woman from the beginning. I understood at once that it could not bring happiness to either one. They did not truly see each other, monsieur, but only the shadow of their own thinking. When I watched them as they stood or walked together, it was as if they stood or walked in separate rooms, and when one spoke, the other did not listen, nor did they ever mean what they said above once or twice when they bluffed with the truth. It was strange to see, monsieur, a comedy where the bruises were not painted. One pitied them even as one laughed at them.'

'Laughed? I think, young man – for so I perceive you – that you take grave risks with your employment. We know our servants laugh at us but we do not care to have them tell us so. What is your name?'

'I am Jarba now,' said Jarba. 'I have had other names.'

'Then, Jarba' – the magistrate smiled mischievously – 'since you have spoken so freely, how in your opinion shall we bring the curtain down? What manner of ending shall we have? I am tempted to order their betrothal. I have such powers, you know.'

Jarba looked at Casanova; Casanova, swallowing his tears, nodded. Jarba said: 'They should be separated as one separates two children fighting in the street.'

The magistrate sat for a minute, cogitating. Above them all, unruffled by disaster but beginning to peel in the dampness of the air, Amicomi's Shakespeare, crowned with laurels, gazed down kindly from the ceiling.

'When I was a boy,' began the magistrate, 'and my father or my teacher pulled me off some other boy, we were offered a choice of being thrashed with a belt or shaking hands and parting as two human beings. Often, of course, one preferred the belt to the indignity of shaking the hand of a sworn enemy. Nothing is harder to overcome than pride. If Monsieur Casanova will give his word that he will not attempt to see or by any means to menace the woman Marie Charpillon, and if he will demonstrate his goodwill by shaking the young woman's hand and begging her pardon, then, upon his being signed for by two householders, I am content to set him at his liberty . . .'

'And you suffered this, signore? You shook her hand and begged her pardon?'

'Signora,' said Casanova, plucking at the edges of his coat as if to pull himself forward in the chair, 'I would rather have been flogged at the back of a cart through every street in London! I would rather have . . .'

'But surely it is very easy to move one's hands, one's lips? The blind judge was magnanimous. Others might have treated you more harshly. Had the judge been a woman perhaps . . .'

'You also take her part! How is it you cannot see what she was? It is enough to make one chew one's thumbs off. What of me? Of my suffering?'

'Is this the time,' said his visitor, with a glance at the candle, the flame skipping on the wick, 'for such complaints?'

'Pah . . .' His head drooped. He had been up for more than seventy years. Such a very long time. He sighed, and when he spoke his voice was no more than a whisper.

'Signora, she took some steps toward me also, so though it is true we did not meet quite in the middle, though it was a little more on her side than on mine, I did not have to capitulate entirely. Her eyes were . . . ah . . . like eyes, like eyes, signora, but her smile was that of someone who has both won and lost in the

271

same instant. What was her future? It was as Goudar had foretold it. Before long she would find herself passed over for younger girls with better skins. Lord Pembroke was her protector, but he would not keep her . . . Yes, I held out my hand to her and when she took it, her grip was more like a man's than that of a young woman, which surprised me, for her hands are small, her fingers very delicate. It must have appeared to those who watched us that we were concluding some business matter, something more purely commercial.'

'And you begged her pardon?'

'Yes, I begged her pardon, and loud enough for all the court to hear it. She did not reply but allowed her hand to rest in mine a few moments more. The magistrate dismissed us. He told me I should find some respectable employment, and that a man should have a family and avoid the perils of mistresses and adventure and all that makes life worth living. I thanked him. I asked Jarba if I should pay a bribe but it seemed that the moment had passed. I wondered also if I might say something further to the Charpillon, who was sat near by, or if in doing so I would violate the terms of my bail.'

'Signore, what more could you have said to her? You had moved beyond each other. Your lives were pointed elsewhere.'

'True. And yet that was the very moment when we might have begun to care for each other. Love,' he murmured, as if summing something up that had been occurring to him, very slowly, over many years, 'love requires a cool head . . .'

He looked towards the window. Night was brewing over Bohemia, and though he did not wish to be the first to say it, the walls of his room seemed to be growing thinner. He wished Finette would move, remind him of where his feet were. He looked at his visitor. In the end, no doubt, she would unpin her veil and show herself – unless, of course, he had been merely speaking to the air.

She said: 'There is still flame enough in the candle to burn the letters. I shall help you if you wish.'

Casanova paused, then answered: 'I think not, signora. Later perhaps?'

8

He was surprised, going out, how light it had become. Though there were still lanterns on the sterns of the boats in the market, he could see the grey pediment of the church on the other side of the square quite distinctly. Martinelli and the great man-shadow were with him, found by Jarba and brought to sign for his freedom.

'Where to, monsieur?' asked Jarba, who had resumed, for the interval, his former style.

'Pall Mall,' said Casanova, shivering and glancing back at the playhouse. 'I believe we – you, Jarba – rescued some of the good wine. And some tea for Monsieur Johnson?'

'No, sir,' said Johnson, 'this is an occasion for wine. It is not frequently that one may assist in rescuing a man from perpetual imprisonment. I shall take a bottle of your good wine with you.'

The waterman kept the boat to the centre of the street so as not to snag his oars on the submerged metalwork of shop signs or entangle them in the fishing lines which, hung with little bells, ran from almost every house. A dog stranded on a rooftop barked at them. A milk girl rowed past with her churns, laughing at them for no apparent reason at all.

'The water is dropping by the hour,' said Johnson. 'In five years we shall not be able to persuade a stranger that we once went by boat through the streets of London. We shall not be believed.'

Rocked by the confluence of waters at the bottom of the Haymarket, they pulled past the Painted Balcony Inn, the Smyrna coffee house, Dodsley's bookshop . . . Then the boatman shipped his oars and Jarba stood to catch hold of the sill of Casanova's bedchamber.

With much effort, and some danger of upsetting the boat, they climbed up into the room. Casanova lit the candles and went on to the landing to call for Mrs Feaver who, in the new humidity of the world, had become almost voluptuous, like a dried apricot soaked overnight in a bowl of water. Jarba closed the shutters against the chill of the river and ten minutes later the Chevalier and his guests, sat on chairs salvaged from the parlour, were armed with glasses of white wine, a '47 Sauternes from the Château d'Yquem. They raised their glasses and were about to drink when Casanova heard, from across the street, the familiar sound of a window being thrust up on its sashes.

'Hush!' he said, standing quickly and swinging open the shutters. 'This fellow has been haunting me for months.'

He looked out over Pall Mall. Jarba, Johnson and Martinelli leaned on the ledge beside him. On the other side of the street, directly opposite, a tall, thin, pale man was stood in a crumpled nightgown framed by the darkness of the room behind him.

'Listen . . . There!' whispered Casanova. 'Always the same. What is it he says? What is his lament?'

It was Martinelli, with the softest of laughs, who answered.

'He says he is happy.'

'Happy?'

'I too have often heard it,' said Jarba. 'It is as you say, monsieur, always the same cry.'

'Happy?'

'He cries "I am happy". Nothing more.'

'Is he insane?' asked Casanova, looking round at their faces.

'Very likely,' said Johnson, 'but it is not an offensive madness.'

'Would that it were contagious,' said Martinelli, resting his hand on the Chevalier's shoulder.

They left the window, left the shutters undone and returned to their wine, filling their mouths with the sweetness of a summer sixteen years past. Outside, the city, this bruised honeycomb of a town, was waking up, inventing itself from the mist of the dawn, its citizens sticky with dreams. And over Venice too the sun was rising and a boy would open his eyes and find himself possessed of a world in which almost anything might happen, like a writer leaning over a sheet of paper, nibbling the feathered tip of his pen, his mind suspended in the intoxication of the possible, that instant before the first line, the first word, the first glistening blot of ink would send him on remorselessly towards the inevitable ending. By nightfall – for better or for worse – nothing would be quite as it had been. Everywhere, new stories were about to begin.

Author's note

In part this story is based on Casanova's *Histoire de Ma Vie*, written down in old age at the castle of Count Waldstein in Dux, on the Czech–German border. Much else, however, is the purest invention.

Casanova – the historical Casanova – died on 4 June 1798 at the age of seventy-three, his great body overwhelmed at last by a lifetime of adventures. He was buried in the graveyard of the church of St Barbara, just outside of Dux. There are no headstones there now, but it is said that for years a rusted iron cross over the grave snagged the skirts of young women who walked on the pathway beside it.

As for Marie Charpillon, she later became the mistress of the English radical John Wilkes, but after 1777 – when Marie would have been only thirty-one years of age – she disappears from the pages of the history books. Her fate is unknown.

Praise for *Ingenious Pain*

'Set in the mid-18th century, at the dawn of the
Enlightenment, and roving through England, Europe
and Russia, it presents James Dyer, a man whose
absence of compassion is physical; he can't feel pain
. . . Gripping throughout . . . a book that gives visceral
pleasure'
Independent on Sunday

'Miller's juxtaposition of the weirdly wonderful with
the harsh reality and brutality of eighteenth-century
life is a powerful vehicle for the themes he has chosen
to explore . . . A dazzling debut'
Observer

'Strange, unsettling, sad, beautiful, and profound'
Literary Review

'Skilfully constructed, reaching imaginative heights
and emotional depths, this fine first novel explores the
question of what it means to be human'
The Times Literary Supplement

'Brilliant and unusual . . . it stands head and shoulders
above most of the novels which will be published this
spring season'
Financial Times

'Dazzling . . . Miller tackles notions of mortality and
humanity to brilliant effect . . . truly wonderful'
Evening Standard

'Exceptionally intelligent and elegant . . . remarkable
for its feeling and its humane sensibility'
The Sunday Times

'An extraordinary first novel'
The New York Times Book Review

A selection of other books from Sceptre

Ingenious Pain	Andrew Miller	0 340 68208 6	£6.99	☐
Cold Mountain	Charles Frazier	0 340 68059 8	£6.99	☐
The Maid of Buttermere	Melvyn Bragg	0 340 42373 0	£6.99	☐
Le Testament Français	Andrei Makine	0 340 68206 X	£6.99	☐
Lives of the Monster Dogs	Kirsten Bakis	0 340 68597 2	£6.99	☐

All Sceptre books are available from your local bookshop or newsagent, or can be ordered direct from the publisher. Just tick the titles you want and fill in the form below. Prices and availability subject to change without notice.

Hodder & Stoughton Books, Cash Sales Department, Bookpoint, 39 Milton Park, Abingdon, OXON, OX14 4TD, UK. E-mail address: order@bookpoint.co.uk. If you have a credit card you may order by telephone – (01235) 400414.

Please enclose a cheque or postal order made payable to Bookpoint Ltd to the value of the cover price and allow the following for postage and packing:
UK & BFPO – £1.00 for the first book, 50p for the second book, and 30p for each additional book ordered up to a maximum charge of £3.00.
OVERSEAS & EIRE – £2.00 for the first book, £1.00 for the second book, and 50p for each additional book.

Name _____

Address_____

_____

_____

If you would prefer to pay by credit card, please complete:
Please debit my Visa/Access/Diner's Card/American Express (delete as applicable) card no:

Signature _____

Expiry Date_____

If you would NOT like to receive further information on our products please tick the box. ☐